LET GO, LET THE RIVER

Canoes in Winter – Book 2

Bob Guelker

Copyright © 2016 by Bob Guelker
All rights reserved. No part of this publication may be reproduced, distributed, or transmitted in any form or by any means, including photocopying, recording, or other electronic or mechanical methods, without the prior written permission of the publisher, except in the case of brief quotations embodied in critical reviews and certain other noncommercial uses permitted by copyright law. For permission requests, write to the publisher at the address below.

Printed in the United States of America
ISBN 978-0-9977457-2-6

Five Pines Publishing
16910 County 13
Nevis, MN 56467
Cover Art by: Amelia Woltjer
Cover Design by: Eled Cernik
Website: CanoesInWinter.com

Publisher's Cataloging-in-Publication data

Names: Guelker, Bob, author.
Title: Let go , let the river / Bob Guelker.
Series: Canoes in winter.
Description: Nevis, MN: 5 Pines Publishing, 2016.
Identifiers: ISBN 978-0- 9977457-2-6 (pbk.) | 978-0- 9977457-3-3 (ebook)
Subjects: Horses--Fiction. | Canoeing--Fiction. | Minnesota-- Fiction. | Love stories. | LCSH Post-traumatic stress disorder-- Fiction. | BISAC FICTION / Romance / Contemporary.
Classification: LCC PS3607.U445 L48 2016| DDC 813.6--dc23

DEDICATION

To the good folks in this little corner of the world--in and around Nevis, Minnesota.

Your encouragement and support has been immeasurable and invaluable beyond anything I ever expected. One particular couple really needs to be acknowledged for their undying, generous support, but I know they'd be embarrassed if I put their names here. You know who you are though. And if anyone comes up to me and asks, I'll tell them!

Again I thank all of you from this wonderful place called Nevis with all my heart, and pray I don't disappoint you with this second book.

CONTENTS

Chapter 1: Canoes With One Good Arm and a Bad Leg...1

Chapter 2: Bigger Fish to Fry........................ 17

Chapter 3: To the Rabbit! 25

Chapter 4: His Name was Samuel.................... 43

Chapter 5: The Courtroom Players 65

Chapter 6: A Lightning Rod......................... 75

Chapter 7: Friends with Benefits..................... 93

Chapter 8: Turd in a Punch Bowl 121

Chapter 9: Questions and Answers 133

Chapter 10: Up in a Tree, Thinking 153

Chapter 11: Baby Boy Ryan 167

Chapter 12: Feeling Cheap and Used................ 175

Chapter 13: The Back Way to Streeter............... 193

Chapter 14: Canoes in Winter...................... 209

Chapter 15: Great to Have You Back! 227

Chapter 16: The Power of Prayer 241

Chapter 17: Peabody's Wheels are Turning.......... 253

Chapter 18: The Baby's Not an "It".................. 267

Chapter 19: Kind of Busy 281

Chapter 20: Mission Accomplished................. 289

CHAPTER 1

CANOES WITH ONE GOOD ARM AND A BAD LEG

Maureen's stern advice might as well have been directed at a rock or a fence post. Sam Ryan was to go back inside his house and soak the deep puncture wound in the palm of his right hand for 20 minutes, and then redress it. Also, he needed to give his left leg a break for at least a couple days, to give the jagged gash running down to his shin bone, which she'd just finished sewing back together with 13 stitches, time to quit weeping.

Even before her car is out of sight, heading down the gravel road toward the bridge, his wheels are turning. Sam steps off the porch gingerly with his stitched leg first, his sound left hand holding onto the porch post. He checks his balance, testing the bad leg with a little weight, then stepping off with his left.

"Oof," he says to himself. He points up at the sky with his bandaged hand, ordering into the heavens through pursed lips, "We need to have a man-to-man, God, and I'm gonna do all the talkin'."

With the limp of a salty pirate dragging along a wooden leg, he sets out slowly across the farmyard gravel toward the barn.

Sam feels 93 instead of 53. He's angry that he's become a waste of the freshest air on Earth, instead of reveling in it like the nicely kept-up 40-year-old many folks guess he is. At the outside barn wall, he stands and contemplates tipping the canoe on its side to keep the rain out. But, once past the balance point, it usually rolls over clumsily, making all kinds of racket from the two paddles, spear, and can grabber slamming around inside, as it thrashes violently back and forth several times.

Feeling the weight of the canoe lean toward him, he lets go. His good leg takes its obligatory first step backward. But his aching leg doesn't respond. Sam winces and prepares himself for the worst, but the canoe falls short of slamming into his injured leg by an inch. He sighs in relief as the canoe bounces, lurching back toward the barn. But on the return bounce toward Sam, a paddle flies out. The narrow wooden edge smacks him right on top of his stitches.

"GODDAMNIT!" He gives God a quick middle finger before bending to examine the damage. Down below his cutoff blue jeans, shiny, fresh, bright red blood is already soaking through the thick layer of bandages that are held in place with several wraps of gauze. He shakes his head in exasperation. "Now ya want me to bleed to death? Whatever…I'm too busy for your bullshit to stand here and watch."

Deja sits on her little fluffy butt 15 feet away. Sam's nearly three-month-old yellow Lab has learned in her three short weeks with him that, when he tips the canoe off the barn wall, something fun is about to happen. But when her master curses, her tail stops sweeping the ground. Her ears droop and her eyes plead. Still, when he limps back across the yard toward his truck, she prances out ahead of him, happily anticipating that he's going to back it up to the canoe and they're going somewhere adventurous.

He opens the truck door, and she doesn't wait to be invited inside. Still too little to make the leap, she places her front paws on the edge of the running board and looks over her shoulder at Sam, tongue hanging out and eyes dancing with anticipation. He cracks a smile and gives her a gentle boost.

They've been working on a command Sam wants to try out now, despite the blood running down his leg. In practice, he's been tossing a small treat into the canoe bottom to get her to scramble into the boat, hoping she'll make the connection with his command. But the treats are in the house, and he's saving his precious few steps.

"Get in the boat!" he orders in a happy, encouraging voice.

And she does! He lowers himself down on his good knee next to the canoe. In the other leg, now bent into a 90-degree angle, the stitches sting as they are pulled taught. He feels a narrow, cool streak as the breeze wafts around his lower left leg. The rivulet of blood has trickled its way to his ankle. He quickly fishes the hanky out of a back pocket and stuffs it into the gap between his foot and slipper, while Deja licks his face like it's covered with honey.

"Good girl! Good girl!" He rubs her all over, up one side and down the other. She's still got that sweet puppy breath that makes Sam smile and reminds him of all the other Labs he's had.

Sam doesn't dare call Maureen for a shuttle like he usually would—for obvious reasons. In the past, he'd ask her to pick him up at the bridge, where he'd leave his truck after delivering his canoe to the dam upstream. Then she'd deliver him and Deja back up to the waiting canoe. But given her strict orders for rest, she'd have a fit if he suggested that today.

Walking those four miles is out of the question today and maybe even next week. The takeout at the bridge is only a quarter mile from his house. He hopes no crawling will be required to get home. But he'll worry about finding help to fetch his truck from the dam and canoe from the bridge when the time comes.

The river, she's a-callin', and of course Sam's answerin'.

Up on the edge of the road by the dam, when Sam lowers the canoe from the truck bed, Deja hops right in and wiggles, looking to be congratulated. It had never occurred to Sam he'd have to also teach her: *Get outta the goddamn canoe!*

He has to drag the canoe down a narrow, poison ivy-lined path about 150 feet to the water's edge. It's a good thing the pup only weighs 12 pounds. Anyway, he'd rather have her in the canoe than running through the pernicious understory. Not a problem, even dragging with his off arm and only one good leg for traction.

Getting into the canoe, however, is a whole other dance. Sam pushes it off the bank into the stream, hanging onto the rope. Pulling the canoe close enough to get a hand on it, he slides off the bank and tosses the rope into the boat. Holding his left leg above the water while lightly grasping the gunwale with the fingers of his bad hand, and using a paddle in his good hand as a walking stick, he hops clumsily around to the other side of the canoe. His spastic hopping and flailing reminds him of the old joke about the one-legged man in a butt-kicking contest.

He finally finds decent footing, aims his rear end at the seat, pushes the canoe tight to the bank, and lets himself fall in, butt first. The canoe rocks precariously almost to the gunwale, just an inch short of taking on water. He has a strange feeling he's not alone and glances around to make sure nobody had seen him getting into his canoe like a three-legged cow on roller skates.

Reaching behind the seat, he fetches the plastic soda bottle full of wild grape wine and positions it in front of himself at arm's length. Deja is standing on all fours, as close as she can get to the front, peering across the river as if she sees a grouse or a red squirrel, ears on alert and tail whipping excitely.

Sam shakes his head, thinking that's something else they need to work on when she gets a little bigger: *Stay in the middle of the goddamn canoe!*

He picks up the paddle for a test and instantly discovers he can't press the end into his bad palm without causing eye-watering pain. He switches hands. Yup, that'll work, if he's careful. There will be no extreme paddling this day, for example, to dig deep into the water and swing the canoe 180 degrees and reverse course, as he often does to snatch a can, bottle, or bison bone from the riverbed.

With the tip of the paddle, he deftly directs the canoe out into the current. In a few yards, he's floated safely beyond the two downed beaver trees whose tops almost meet in the middle of the river. He unscrews the cap from the wine, points the bottle to the sky, and says, "Remember me? Sam Ryan? I need a word with you."

He takes a big swig and sighs, wiping his lips with his forearm. Again, he looks around to make sure no one is eavesdropping on him. He can't shake the feeling that he's not alone.

Sam simply thinks quietly as he floats along lazily in his river. It's his nature to take his time. Even when Deja gets her two front feet up on the gunwale and looks as if she's going to leap out, he commands in just a whisper, "No, girl! Sit! Preferably in the middle." He gently nudges her to the center of the boat with the tip of the beer can spear, which is almost too dull to stab even an aluminum can. She glares at him like she'd just been run through with a lance.

Sweetly, he asks, "Come?"

She forgives her master, happily scoots under the two thwarts, and wiggles up to him for pettings. He'd taken his new puppy for three short canoe rides on Fox Lake, just to get her used to behaving in the canoe—plus their two-night river trip, which she mostly slept through. Never before today had she acted like she'd consider going overboard. Or given him that pathetic look after being touched with the dullest of fish spears, which could surely bring the ASPCA down on his sorry, pet-abusing butt in a heartbeat.

He grins as he jostles her ears lightly. "Thank you, my God, for this puppy. I know, I know, Sally bought her for me…back before she… But I don't wanna think about that anymore. I'm orderin' you, everyone else's God, to butt out and let Deja and me live happily ever after, just the two of us."

To Sam's way of thinking, the "whatever it is up there" that nearly all other folks refer to as God pulls strings like a puppeteer, sometimes to the followers' apparent benefit, resulting in faithful devotion and a bump up in the collection plate. But, just as often, the tangible effect is tragic, painfully nonsensical, illogical, and hellish.

That particular god, according to Sam, is absolutely not to be trusted, adored, revered, or respected, as anything resembling the proverbial *Beginning* or the *End*. But boy, does he know how to mess up everything in between!

Sam Ryan speaks his truth from over five decades of in-depth personal experience.

Sam's god is the universe. Like many other unconventional former church types, to him, his god is everything beautiful and truly loving and has not a damn thing to do with religion. His god is the miracle of birth, a gorgeous sky. It's loving one another for love's sake with no conditions and the whistling of swans' wings. It's puppy breath, it's déjà vu and spiritual healing and those rare glimpses through the crack into the universe, where everything makes perfect sense and you get that fluttery feeling up and down your spine.

And it's one more thing he'd discovered five weeks ago, watching Sally Hunter ride her horse. Running hellbent in a game, walking, or simply sitting still in the saddle…it didn't matter anymore. Sally's gone. Once and for all…for good.

"But now back to you, string-pulling puppeteer, God. No way, I'm not thankin' you for last night. I should probably blame you. After my god saved her horse's life, then Sally informs me she's gonna stay with her idiot, abusing, philandering husband—Bill the Pinhead—forever, and she'll never be back.

"But then in my bedroom, we undress each other and make love. And like nothin' I've ever experienced, not even with Karen. I could tell Sally felt the same way. I never had anyone hold me so tenderly, so lovingly... never had a woman cradle my face as her tear fell onto my cheek. I never felt so *right* with anyone, ever. Even though we both knew she was goin' away for good.

"And she knows that I know—and I know that she knows—that hubby Bill is the one who tried to kill Dakota by stickin' a big syringe needle in the horse's flank. Then the idiot broke it off in there, ruining his perfect crime.

"Ya know, it just occurred to me I should give you—the God who loves to manipulate, who contrives drama down here rather than rent a movie for yourself and leave us alone—a nickname so you two don't get mixed up about who I'm talkin' to. How 'bout *Everyone Else's God*? 'E God' for short.

"Heh, heh...perfect. Sometimes I don't know where I come up with this shit..." Sam mumbles and smiles to himself.

Sam takes note of his river bearings and stops giving E God hell for a moment. Out of the rice bed and back into the forested part, he dips his paddle and pulls backward to steer away from a tree that's fallen into the stream, its top branches spanning all but 10 feet of the little river's width. He remembers how the brilliant sun had struck Sally's golden hair right in this same narrowing, when she'd leaned her head back and let her ponytail swing freely, how it took his breath away.

Sam asks himself and anyone who might be listening up there, "Will I ever be able to canoe this beautiful river again without being haunted?"

He had brought Sally canoeing the day after their fateful meeting in the gravel pit. Sally, his neighbor Maureen's younger sister, had stumbled into his morel mushroom Shangri-La and really cleaned up. There she was, he didn't know who at first, sunbathing naked down in the gravel pit. As he lay out of sight at the precipice of the near-vertical bank, lurking 50 feet above the sunbather, and contemplating a covert retreat (after one more look), a huge hognose snake, with its head flattened like a cobra's, was hissing six inches from his nose.

"Both of you know I'm terrified of snakes!" Sam snarls under his breath. "E God, I know that was you. I coulda stroked out right there! Why scare me with a goddamn snake? I know…I know…you're so damn famous for usin' snakes to tell your ghastly parables and make your disturbing God-fearin' passive-aggressive threats. Remember? I'm a *recovering Catholic.*

"And even when I was a kid you couldn't suck me in, because I was already positive *God's Word* was just so much fiction…really bad fiction, but the snakes still freaked me out. The snake was overkill. So was compelling me to scream like a woman and jump to my feet, only to have the bank give way and send me tumbling down the pit to slam into Sally, who was wearing only a hat. My God, I'll give you the credit for that one. E God, you get the credit for my head hittin' a rock on the trip down and splitting open.

"Maureen and even Sally's father-in-law, Pop, had suggested to both of us we should meet someday, and neither of us had a clue who they were talking about. And neither of us gave a crap if we got set up or not; our lives were already settled." Sam shakes his head.

But they had met once, three weeks before, briefly. In the insurance office where Sally had worked when Sam was paying his bill. And then he became compelled to make a second trip all the way back to Park Rapids that day to bring her two bottles of his homemade wild grape wine.

"In all honesty, my God, I just wanted to make sure I wasn't dreamin'. Something about her, besides the obvious. Even if I made a goddamn fool outta myself and she busted one bottle over my thick skull and threw the other one at me as I bolted out the door…"

And early the next morning, with Sally just a brief, pleasant diversion along his concrete life's path, he'd left his home in the northern Minnesota hills, aiming his old pickup truck at Boise to be at the birth of his second grandson, and stay for a month afterwards to help out. He never gave her a thought during the trip.

Out there, for the third time in a little over two years, unforeseen circumstances drafted Sam into emergency midwife duty, when his grandson decided being born at home in the middle of the night on the bathroom floor would make for a more memorable journey to Earth. The second delivery, the fall before, he was having drinks with friends in the muni one evening and the bar patrons heard ear-shattering screams coming from the ladies' restroom. The woman didn't even know she was pregnant. She thought the greasy bar pizza rolls were cramping her up and she went to use the restroom. Already famous, at least locally, for delivering the baby girl on his school bus two years before that, the crowd drafted Sam to perform the duties.

Sam wasn't supposed to be home from Boise until at least two weeks after the season's morel mushrooms had disintegrated into mush and melted into the forest floor. And then in Boise, *it* struck. He'd never seen it coming—a family fight with his estranged older brother about the Vietnam and Iraq wars. And the skeleton in Sam's closet had busted out. He'd left Boise, disgraced, in the middle of the night after wandering the town like an insane bum for two whole days and nights, maybe three. He couldn't remember. A physical and emotional train wreck.

"My god, thank you for guiding me home safely. I don't know how you did it; it was the worst attack ever. But no thanks, E God, for the PTSD or whatever it is, and no thanks again for what the neighbor did to me when I was a kid. And as long as we're talkin' about somebody getting screwed, go fuck yourself, E God. TWICE. The second time for the other stuff my therapist says we need to work on—the family crap."

Sam's canoe enters a faster stretch of water with a few boulders lurking just below the surface. He has to pay attention to the river and use his paddle as a rudder, steering around the obstacles. With only 100 feet or so left of the riffle, and on a good course, he rests his paddle across the gunwales in front of him, grabs his bottle and takes a swig.

As he twists the cap back on, he continues, "Sleeping with Sally was never the point! Being her friend was first and foremost. Now I wish we hadn't gone there last night. It's like the memory of being with her is more punishment for breakin' my own damn rules and gettin' involved with a married woman…again.

"Yup, I admit I really did it this time—a real SIDAS WAPBO, a Self-Inflicted DumbAss Situation With A Predictable Bad Outcome. I should get that tattooed on my forehead backward, from temple to temple in big gaudy colors, so every time I look at myself in the mirror, I'm reminded to keep my own rules."

The hairs on the back of his neck stand up and tickle him. It's that special fluttery feeling he gives his god credit for. Again, he glances around self-consciously, hoping nobody heard him, even though he's in the middle of nowhere and alone on the river.

"My god, please, how am I gonna get her outta my mind?"

Sam closes his eyes and sighs deeply, as if she were still lying next to him and he could feel her breathing, when actually he should be paying attention to where his canoe is heading. He even forgets for a moment that Deja is with him. That is, until he feels the canoe listing to the side.

His eyes blink open just in time to see Deja up front out of reach, balancing all four feet on the right gunwale, gazing intently out over the river, poised like an Olympic swimmer waiting for the starting horn.

"No! Deja, NO!! Come here!"

His puppy tilts her head at him, ears alert and tongue out, and Sam is hopeful for half a second that she's going to fall backward onto the canoe seat. But the front of the boat clunks into a submerged rock, she loses her balance, and SPLOOSH!

Deja falls chest first into the rushing stream. Suddenly she's splashing spastically, standing on her hind legs.

The irony completely escapes Sam that his question about how to forget Sally only took three seconds to get answered.

"It's okay, girl. You know how to swim." He pats the water with his injured hand, forgetting he's not supposed to let it get wet.

Leaning to the side turns the canoe a few degrees and allows the current to catch the upstream side and send it swiftly swinging around, the front still firmly lodged on the rock. Sam realizes suddenly that Deja's right in the boat's path. He instantly drops to the canoe floor on both knees, his left shin crying out in excruciating pain. He's got a mere two heartbeats to snatch her out of harm's way.

Deja is still splashing frantically. When she's just within reach, Sam manages to slip two fingers under her collar and slide his other hand under her belly. Legs churning, she gouges his left wrist with the razor-sharp claws of her hind feet.

He lifts his dripping puppy over the gunwale and holds her close to his chest, disregarding the ill-advised soaking he's receiving.

"It's okay girl," he whispers to his wiggling puppy, who seems to be trying to escape his embrace. He kisses her on top of the head. "Whew. That was too damn close…"

He lifts her over the thwart and sets her down on all four feet. Like any dog does, Deja shakes violently.

"Go ahead, girl. I can't get any wetter."

Deja seems to have recovered from the experience already and hurries to duck under the next thwart, headed for her station, a boat cushion, near the front seat. Sam directs his attention to the scratches on his wrist, three narrow streaks turning red with blood.

He has to use both hands on the gunwales to help get off his knees. The bandages on his left leg are soaked and bleeding through again. Three of his four limbs are screaming at him. He squeezes his eyes shut and is grateful the canoe is still handily stuck on the rock for now while he gathers himself.

Then the canoe lists like it had a minute ago. His eyes fly open, and there's his puppy, ears erect, eyes fixed out over the river, all four feet on the gunwale.

"No! Deja, no!"

"WOOF!"

SPLOOSH.

"Sam Ryan, you're busted!" Maureen shouts from the bridge rail as he steers the canoe around the last bend.

Deja, who'd been curled up sleeping on a boat cushion, stands, stretches, and yawns, letting out a little puppy sigh. Her tail wags slowly at the sound of a friendly voice.

"I knew you'd do this…" Maureen shakes her head and wags a finger. "And you're soaked! What the hell?"

"Just needed to get out of the house," he offers innocently as he nudges the canoe into a slot next to the bridge pilings. He shrugs sheepishly as he pulls his soaked t-shirt loose from his chest.

Maureen sidesteps off the roadbed down the steep ditch bank into the little parking area. Deja scrambles out onto the ground and sidles up to Maureen.

"Just hang on," she orders sternly as she bends to jostle Deja's ears. "Lemme hold the canoe so you can walk up to the front and stay outta the water. Not that you could get that leg and your hand any wetter…"

"Turns out Deja wants to be an Olympic diver! Strangest thing—it was like she was trying to catch something in mid-air. She did that at least 10 times between the riffle just below the rice bed and the double horseshoe bend. And shook off all over me every time I lifted her back into the canoe. Wouldn't ya think at 11 weeks old she'd mind better?" He flashes a grin.

Maureen sucks in a loud, exasperated breath as she steadies the canoe by leaning most of her weight on it. "And wouldn't ya think at 53 years old, *you'd* mind better?"

Shaking her head again, she admits, "Just had to check. I knew you'd do somethin' goofy after…yesterday. Drove back to your place 20 minutes after I left there. Drove up to the dam, and wasn't surprised one bit to see you were parked there. Come on, let's go get your truck, then we'll disinfect and redress your leg and get that hand soakin'. This time I'm not leavin' your house 'til it's been 20 minutes in the solution. Could use about 20 minutes of wild grape wine with my neighbor anyhow."

She offers Sam her arm as he gingerly steps out onto the bank.

"You're the best, Maureen, you really are. If only things were different," he teases her, like he often does. "I'm sure Joan could find somebody else if you and I… you know…ran off!"

"If you were the *type* to be on my radar, I'm sure you'd be adequate with the love and honor part. But you'd need some serious work when it comes to the *obey* business!"

CHAPTER 2

BIGGER FISH TO FRY

Sam tells his therapist, Laura, about helping to save Dakota's life—what he can remember of it. He confesses about sleeping with Sally.

She looks directly into his eyes for a clue about his mental state. "So, Sam, what does it feel like?"

"Like shit," Sam growls. "This hand. My leg. I got what I deserved. But if you're askin' about the other stuff, I've slept in my own bed every night since. But against Maureen's advice, I did canoe the river the morning after. Had one of my patented talks with God. I'm not angry. Actually, believe it or not, I'm glad the deal with Sally is over. The drama, the uncertainty, having that fuckin' Bill pullin' the strings of my life. Who needs any of that crap?"

"Your old pattern," Laura reminds him. "I think you are making some progress with that. This final breakup with Sally could have been a classic trigger and sent you to the edge. Any idea why that didn't happen this time?"

"You're gonna think I'm nuts."

"Try me."

"It's little Sammy inside me. He reminds me we got bigger fish to fry, like that fucker Sparky! Let's make him sizzle like droppin' a battered crappie in hot oil! The little guy's actually growin' on me. And he's become way stronger and feistier than I thought he could ever be. I hope that rubs off on me."

Sam shakes his head, looking puzzled. "Man…have I gone off the deep end? It's probably okay to do that here in my shrink's office, but I find myself talkin' to 'im at least 10 times a day lately! Even askin' for the little guy's advice…out loud!"

Laura smiles. "It was my idea, remember? Sometimes it can help to find the real truth by stepping back, getting outside our normal reality. What else has Sammy said to you lately?"

"Well, he vowed that from this day forward he's not gonna be the little abused kid who's afraid to tell someone about stuff that happened. Does that make any sense? Gosh, it's almost like Sammy…like he…really isn't me."

"Oh, he's you alright. It's just taken you a while to remember that. So you are thinking about actually confronting Sparky?"

"Just started thinkin' about it right now. I've never been one to seek revenge. That's what this feels like. Terrible anger, like I got an angel perched on one shoulder whisperin' in that ear, and Sammy on the other one. I've been angry enough this life already. What if Sparky's got a great life now? He sure doesn't need me waltzin' in and diggin' up the past. Maybe I was the only one he did that to. At this point, does he deserve havin' it waved in his face?"

"Confronting him is not revenge," Laura corrects. "It's simply taking back what was stolen from you. It's also possible he wants a chance to be forgiven. But don't count on that. It's not up to you to filter his personal outcome. I'm not saying you must confront Sparky in order to heal. But *not* confronting Sparky out of your consideration for him once again makes you his victim, the keeper of his dirty secrets."

"But isn't confronting him like saying, *You won. You fucked up my life*?" Sam throws his arms wide.

"You needn't be judge and jury to sort out how this might affect Sparky. You're simply a witness telling your side of the story."

"I'll take that under advisement."

"And Sam, if you do decide to go see Sparky, let's talk beforehand about how it might go and what to expect."

"Yup," Sam agrees. "I want my head screwed on a little straighter about a lotta things before I go there. Week after next? Same day, same time?"

Laura checks her calendar. "Would it be okay if I penciled you in every Wednesday for a while? You can always cancel if something comes up."

"I think I need a week off. I'll be alright—don't worry."

"Yup, we've covered a lot in a month. The week after next, okay?"

Sam pauses at the door and turns to Laura. "One more thing. What about Pop? We've become so close. He's the person I chose to tell about Sparky. He'll wonder what happened. I don't want 'im to think I took that wonderful gift of his team of horses and just ran off with 'em."

He squeezes his temples as if to hold off a difficult emotional response.

"Why don't you visit Pop at the hospital during the day. I'm guessing he misses the hell out of you."

Maureen calls Sam that night and tells him that when Pop is eventually discharged from the hospital, Sally will be taking a leave of absence from her job to care for him. Maureen assures Sam that Pop isn't cutting him loose either.

"You know," Maureen says, "It means more than the world to Pop that you let him give you the team. He's been worried sick since his stroke they'd end up in the wrong hands. You know who I'm talking about, Bill and Robert. He loves you like a son, Sam."

On the other end of the line, Sam bites his lip and can't find any words.

Maureen continues, "He said he wishes there'd been more he could give you. He said, 'Two outta three of who I love more than anything, if that's the way it has to be.'"

"That's the way it has to be," he agrees softly.

"Pop wants to talk to you at least twice a week, to ask how Elvis and Roy are doing. About the grape crop. If you helped deliver any more babies." She chuckles. "It's all set then—Pop said he'll do the dialin'."

On the Fourth of July, there's a bull ride event, with the women barrel racing at halftime. Sam is certain that Sally will be competing to defend her title.

He'd planned to have a few drinks with friends that night, and listen to a band at the Eagles Club. Instead, he drives past the club toward the rodeo grounds, pulls into the parking area, and buys a ticket. But he vows to stay out of sight. He just wants to see how Sally's doing and whether her mare, Dakota, is back to her old form.

Somehow he expects he'll be able to tell from a distance how sad and sorry she is for dumping him and deciding to stay with her snake of a husband. And then he'll slip away, smug and satisfied.

The first round of bulls is almost over by the time Sam makes his way into the rodeo grounds. Sure enough, from the pavilion where he buys a beer, he can see Sally across the way exercising Dakota behind the bull pens. Her form is unmistakable, her straight posture in the saddle, the way she holds the reins, her concentration, her perfect figure.

She's wearing the same clothes Sam had helped her pick out for the other rodeo, the first one he'd attended. The one where he'd fallen for her…hard. He wonders if her outfit is a coincidence. More than likely, it's about being superstitious.

He takes a deep breath. He's decided he's going to say hello, maybe ask her how Pop's doing after his stroke that had come on the day Bill had tried to kill Dakota. Although he knows, because he talks to Pop all the time. Maybe he should just wish her good luck. Both bad excuses. For sure, he'll be friendly toward her, like she's just another cowgirl whose acquaintance he's made. He begins thinking *To hell with it*, but then reasons he might as well get this first time over with.

He takes a step, and Sally suddenly turns her head and stares intently toward the parking lot. Still anonymous within the crowd, Sam can see her face light up. He imagines that wide smile, the perfect teeth, those dancing blue eyes.

A cowboy walks over to her. He wears a black hat that's too big—low on his forehead with his ears tucked under it. It looks brand new, the kind with the front smashed in like the outlaws wear in movies. His black Western shirt with mother of pearl snaps and buttons is freshly starched. His jeans are fashionably too long, wrinkled over his boots in the front, hanging over his heels to the ground in the back.

When he holds a beer out to Sally, Dakota shies and grunts. The cowboy jumps back. From six feet away, he speaks softly to the agitated mare while opening the beer. Sally pats and assures her horse everything's alright. She leans down to kiss the cowboy. Dakota is having none of it and jumps sideways. Sally dismounts. The man takes his hat off to accept a kiss.

No wonder the cowboy's hat was down over his ears. It's Bill the Pinhead.

He gives Sally a very public butt squeeze. She laughs and doesn't make him remove his hand. He gives her a second squeeze.

Sam slips away from the glare of the arena lights, making sure they won't see him. He scolds himself for wasting $22 to impose upon himself another SIDAS WAPBO. By the time he reaches the other end of the grounds, the tractor has finished dragging the arena, and the barrel setters are taking their places. From the shadows between the bleachers, he peers through the dark into the arena. Down below him, Bill leans against the fence near the third barrel, one boot resting on the bottom rail, his hat cocked back and to the side a little, like he owns the joint.

Sam turns and heads for the exit.

But right then, the announcer hollers Sally's name and hometown. She had drawn the first position. Sam hurries back to the shadows to watch.

The crowd roars to life as Sally and Dakota fly out from the alley to Hank Jr.'s "Born to Boogie". There's a collective sigh as they turn the first barrel so tight they bump it, but thankfully it doesn't tip over. The second barrel is clean and very quick. Up and down his spine, Sam can't help but feel the thrill of another great ride. At the rate Sally and Dakota are running, he knows they are going to set the bar pretty high for the other riders.

Maybe the crowd doesn't notice, but shortly after the second barrel, Sam sees that Dakota isn't on course to turn the third barrel as directly as she should be. Sally pulls hard to direct Dakota back on line. But the mare is running right at Bill—head down, mouth open, ears back. Sally sits back and pulls Dakota up, with Bill barely out of range of the mare's flailing hooves. She grabs onto the saddle horn with one hand, to keep from falling off. Bill is stuck in his tracks. The crowd goes eerily quiet.

Sally yells at her mare, "Stop it! STOP IT!"

She regains control, spins Dakota into three pivots on her hind legs, then makes the mare back up a good 20 feet, to show Dakota who's boss. The horse shakes her head the whole way, her mane tossing. They lope toward the third barrel. Dakota shakes her head furiously in Bill's direction and runs into the barrel with her chest. Sally lopes her horse out of the arena and down the alley into the half-light.

Bill walks shakily a few yards into the arena and waves his hat to the crowd like a rodeo clown. The crowd roars their approval, not realizing that he isn't some fearless stud cowboy, but instead just a runty coward who beats his wife and who'd been frozen in fear for his life. And who'd just shit his brand-new cowboy pants.

CHAPTER 3

TO THE RABBIT!

On the Saturday morning of Fourth of July weekend, Sam's son, Matt, and his girlfriend, Marsha, arrive at his dad's place. Two things are new on the farm since their last visit: the team of horses and little Lab puppy, Deja.

Marsha isn't feeling well. When she excuses herself and disappears into the bathroom, Matt hustles Sam outside.

"Dad," Matt whispers excitedly. "We were with Marsha's folks last night, at a cabin over on Leech Lake, with her brother and sister and a few other folks." He smiles and rubs his hands together. "I talked to her father. Invited them over for a picnic and campfire this evening. Hope that's okay. But Marsha doesn't know they're coming."

Sam replies, "Of course, son! That's fine. Ever since you and Marsha and your friends camped up here last summer, and you two crawled outta the same tent the next mornin', I've been wondering if I'd get to meet her family."

Matt rolls his eyes and whispers, "Here's the plan. The horses and wagon, that'll be perfect…"

The three of them and Deja drive the team to the campfire for what is purported to be their own little picnic. The fire ring had been built by Sam and Matt during Sam's first summer on the place six years before. It sits in a beautiful niche within Sam's high woods, between three giant white pines, overlooking the distant river valley.

Sam and Sally had brought Pop to these woods to pick yellow morel mushrooms two weeks after they'd officially "met" at the gravel pit. Pop had fallen in love with the place. It was there, right on the spot, sipping Sam's wild grape wine, that Pop had given Sam his team of Percherons. He'd told Sam that all he wanted out of the deal was to be able to come up and drive them once in a while, and for Sam to deliver him to his final resting place in his wagon pulled by the team. Pop had also imagined, once the winery was up and running, Sam giving folks rides in the wagon, from the winery to this very spot.

They unload the cooler and the picnic supplies from the wagon. Matt builds the fire. Sam opens the wine. He gives Marsha a sharp knife and points her toward the hazel brush patch to cut some sticks for roasting sausages.

"What's the deal with the jack pine, Dad?" Matt asks.

"You don't wanna know, son."

"Does it have something to do with the new axe handle?"

Sam sighs heavily. "Let's just say you were right about Sally. I hate to say it, but I feel a little used. It's over, but it's okay. We're both okay with it."

"That's too bad, Dad. Well, hey—you got yourself a strawberry blonde with brown eyes to sleep with instead." Deja's curled up by the fire.

Marsha finishes whittling the roasting sticks to sharp points. Sam checks his watch.

On cue, he says, "Oh shit, I need to make a phone call about a summer bus trip. Be right back…"

Matt winks at his dad as Sam climbs aboard the wagon, and clucks the team into a walk.

Marsha's family has just pulled into the yard. Introductions are made all around. Marsha's parents, Gary and Amy, are about 10 years younger than Sam. Her little brother and sister are twins, about 13 years old, and they each have a friend along. They all run off toward the golf cart and jostle over the driver's seat.

A second car pulls in as they're loading chairs, coolers, and boxes into the wagon. It's Marsha's mom's sister, Carolyn, and her two kids, a boy and a girl about the ages of the others. When Sam sticks out a hand in greeting, Carolyn grabs it with both of hers. He wonders if she isn't trying to display her lack of a wedding ring. She's kinda pretty, in an aging-bombshell sorta way.

They load Carolyn's chairs and picnic goodies into the wagon. The top slides off one of Gary's coolers, revealing two bottles of champagne and a bottle of sparkling grape juice, all on ice.

"What's goin' on?" Sam whispers to Gary.

"Oh, I dunno," Gary lies. "Heard so much about you from the kids. Just glad to finally meet you! Hey, we're on vacation, right?"

It's decided that the twin girl and her friend, along with Carolyn's daughter, will have first dibs on the golf cart and the boys will drive it back after the picnic. The caravan heads back to the fire pit site.

Marsha hears the wagon and crowd coming up the hill before they come into view. She and Matt hurry halfway down the hill to greet the entourage. They climb up onto the wagon.

"Hey, everybody! Wow. Matt, what's this all about? Why didn't you tell me?"

They all unload from the wagon and the golf cart near the wood pile.

Amy's next to ask, "Yeah, what's this all about?"

"I'm wonderin', too," Sam adds.

"Just a nice picnic at my dad's place! Glad you could all make it." Matt grins.

Gary's already lining up the bottles of champagne and the sparkling grape juice. "Give me a hand, will you Matt and Sam? Ma, please put the glasses together."

Plastic corks pop into the air. Carolyn helps Amy attach the bases to the tops of the plastic champagne glasses. Matt does the honors, pouring for the adults. Gary pours sparkling grape juice for the kids.

"Ahem!" Matt climbs atop the wagon to get everyone's attention. "They say you have a love like I have for this woman only once in a lifetime." Matt holds his glass aloft, smiling down at Marsha. "Or in my dad's case, two times…and in Aunt Carolyn's case, three times!"

Everybody laughs except Carolyn's daughter, who asks innocently, "Mom, I thought it was four times?"

"No, honey," Carolyn whispers. "Just because he stayed overnight doesn't mean we're in love!"

"That's a little more information than we need, Aunt Carolyn," Matt teases. "Please let me continue."

He climbs down and kneels in front of Marsha. Everyone gasps.

"Gary," Matt says seriously, "first of all, thank you for givin' me your permission."

"Thank you for asking," Gary replies, as he dabs at his eyes with his hanky.

Matt sets his champagne down on a rock chair. He fishes a ring wrapped in a purple velvet cloth from his pocket and holds it with a slightly shaky hand up to Marsha.

"Marsha, my love, will you…"

"Yes! Yes! Yes!" Marsha cries.

"…marry me?"

Her hand trembles as Matt slips the ring onto her finger.

There's hooting and cheering. Sam makes himself heard over the crowd. "This calls for a toast!" He holds his glass aloft. "To my wonderful daughter-in-law-to-be, Marsha, and my incredible son, Matt!"

Everyone holds their glasses up, "Here! Here!"

"Wait a minute," Marsha says.

The crowd goes silent and still. She walks to the line of adults and pours a little of her champagne into each of their glasses until hers is empty, then pours herself some sparkling grape juice.

"Whatcha doin', honey?" Matt asks.

Marsha raises her glass and finishes the toast. "…and to the rabbit!"

"Huh? What rabbit?" Matt asks.

"The one that died!"

The little kids haven't a clue what that means. But the old folks quickly cheer and drink up. Hugs and back pats and high fives ensue. Tears of joy stream down faces.

"If you hadn't asked me pretty quick," Marsha laughs, "I would have asked you!"

They do the math. It will be a March baby.

"Here are your instructions, son," Sam orders. "Now that you got it workin', you don't quit until you get me at least one baby boy to carry on the family name, or I'll do that deed myself!"

Carolyn's face immediately lights up. "I'll help you, Sam!"

Sam laughs. "So what would that make our kid, Carolyn, to the rest of these people? Uncle-in-law? Brother/cousin? We'd have to go on Dr. Phil and have him figure it out!"

"Come on, sweetie!" Carolyn grabs Sam's arm and directs him to the woods. "We got nine months to figure that shit out!"

They party around the fire until after dark. The kids run the golf cart until its batteries go dead. They never do figure out all the possible familial relationships a product of Sam and Carolyn would have to those attending that night.

Back at the house, after everyone else has gone and Marsha's asleep on the couch, Sam and Matt lean on the rail fence near the horse waterer.

"Dad, I'm inviting Grandpa to the wedding. He and I talk once in a while."

"That's fine," Sam answers.

"Grandpa asked me (of all people) if I thought you'd give him another chance."

They both stare straight ahead, into the dark pasture. "I know about some of the stuff that happened when you were younger. He told me, and said he hopes to make it right if he can. And Grandpa says he's pretty sure you've forgiven him, because of the letters you write, keeping in touch even after he disowned you. He says he wants to ask for your forgiveness."

"Where the hell did that come from?" Sam asks. "He's never admitted to being wrong, or apologized for anything in his life."

Matt smiles. "Said he had a dream (pretty sure it wasn't a stroke or anything) and wondered at first if he'd died in his sleep. Grandpa swears an angel told him it's time to quit being judge, jury, and executioner. And the angel assured him it would be alright. And when he suddenly awoke and bolted upright, the bedroom curtains were fluttering, even though the night was completely still."

"Hmph! My dad…divine intervention. Always figured that's what it would take!"

"Dad, remember you and I had the same kinda talk, right after Karen died," Matt reminds his father quietly. "That meant the world to me, that you cared enough to ask my forgiveness, and that you'd accept mine. It's a two-way street, you know. And it works, if you let it."

Since the rodeo two weeks before, Sam had finished fixing the fence around the 23-acre pasture for Elvis and Roy. Pop had bought the lumber and the hardware for the two stalls, which Sam lined with inch-and-a-half-thick pine tongue and groove. Sam put the sliding doors together himself. They talked about getting Pop up here to see Sam's handiwork and so he could drive the team again for old time's sake. Pop lamented that he wasn't bouncing back from this last stroke like he'd hoped, so he'd stick pretty close to home for a while longer.

Sam went to sweep out the wagon one day and ended up sanding all the metal on the wagon and painting those parts shiny black, including the wheel rims. The wood of the box was restored to its original two-tone affair, freshly painted dark green with dark brown highlights. He cleaned the tires with Armor All, inside and out. The wagon certainly was handsome. Once again, it was suitable for parades and other special events, like his son's wedding.

Deja was his constant shadow. Lord knows there's no end to the things a puppy finds fascinating and irresistible on a farm, especially Sam's tools, brushes, and sandpaper when he was working on the wagon. Also, his slippers and shoes, the telephone cord, any clothes lying around, and the garbage. She became the light of his life, a source of constant company and amusement.

Deja gathered a collection of toys and other interesting objects, pieces of wood and bark, old tin cans, little chunks of concrete, and a dead baby robin, all of which she placed on the front stoop, handy for when Sam let her out. Sam wished he'd seen the little pup tear the pages out of the old Sears catalog from the outhouse, and spread those pages on the porch quite neatly in three rows about six inches apart.

Most evenings, they went to the bridge and played in the water. Sam always laughed when she'd play stand-off with Elvis and Roy—crouching, barking, growling—only to run and hide between Sam's legs and whimper when either of the giants would lower its head to sniff her.

Sally doesn't let Pop out of her sight during his waking hours. When he naps, sometimes she goes outside to visit the horses. The last race she'd been to was two weeks ago, on the Fourth of July.

Bill's brother, Robert, had been puttering around quite a bit recently, cleaning up after the four-wheeling campers and poking around the farm buildings. He never once checks in to see how Pop is doing. A couple of times Sally had seen Robert in the barn, as if he was looking for something.

Quite the opposite of his scrawny older brother Bill, Robert is stocky, with a prominent brow remindful of caveman drawings. He did terribly in school and never did graduate. The only work he seems capable of is that which doesn't take much thought. He had been married briefly once, to a woman of similar mental and social capacity. She'd accused him of molesting her two grade school-age daughters. Since then, he'd gone back to lurking alone around the perimeter of life like a stray mongrel dog.

His leers at Sally, usually directed below her neck, give her the creeps. She wonders sometimes, when she's home alone at night or when Pop is sleeping, if Robert is outside her house. Sheba, Sally's chocolate Lab, must wonder the same thing. At those times, she growls toward the windows the same way she growls at Robert in broad daylight.

Pop is napping in mid-afternoon, so Sally heads to the barn. She isn't feeling well and needs some air. She wonders what Robert had been looking for. There doesn't seem to be anything out of place.

As usual, Robert's damn cats are all over hell. They aren't Sally's problem though. She dislikes cats in general, and really hates this litter, which was bought in by Robert and Bill to keep the mouse population down. The only grain on the farm now is for the horses, and Sally keeps it tightly sealed in a metal bin so the damn cats don't try to use it as a litter box. The felines are messy and smelly, in terrible health, and regularly dying off where Sheba can find them and drag their rotting carcasses up to the house.

One particular kitten is off by itself in the last stanchion, across the alley from the horse stalls. It's rolling and playing with something in its paws. The object is white and cylindrical, about four inches long. Sally walks over and the kitten hisses and runs off, leaving behind its toy. A cattle syringe.

It isn't unusual to have a cat playing with a cattle syringe. Bill and Robert left them lying all over while the cattle were still on the place. They had always removed the needles though, ever since Bill had stepped on one and it went through his boot and gave him a nasty foot infection.

At first glance, the kitten's syringe appears also needle-less. Sally isn't sure why, but she's compelled to examine it closer. The screw-on metal collar is still on the plastic tip of the plunger. The needle is busted off just below the metal collar, a jagged remnant.

Sally grows faint, the memory washing over her in a hot wave. The day Bill couldn't lead Dakota out of the stall because the horse had been rearing and hollering. That night when Dakota was dying, and Sam had found the big needle in her flank.

Sally had been holding out for the faintest hope that there was another explanation. She kneels in the stanchion and vomits. The sickly cats quickly gather to fight over her lunch.

Somehow, after making it across the yard, into the house, and down the hall to her bedroom, Sally absently stumbles into the end table. The lamp's glass base smashes onto the floor. Sheba comes running and barking from Pop's room.

Pop wakes with a start. "Sally! What's goin' on?"

She sucks in a big breath. "Nothin', Pop. Just dustin' in here, knocked the darn lamp over. Sorry for wakin' you."

She lies down on the bed, still faint, pale, and sweating.

Pop, pushing his walker, appears in the doorway with messy hair and rumpled clothing. He sees the syringe and broken needle lying in the bed next to Sally.

"Oh my God! Where'd you find that?"

She points out the window toward the barn. "A kitten was playing with it."

"Son of a bitch! I'm so sorry, Sally…"

Tears run down her cheeks.

Bill calls at suppertime to inform Sally he won't be home from Grand Forks until late that night. He's slurring his words. Robert comes and goes, after wandering around in the barn for several minutes. Sally assumes he's headed over to the campground, once again without even bothering to check in on Pop.

That evening, the mood is as if someone has died. Pop doesn't try to fix it. He knows he shouldn't, although he could if he wanted to. One phone call to his banker and he could send Sally and the horses far away, set them up with a new life.

They sip wine and play cribbage until it's time for Pop to take his pills before bed. Sally kisses him goodnight on the forehead.

"I love you, little lady," Pop whispers. "Thanks for everything."

"I love you, too, Pop." She kisses him again.

Faithful watchdog Sheba assumes her post at the foot of Pop's bed. Sally turns off his lamp, then wanders slowly throughout the house, turning off the rest of the lights, except for the nightlight in the hallway. She undresses, puts on her nightshirt, and lies in bed on her back, staring into the darkness. She rolls onto her side to look out the open window. The barn spotlight is abuzz with insects. The usual loud music, revving engines, and shouting drift over from the nearby campground. Two barn cats are playing with a mouse they caught.

Despite the distractions, the tears fall again. The knot in her gut keeps tightening. She isn't angry. She isn't sad. She is afraid, though.

When Bill pulls in, it's after 1:00 a.m. She can see from the bedroom window that he's very drunk. He wobbles up the driveway, kicking a cat and sending it flying into the lilac bushes. Opens his fly and pisses from the edge of the sidewalk into the flower bed.

With every inch he staggers closer, Sally feels her panic build. She becomes light-headed again. Stumbling to the bathroom, she kneels over the toilet and wretches, but nothing comes out. She heaves again and again, her stomach tensing.

Suddenly she jumps, feeling Bill's clumsy, rough hand clamp her shoulder.

"Come on," he slurs. "Let's get to bed. Gotta present for ya…" He grabs himself crudely.

"No! Get off me. I don't feel good."

He grabs her nightshirt and yanks her roughly away from the toilet.

"If you want a kid so goddamn bad, you better get in there…"

Sally sobs, "I can't…I can't…"

Bill grabs his wife by the hair. She shrieks in pain. Sheba lunges from behind Bill and locks her jaws on his calf.

"Fuckin' goddamn dog! Get 'er off me!" He kicks Sheba in the throat with his other foot.

Sally begs her pup, "No, no girl! Go find Pop."

Sheba lets loose of his leg, but stands her ground, growling and showing her teeth.

Sally scrambles to her feet. "It's okay, girl…"

She leads an angry Sheba by the collar back to Pop's room. He has slept through the whole encounter. She kisses him and shuts the door behind her until it latches. She usually leaves the door open a crack so Sheba can come get her when Pop gets up in the middle of the night. But tonight, Sally knows she won't be sleeping anyway.

"Ya comin'?" Bill shouts.

He is lying on his back, wearing only a t-shirt. Sally nervously steps out of her panties and lies next to him, pulling her nightshirt up around her neck. He pushes next to her, smelling of stale booze, chewing tobacco, and body odor. He gropes her breasts with a clumsy, rough hand. Sally closes her eyes.

Bill slides his hand between her legs, but Sally clamps them tight.

"Jesus Christ! Aren't you glad to see me?"

She spreads her legs, trembling. He rolls onto her, one of his hands squeezing onto her breast for support. Sally winces at the pain. He slumps onto her, flaccid against her thigh.

"Hey!" Bill demands. "A little help here."

He grabs her hand and places it on his penis. She tries to make him hard, but he's too drunk.

"Come on, goddamnit!" Bill hollers.

Sally turns her head and begins crying. She lets go of him and curls into a defensive position.

"Come on! How we gonna get a baby if you can't even make me hard?"

Sally pushes him off and jumps from the bed, bolting toward the bedroom door. She fumbles with the doorknob. Bill catches her and spins her around violently, slapping her face hard enough that she'll have marks in the morning. He throws her back down on the bed.

Sheba begins barking and furiously scratching at Pop's bedroom door.

"It's Pop!" Sally cries.

Bill holds her by the wrists, a snarl on his face. "No, it ain't. Your goddamn dog just wants another piece o' me."

"No! No! I know that bark," she struggles to break free from his grasp. "Something's wrong with Pop!"

Sally frees one hand loose and shoves her drunken husband aside. Frantically, she again tries the doorknob. Chancing a quick look over her shoulder, she's relieved to see that Bill is lying still, muttering, and close to passing out.

Sheba's still barking furiously. Sally tries to open Pop's door, but there's something in the way, so she can only push it open about an inch. Sheba whines and paws even more frantically at the door from the other side. Sally switches on the overhead hall light. Through the crack in the doorway, she sees Pop's hand on the floor.

"Pop!"

She braces herself against the far wall, with her back against the door. With great effort, she pushes the door open a foot. Sally scrambles to her feet and shimmies sideways into his room.

Pop isn't moving. He isn't breathing. His eyes are open, pupils dilated. His skin is ashen and he is cold to the touch. Sheba whines and licks at Pop's face. Frantically, Sally begins CPR. She yells to Bill at the top of her lungs again and again, as she switches from breaths to chest compressions.

"Bill! Please! Call for help! Pop's dyin'…"

When Bill doesn't respond, she hollers and cries at the window and into the night for help from anyone. Sheba lunges angrily at Pop's window and growls.

Sally finally runs out of strength and collapses onto Pop's body. She stumbles to the living room and dials 911. Then she calls Maureen, sobbing over and over, mucous running from her mouth and tears streaming down her face, "Pop's gone…Pop's gone…I couldn't save him…"

The deputy sheriff and ambulance attendants assure Sally that she had done all she possibly could have. But their words are no consolation. Bill is still passed out in their bedroom. Sally asks the rescue personnel to lift Pop back onto his bed. There won't be any need to take him to the hospital.

Maureen and her partner, Joan, with Sam following behind, arrive just as the sun is rising. All three of them rush into the house. The deputy is still there. Sally has dressed, but her face is a mess of grief and bruises. She sits at the dining room table, sobbing. When Sam sees the marks, his blood boils.

"Where's that fuckin' goddamn asshole?"

"What?" Sally lifts her head, confused.

"Bill?"

The deputy points down the hall, not realizing what is about to transpire.

"No! Sam!" Sally yells, standing suddenly as he stalks down the hallway. "Somebody stop him!"

But Sam has already entered the bedroom, grabbed Bill by the undershirt and set him up, cocking a fist. The deputy grabs Sam and gets him into a hold from behind. Bill flops lifelessly back onto the bed, then slowly comes to. He runs his hand through his hair, and raises himself to a slumped-over sitting position.

"What? Who are…What are you…doing here? What's happening…?"

The deputy whispers sternly to Sam, "Not here. Not now."

Then he orders Bill, "Put your pants on. Your father is dead."

"Oh." Bill simply blinks as he runs his hand through his greasy hair again.

Joan hurries down the hall. "Jesus. Take him in! Test him. He was drunk when he got home! So goddamn drunk, Sally yelling from the next room couldn't stir him."

"I was not. Mind your own fuckin' business, dyke. I work hard. I sleep hard."

"Sally," Joan implores, "Tell the deputy what happened to your face, what kinda condition he was in last night."

"I…I did it getting Pop's door open. I was asleep when Bill got home. I don't know…"

Everyone in the house knows she's lying. But nobody knows why.

Maureen vows, "I'm not leavin' this house without you."

CHAPTER 4

HIS NAME WAS SAMUEL

Sam learns of the funeral arrangements from Maureen.

It's a little over 20 miles from Sam's house to Streeter, where the funeral home and church are. Sam has to ask Pop's old veterinarian, Johnny, how long it will take to drive Elvis and Roy down there. The vet says about three miles an hour. Johnny offers to haul Elvis and Roy. Mack, from the dealership, offers to haul the wagon to town on a flatbed. Sam takes them up on the offers, agreeing that after three years in the pasture and only a couple of short jaunts around his place, the older horses probably aren't fit for a round trip of over 40 miles in one hot summer day.

Sam spends Tuesday readying Elvis and Roy. He bathes and curries them, removing the tangles and burrs from their manes, tails, and fetlocks. He buys polish for the rigging and makes the silver shine. He gets Pop's farrier on short notice—a trim and new shoes for both boys. The farrier won't accept any payment. Sam will coat their hooves with hoof oil just before they go into the trailer Wednesday morning.

The visitation is Tuesday evening at the Streeter Funeral Home. It's hot and muggy, as late July can be in Minnesota—like a sauna, with insects. The doors to the funeral home are propped open. Fans hum from every corner.

Sam doesn't recognize anyone when he walks in. But a group of four men who are off in a side room eye him suspiciously. He signs the guest register and takes a folder. Sam had never known Pop's real name. It was Samuel. A lump forms in the back of Sam's throat.

Bill and Robert visit people among the chairs. Maureen and Sally do the same with folks near Pop's casket, which is surrounded by at least a dozen flower arrangements. Sam stands uncomfortably at the back of the room, not sure of his place in all this. Robert sees Sam and nudges his brother. They immediately walk over, with some men from the side room in tow.

Sam says, "I'm so sorry about your dad."

"Yeah, I'll just bet," Bill snarls. "After you drop Pop off at the cemetery, you're gonna drive the team to the farm."

Robert pipes in, "Yeah, you got no right…"

Sally interrupts, "Come on, Sam." She takes his arm and escorts him over to Pop. When Sam bows his head and covers his eyes, they cry together, arms around each other's waists in comfort. Maureen and Joan join them, one on each side.

Bill approaches the four, jaw set and eyes narrowed, as if he's going to take a swing at someone. Johnny and Mack step between the four mourners and Bill, drawing the attention of everyone in the funeral parlor. Robert and the other men in the back are pacing, their fists clenched, like they're itching for a fight. The town folk and relatives, who know Pop's boys well, aren't surprised at their behavior. Many simply shake their heads and drop their eyes in embarrassment.

Wednesday promises to be hotter and muggier than Tuesday. Even at 7:00 in the morning, when Johnny arrives with his horse trailer, and the dealership hands pull in with their flatbed, the men are soon dripping with sweat.

"Are the boys gonna be okay in this heat?" Sam asks the vet.

"I got a feeling," the vet offers, "the sky's gonna open up this afternoon, and they'll be fine."

Sam drives the team from the dealership at the edge of town, down Main Street four blocks, then another two blocks south to the funeral parlor. Folks step outside of stores, offices, and cafés to gaze at the handsome team and refurbished wagon. Some call Sam by name, complimenting him on his work. He doesn't know any of them. Expressionless, he nods his appreciation.

Sam wears all black, a long-sleeved Western shirt, jeans, and a well-worn Western hat. The hat had been Pop's. Sally had asked him to wear it. By the time Sam and the team reach the funeral parlor, he has sweated through his shirt. Streams of sweat also run down his face and neck.

Johnny is waiting at the funeral parlor. He places two five-gallon buckets of water on the pavement for Elvis and Roy. He tells Sam that he'll have his son, Mike, water them at church as well, watch the team during the service and give them oats, and clean up after them. Those are all details Sam had overlooked. He thanks the vet.

"Shit. I hadn't even thought about water for myself."

"Got that covered, too," Johnny assures Sam, tossing him a water bottle.

The men who'd been with Bill and Robert the night before are cousins, and serve as four of the pall bearers. The other two are Johnny and Mack.

A heavy, pungent odor of stale booze emanates from the cousins, as the six men lift the casket off the dolly and into the wagon bed. Bill is obviously hungover. He has bed hair, and clearly hadn't showered. He hovers close to Sally at the funeral home, like a junkyard dog by his dish.

Sam's surprised to see Sheba outside the funeral home.

"How sweet. She beat us here," Sally says, with the only hint of that incredible smile that Sam will see this day. Once the casket is loaded, Sheba leaps up onto the wooden seat beside Sam. The dog sits quietly and looks straight ahead, panting in the heat.

During the two-block procession to the church, Sally, Maureen, and Joan choose to walk behind, as do Johnny and Mack. Bill, Robert, and the cousins jam into two four-wheel-drive pickups with huge tires and mud all over them. They quickly detour around the cortege, passing so close to the team of horses that Elvis and Roy shy momentarily. Bill, Robert, and the cousins toss empty beer cans into the back of the trucks when the cortege arrives at the church.

The mourners trickle in. Sam stands beside the wagon. Johnny's son, Mike, stands in front of the church. Sam recognizes him as the young guy who had been directing traffic at the rodeo. Everyone admires the team and wagon. Sam learns that Roy and Elvis are Pop's third team. There are stories about parades and pulling contests. And about the time Pop drove a team for Johnny's dad's funeral.

Sally isn't feeling well, and rests on a bench outside the church with Maureen. Sam approaches, a questioning, empathetic frown creasing his face.

"I think I could use a little help from you two," Sally says. "Just to get me through this."

"Done," Sam responds.

He walks away, to stand under a sprawling white oak, Pop's hat in his hands. When he returns a few minutes later, Sally's up and greeting mourners. She looks as fine as any daughter-in-law who'd lost someone like Pop could possibly look.

When the cortege leaves the church, it is 11:00 a.m. and already pushing 90 degrees. The American Legion drum corps taps out a slow, steady rhythm. With the horse-drawn wagon, it is reminiscent of a military funeral procession a century and a half before. The Legion Color Guard is stoic and proud, a mixture of men from several wars and generations. Only the same five walk behind the wagon, as they did to the church. The procession turns west onto Main Street. Folks again watch from the sidewalks. Hats are removed, children are shushed, salutes are given, and eyes are dabbed with tissues.

The Legion Auxiliary waits along the block just before the state highway, three blocks down Main. The color guard commander gives the order to halt. All those walking—the five mourners and the color guard—are given water.

Sally accepts a water bottle, but before she can get it to her lips, she suddenly buckles. Maureen and Joan catch her, then Johnny and Mack help her to a bench on the sidewalk. The auxiliary ladies hover nearby and fan her with their hats. Bill watches from the air-conditioned confines of his cousin's truck.

"Maybe you better ride?" a lady suggests, pointing to the funeral sedan behind the wagon.

Sally nods. Mack and Johnny begin leading her to the car. Sally shakes her head and points to the wagon. Pop's two old friends help her up onto the seat next to Sam. Sheba moves into the box right behind them, her head between them on the seat. Bill jumps from the pickup truck and runs past the sedan, toward the wagon.

"Just a minute!" He suddenly wants to ride along. He's carrying a partially drunken beer.

Sheba stands at the front corner of the box where Bill tries to climb on, growling, her fur standing on end.

"Come on, then," Sam invites, without looking at him. Bill takes a seat next to Sally.

"Get ridda the beer," Sam orders Bill quietly, again without looking at him.

Bill slams down the rest of the beer, then tosses the can over his shoulder into the box. It hits the casket, leaving a small nick in the finish. Droplets and foam run down the side of the casket. Everyone, including the color guard and drum corps, is watching. Sam pinches the bridge of his nose with his thumb and forefinger. As much as he'd like to get out of the wagon, grab Bill by the shirt, and throw the idiot to the pavement, he won't make a scene at Pop's funeral.

Sally motions to Sheba, who grabs the can in her mouth and jumps from the wagon. She finds a garbage can on the sidewalk, puts her feet up on the rim, and drops the can. She leaps back into the wagon, and sits stiffly on guard, directly between Bill and the casket. The cortege moves on.

Storm clouds are building in the west, the kind that are huge and high, with their tops sheared off by the jet stream, so they resemble an anvil. The kind of clouds that can spawn torrents of rain, lightning, hail, terrible winds, and even tornados. No thunder can be heard yet, so their fury is at least an hour away. Thankfully, it's only another 15-minute ride to the cemetery and the graveside service will be brief.

Halfway there, Bill, thirsty for another beer, jumps down from the moving wagon and returns to his cousin's pickup truck. He fishes one from a cooler in the back and slides into the front seat. Sally remains close to Sam.

The two cry softly as they ride along, but don't speak. Typically, this would be a moment for gentle touches—the back of a hand, an arm, a shoulder. But Sam's hands stay on the reins, Sally's folded in her lap.

Sam remains in the wagon during the graveside service. Sheba follows Sally and obediently stays by her side. The service ends with a gun salute. A kid from the high school plays "Taps" from a ways away, near the veterans memorial.

When it's over, Mike motions Sam to drive the team over to a pickup truck. Sam clucks the team into a walk.

His eyes find Sally in the crowd. She gives Sam a long look and mouths the words, "Thank you." Bill notices his wife gazing in Sam's direction and quickly hustles her away toward a funeral parlor sedan.

Mike approaches Sam and says, "Dad says we can haul the horses and wagon back to your place if you want."

"Thanks. But I'm okay."

"Dad made a map, marked farms where you can pull in if the storm gets bad."

Mike hands the map to Sam. Then he lifts the two five-gallon buckets half full of grain into the wagon box, plus a pail with a lid on it filled with water, for Elvis and Roy. Mike slides a small cooler onto the seat next to Sam.

"What's this?"

"Lunch. Somethin' to drink. From Sally. She knew you'd wanna drive the team home yourself."

The kid tosses Sam a plastic bag about the size of a cigar box. A rain poncho.

"I think you're gonna need this."

Sam reaches for his billfold.

"Nope," the kid says, holding his hands out.

"Tell your dad thanks. I'll be in touch."

The first distant roll of thunder echoes across the still, steamy countryside. It isn't quite noon. Sam slides the cooler open to find two sandwiches, four or five cookies, and eight cans of beer. Plus a note.

I have to do this myself. Thank you, sweet man...for everything. I'll never forget you. God bless you.

Sam chances a look back at the crowd leaving the gravesite. Sally ducks into the funeral car with Joan and Maureen. She doesn't look back at Sam, but Bill's staring right at him, smiling and nodding.

Sam checks the map, and takes a left on the county road. The horses' shod feet *click, click, click* in a slow, walking rhythm. The wagon rocks a little. Sam fishes a beer from the cooler and pops it open. He drinks the first one in two swigs, the second one in four. He lets them sink in for half an hour. When he pops open the third beer, lightning strikes out in front of him and the team less than a mile away. The leaden sky opens up like a dam bursting.

In the din of the downpour, Sam doesn't notice a vehicle approaching from behind. Suddenly one of the cousin's pickup trucks pulls alongside. The horses shy two steps toward the shoulder of the road. Bill rolls down the passenger window.

"Hey, old man!" he yells through the downpour. "You're headin' the wrong way! We come to get our horses and wagon."

The cousin gooses the engine, then slides the truck to a stop crossways in the road, blocking the wagon. In one slow, fluid motion, Sam sets the brake, reaches under the seat for a two-pound hammer, and steps down from the wagon seat. He stalks to the tailgate. The first swing of the hammer shatters the passenger-side taillight. He saunters forward. The second swing takes out the rear window.

"What the hell?" Bill screams through the hole where the back window used to be. "Are you crazy, motherfucker?"

Sam keeps moving forward. The third swing shatters Bill's side window, which he'd gotten only halfway closed, forcing him to jump into his cousin's lap, like they're parked after a date. The fourth swing is to the windshield, pulverizing the glass on impact and sending spider web cracks across it. Only after Sam demolishes the right headlight is the dumbstruck cousin able to get his truck in gear.

Elvis and Roy watch calmly. In his frightened state, the cousin drives into the steep ditch, nearly rolls the truck when turning it, and has to gun the engine to get it back up onto the road. Tires squeal and Bill shouts, "I'll kill you. I'll kill you, crazy motherfucker!"

The wrecked truck disappears over a hill.

"Crazy?" Sam says aloud to himself. "Oh shit…I forgot my appointment with Laura today."

Sam stands in the pouring rain, feeling nothing, except a little drunk. There's no knot in his stomach, like when he'd gone into rages before. He feels as benign and emotionless as if he were doing dishes. He kicks aside the glass on the roadway before hauling himself back up into the wagon seat. He grabs another beer from the cooler.

An hour up the road, Sam realizes he'll need more beer to get home. He stops at a little joint in a village named Halfway. The smashed pickup truck is there, the only vehicle in the parking lot. Sam takes the hammer in with him, just for the fun of it. He's drunk enough and he knows, like Pop said, that they're all chickenshit.

He walks into the bar, announced by a metal bell, rain dripping off his hat and poncho, and looks around. Sam stands in the shadow of the entryway tapping the hammer into his palm. Bill and the cousin turn to see who's entered.

Sam's silhouette is apparently too similar to Clint Eastwood's *Man With No Name* for the wannabe horse thieves. Bill and his cousin knock over their table and beers, frantically escaping out the back door and into the pouring rain. Sam pays for a six-pack to go. Then he plunks down another $10.

He instructs the bartender, "When they come back, make 'em each a Shirley Temple…and keep the change."

The day after the funeral, Maureen isn't able to stay with Sally at the farm. She has to get back to work. Maureen can't convince her sister to stay at her place, so she programs Sally's phone to speed-dial the police and her own number, in case there's trouble.

But after the funeral, Bill suddenly seems to have mellowed. Nobody knows exactly why. That is, except for the cousin and Sam. The cousin has already reported the damage to his insurance company. The police report reads: "Vandalism by unknown persons at the campground."

Sally had planned to return to work Monday, but decides to request another week off. Bill has also decided to take another week off, to work on plans for expanding the bar and campground across the pasture—using his, Robert's, and Sally's inheritance.

A bid comes through that Sam had put in to install fieldstone on the front of a house. He tells the homeowner he'll begin the job Monday. It will take him about three weeks of good weather.

Monday mid-morning, Sally's engrossed in a phone call. When Bill walks up behind her suddenly, she quickly ends the conversation.

"Who was that?" Bill demands.

"Oh, just work. They're wonderin' how we're doin'."

Bill sighs deeply. "We been doin' just fine. Why can't you tell 'em that while I'm here?"

"I dunno," Sally says, rubbing her forehead.

Bill points a finger in her face. "Don't fuck this up, Sally. I been tryin' real hard. But you're lyin'. Who the hell were you talkin' to?"

"I told you! Go ahead. Call Gina and ask her!"

She throws the phone at him and stomps into the bathroom.

"Damn right, I will!" Bill growls. "I know you're lyin'. I can always tell when you're lyin'."

But instead of dialing the insurance office number, he pushes the redial button.

"Planned Parenthood of Hennepin Park," the automatic recording announces. "Please stay on the line…"

Bill slams the phone onto the end table.

"Planned Parenthood!" Bill shouts through the bathroom door. "What the fuck is that all about?"

Sally reluctantly opens the door. She shows Bill an early pregnancy test.

"Is that what I think it is? You're pregnant?"

Bill's livid. His right hand slowly clenches into a fist. He strikes Sally in the solar plexus with an uppercut. She drops to her knees and wretches.

He grabs her under one armpit and by her hair and yanks her to her feet. She sets her jaw and stares him in the face.

Sally, catching her breath, growls defiantly, "I can't… do it. I won't…have a kid with you."

Bill slaps her face with the back of his hand. Blood gushes from her nose.

"Damn right, you can't!" He hollers so close to Sally's face, she can feel the heat from his breath. Bill spits his wad of tobacco onto her cheek.

"And you ain't gonna have this farm with me, either! Or anything else! Git your goddamn horses and dog and the resta your shit and get the hell out!"

Sally can't get out of the bathroom; Bill has the doorway blocked. He punches his wife in the gut again. She wobbles, but doesn't lose her feet. Her eye is swelling shut from the first blow.

"Go ahead and kill me," Sally dares. "You killed Pop. And so did Robert. I know he was outside when I was hollerin' for help, when you were passed out."

Bill hisses with his jaw set firmly, "You'll be hearin' from my attorney."

She finally brushes past him and bolts for the back door.

Bill stalks her, but then stops at the door. "You fuckin' goddamn whore!"

He rummages through the kitchen drawers and finds a box of large trash bags. He shuffles to their bedroom and hastily empties drawer after drawer into the bags. Half the contents miss the bags, and he leaves those articles on the floor. He ties the bag tops in knots then, from the sidewalk, throws the bags at Sally's trailer—six in all. All but two burst open on impact against the side of her horse trailer. He stalks back into the house again and comes out with Sally's purse, which he throws at the trailer. The contents scatter over the lawn and into the lilac bushes.

Sally comes from the barn with both horses and Sheba in tow. The horses load obediently. Sheba stands over her while she hastily gathers her dresser things and tosses them helter-skelter into the living quarters of the trailer. On her hands and knees, she scrambles to gather the things from her purse.

The back door slams and Bill comes toward her, leveling a pistol. Sheba lunges at Bill, who fires instantly, shooting the dog square in the chest. Sheba falls limply at his feet and doesn't move.

Sally runs to her, crying and swearing at Bill, as she embraces her dead dog. She has never seen her husband so cocky, so evil. He opens his free hand. He has the needle and syringe.

"You forget somethin', honey?" Bill taunts, with an evil grin.

He waves the pistol toward the road. "It's time for you to leave. You ever show up here again, you'll be joinin' your goddamn dog."

Bill stumbles back to the house, one hand holding his pistol high in the air, the other holding the syringe and needle.

Sally backs away toward her truck, sobbing and stumbling. "Sheba…Sheba…" she cries into her hands.

Bill has the pistol leveled on her as she stumbles toward her truck and gets in. She speeds down the driveway. Bill fires one shot at the trailer, hitting it in the roof above the horses.

Maureen doesn't receive the mid-afternoon call from Sally that she'd promised, and is worried. Sally doesn't answer her phone. She dials the farm number.

Bill answers. "Consider this your last call here ever again. Don't know where she is? Left here this morning. For good, I hope."

"What do you mean?"

"We had a little *disagreement*. I tossed her stuff out in the yard. She loaded her goddamn horses and took off, and that's the last I seen of her. The last I ever want to see of that whore and her fleabags."

"You son of a bitch! If you hurt my sister…" But the line has already gone dead.

Maureen frantically dials Joan's number. They agree it's best to call the sheriff and get out there. For all they know, Sally's lying there hurt—or worse.

They meet the deputy in Streeter—the same deputy, Marcus, who came the night Pop died—and drive to the farm together.

Bill stands looking through the screen door. He'd been napping when he heard the two vehicles drive in. He's wearing only a rumpled tan t-shirt, stained with smears of blood, saggy white boxer-brief underwear and black socks, one of which has fallen down to his ankle.

The deputy walks up the porch stairs and approaches the door. From three feet away, he can smell the stale alcohol emanating from Bill.

"You assholes git off my property!"

"No, Mr. Hunter," Deputy Marcus replies sternly. "I need to check on the welfare of your wife. I've got probable cause to believe she might be in danger."

"Probable cause, my ass! Those two dykes worryin' ain't probable cause for shit! Now get the hell off my place."

"Have it your way, Mr. Hunter. I've already got a warrant in the works."

"You can shove that warrant up your ass!"

Marcus speaks into the radio clipped to his shirt. "Thompson, how long before you get here with the warrant?"

The radio crackles, "I'm in Streeter. Two minutes."

Maureen discovers a pool of blood in the grass near the sidewalk and gasps.

"What's this, Mr. Hunter?" Marcus demands, pointing at the blood.

"Her goddamn dog attacked me. Self-defense—ain't no law against defendin' yourself from a mad dog on your own property."

Bill motions toward the pasture beyond the barn. A flock of ravens and crows is jostling over something on the ground. "Go see for yourself. Had to shoot her in the chest just before she got me by the throat."

When Thompson arrives with the warrant, Bill still refuses to allow them into the house. Maureen and Joan watch from the driveway as he argues with the deputies through the screen door.

"Are you sure you want to interfere with a legal search, Mr. Hunter?" Marcus asks.

"You ain't gettin' in here without a fight," Bill growls.

Marcus pulls the screen door open. Bill lunges at him. Thompson catches Bill from behind and quickly wrestles him off the deck and onto the ground. Bill is handcuffed within seconds, but still thrashes and curses at the deputies.

"You motherfuckers! I want my attorney, right now!"

The deputies call for backup. Another car that was already on the way arrives in less than a minute. That deputy, Swenson, guards Bill sitting on the ground near the pool of Sheba's blood.

Marcus and Thompson search the house. Bill's pistol lies on top of the freezer in the entryway. Blood is spattered on the bathroom floor, the wall, and the door, with more droplets leading throughout the house and onto the deck. Bill hadn't cleaned the mess in the bedroom, so the dresser drawers are strewn about as are Sally's things that missed the garbage bags. Maureen and Joan aren't allowed into the house during the search.

Calmer, Bill offers to Swenson, "Hell, she left here on her own. Yeah, we had a tiff. Not a big deal. Lotsa couples fight! She wasn't the only one who got hit! I'm gonna press charges myself."

Marcus returns to the porch. "Can you call her cell phone, Maureen?" The deputy glares at Bill. "You'd better hope she answers."

A phone rings from the nearby lilac bushes. Joan finds it among the greenery and picks it up, her hands shaking. Maureen rushes at Bill, and Swenson grabs her by the shoulders as Bill rolls onto his side.

Bill spits. "Look in the bathroom trash. A goddamn pregnancy test. That fuckin' Sally's on her way to get an abortion."

"Where?" Maureen demands, her teeth gritted.

"Said she wasn't gonna have a kid with me," Bill whines pitifully. "We been tryin' so hard to have a kid. She took a coupla swings at me. I can't help it if she hurt herself tryin' to get at me."

Maureen screams right into his face. "Where…did…she…GO?"

"I don't know. Hennepin something."

"That has to be in Minneapolis!" Joan says.

"We gotta call 'em. See if she's okay," Maureen says as she heads into the house.

"Won't do a bit of good," Joan laments. "They won't tell us if she's there or not. They won't even take a message for her. They won't give information to anyone without a court order."

"How ironic," Bill chortles, "A fuckin' women's clinic that won't even talk to women. Ha, if that's what you two are. Already talked to my attorney. He's startin' the divorce papers as we speak. Says she's not gonna get a nickel after what she done to me."

"Deputy," Joan says, "first thing in the morning, I'll be filing for a temporary order on Sally's behalf, to make sure Bill doesn't mess with her possessions, or make off with any assets."

"I demand to call my attorney!" Bill hollers. "I'll have your badge! And everythin' those two dykes own, and most of your shit, too, cop!"

The other two deputies drag Bill to Thompson's patrol car, and stuff him into the backseat. Bill finally realizes he's in his underwear.

"At least lemme get some pants on!" he hollers.

Thompson says calmly, "Don't worry about it. I bet they have a nice orange jumpsuit at the jail just your size."

"One more thing," Maureen points to a car pulling into the drive. "His brother, Robert. How you gonna keep him outta the house?"

"I know Robert," Swenson announces with a sly grin. "This won't be difficult."

The deputy approaches Robert as he parks by the barn and begins talking to him. From inside the patrol car, Bill shouts, "Robert! Don't say nothin'! It's a trap!"

Robert immediately lunges at Swenson. It's a two-second fight, with Robert ending up on the hood of his old car face down, nose bleeding.

"Threatening an officer," Marcus says. "Works every time."

The investigator, Jerry Blaise, calls Planned Parenthood in Minneapolis. Joan is right. They aren't going to cooperate, no matter how dire the situation might be. When Jerry threatens he'll have the Minneapolis police there with a warrant, the Planned Parenthood representative tells him, "Don't bother. Here goes my job right out the window if anyone finds out I talked to you. Yes, Sally Hunter called. But she didn't make an appointment with us. I only told her there's a 24-hour waiting period after her first contact with us or any other clinic in Minnesota.

She said then she'd go to the folks she talked to the day before. But she didn't say who that was."

Maureen takes the home phone and runs back through the previous outgoing calls. The call to Minneapolis is the only one out of the ordinary.

"Her cell!" Maureen suddenly cries. "Let me check her cell."

Maureen scrolls through Sally's outgoing calls. The only odd call is to a number in North Dakota that was made the afternoon before. She calls the number.

"Eastern Dakota Women's Clinic."

Just then Thompson comes into the house and announces, "Wherever she went...the truck and horse trailer tracks...she took a right out of the driveway, heading west."

Maureen sobs as she tells Sam the whole sordid story over the phone.

Sam feels like some demon has reached down his throat and pulled out his soul. He feels as if he'd failed Sally horribly and somehow made it worse for her with Bill.

In the fading evening light, he drives to Sally's farm and collects Sheba. He digs her grave in the dark, on the west slope below the fire ring.

Back home, he gives Deja a kiss on the nose and settles her into her kennel crate. Then he delivers the canoe upstream to the dam, drives back to the bridge and parks his truck. He changes his mind about Deja and lets her come along. They head out on foot cross-country in the dark the three miles back to the canoe, the last mile his puppy sound asleep in his arms.

Sam will listen quietly to the river this night, his Deja snuggled asleep at his feet on a boat cushion, covered to keep warm with Sally's shirt she'd left the night after Dakota was sick.

CHAPTER 5

THE COURTROOM PLAYERS

Jack Peabody is Bill and Robert's lawyer. Mr. Peabody is renowned for dealing just under the Judicial Ethics Board radar. Rumor has it, the board in St. Paul needs an entire three-drawer file cabinet to house all the complaints against him.

But the worst offense he'd ever been convicted of was arranging a lease for one of his clients, an elderly spinster, as a favor for his business partner. A 99-year lease for 95 prime acres at $100 a year, and she'd pay the taxes. The partners had planned to open a gravel pit and road pavement plant there, until the spinster's long-time, young male companion returned from Mardi Gras and blew the whistle on Peabody. Still, that one had only cost him a 30-day suspension of his license and a token fine.

Peabody's a large man of nearly 50. A few inches over six feet and imposingly broad across the shoulders. He shaves his head, but has an unruly full, black beard and a moustache that covers his upper lip. The very picture of a professional wrestling villain. He has a booming voice to match his imposing stature.

Peabody loves to intimidate whomever he can—the judge, the bailiff, the court administrators, and of course the opposing counsel. Even the guy who fills the pop and candy machines. But he's planning a different attack this morning.

The long-time sitting judge, Elmer Friday, had been hit square in the forehead with a hockey puck at a University of North Dakota game that spring. There was no apparent injury, but his UND alumni buddies became alarmed when the good judge began cheering wildly, running up and down the aisle giving high fives and shouting, *Rah Rah Rah, Sky U Mah!*, the Minnesota Gophers fight cheer, after they scored a short-handed goal in overtime.

Subsequently, after three months of court administration keeping track of Friday's ramblings from the bench, which had grown from the usual 10- or 15-minute pointless tale before the hockey puck hit him to (after the puck hit him) stringing together three or four such tales and making a mess of the court schedule. Also, the clerks had begun timing his naps on the bench, which also had grown considerably in duration. However, the review panel concluded that Friday's behavior was not unusual for a judge, and therefore not punishable by a forced vacation from the bench to get medical treatment.

It wasn't until the next round of official complaints against the judge that they removed him. It seems that in his chambers, the judge thought he was getting undressed for bed. Stripped down to his underwear and socks, put his robe on like a nightshirt without bothering to zip it up, and walked into the courtroom that way. The word around court was that the only reason the review panel gave the judge some time off was because his socks were mismatched.

Peabody hasn't heard that Judge Friday is on vacation. He relishes baffling Friday with bullshit. That is, if he can't impress upon the party-line Catholic judge the unthinkable evil of Sally Hunter leaving town for an abortion. That is, after she was so disobedient her husband had to slap her to her senses to save the life of the baby.

Bill is led into the courtroom, wearing a jail-issued orange jumpsuit and tan sandals, his hands and feet shackled. He glares at Sam and Marcus, who are sitting in the gallery. The bailiff escorts him to Peabody's table. Maureen and Joan already sit at the other. Bill glares at them, too.

Peabody and Bill smile at each other and conspire like two naughty boys who are about to pull the head off a baby bird they just stole from its nest.

"Piece of cake," Peabody says, loud enough for Maureen and Joan to hear.

"All rise," the court administrator announces loudly.

Peabody and Bill stand, still in conversation.

"Please be seated," Judge Riley requests.

Peabody's head snaps toward the bench so fast, it's amazing he doesn't dislocate a vertebra. "Who are *you*?"

"That's 'Who are you, *Your Honor?*'," the judge corrects.

Peabody doesn't know a thing about Judge Riley, a retired judge who'd sat on the bench in Hennepin County for 24 years. The judge is about half the size of Peabody, with a no-nonsense look about him, a gray crewcut, tanned and lined face (likely from fishing or golfing), and reading glasses sitting down his nose a ways.

"I'm Judge Riley. Let's get started." He turns to Joan. "Ms. Adair?"

Peabody leaps to his feet with his hands out. "Your Honor! There is no legal basis for a third party to file such a motion on behalf of an absent party!" He pounds the table. "Miss Adair DOES NOT HAVE POWER OF ATTORNEY ON MRS. HUNTER'S BEHALF!"

The judge frowns. "Mr. Peabody, please be seated."

Judge Riley motions for her to present her case, and Joan stands.

"Your Honor, thank you," Joan responds. "Considering the circumstances of Sally Hunter's sudden disappearance and Bill Hunter's statement that he is beginning divorce proceedings, Maureen Novotny believes it is in her sister's interest for the Court to ensure protection of Sally Hunter's share of the joint marital assets. The Court has the affidavits from myself and Ms. Novotny, who is sitting next to me. I am prepared to have Deputy Marcus Hiliger testify as to the accuracy of the affidavits.

"Unfortunately, nobody here knows the whereabouts of Mrs. Hunter at this time. She was apparently beaten so brutally, she fled the farm she lives on with Mr. Hunter. This is not the first time Sally has been beaten by her husband."

Peabody jumps to his feet and hollers, "I object!"

"On what grounds," the judge asks.

Peabody holds his arms wide, pleading, "This is not a trial! This is all conjecture and sounds like an opening statement at a trial!"

Joan interrupts Peabody, "Mr. Hunter admitted to us that there had indeed been an altercation yesterday morning. He admitted that it is his wife's blood throughout the house. Mr. Hunter also admitted he shot and killed Mrs. Hunter's dog."

"I object again! What about my client's Miranda rights?!"

The judge is scanning the affidavits Joan provided. "It sure looks like your client did some talking yesterday, of his own volition."

"Your Honor! This is not a trial!" Peabody bellows again.

"Thank you for reminding me of that again, Mr. Peabody," Judge Riley responds coolly, obviously agitated. "Now let me remind *you*, Mr. Peabody, that this is an emergency hearing for a temporary order to protect Mrs. Hunter's share of the marital assets. So please sit down."

Peabody obeys. "When do I get *my* turn?"

The judge asks, "What part of the temporary order do you object to? It says right here that neither Mrs. Hunter nor her attorney can help themselves to the marital assets either, without the mutual consent of your client. And it says in the affidavit that your client has already begun talking to his attorney about starting a divorce. That attorney would be you, right? Have anything to add to that, Mr. Peabody?"

Peabody shakes his head.

The judge continues, "I am *not* going to sign Ms. Adair's proposed order as is. She is requesting immediate relief, giving Maureen Novotny temporary possession of her sister's personal property, until Ms. Hunter's whereabouts and wishes can be determined. I will have my clerk *add* to Ms. Adair's proposed order that Maureen Novotny is also granted the power of attorney on behalf of Ms. Hunter.

"Mr. Peabody, thank you for reminding me to add that part. As you know, power of attorney will give Ms. Novotny all the rights and powers as Mr. Hunter's wife."

Bill tugs furiously at Peabody's coat sleeve.

"Please give us a minute, Your Honor," Peabody requests. The two confer in whispers for a minute.

Peabody finally stands and exclaims. "Do you realize what you've just done? If my client needs to raise bail for the pending charges against him, he'll need Ms. Novotny's permission to get the money out of the bank!"

"Now you're catching on, Mr. Peabody," Judge Riley agrees. "I'm sure she'll be reasonable. If she's not, you'll let me know, right?"

Joan stands, "Your Honor, Deputy Hiliger, who is sitting in the gallery, has volunteered, on the Court's behalf, to inventory Mrs. Hunter's possessions."

"So ordered," Judge Riley agrees.

"Your Honor! I object!" Peabody bellows. "We want someone there from our side, too! The deputy is obviously biased against my client!"

"Because the deputy arrested your client for interfering with a legal search—on a warrant I signed? Sit down, Mr. Peabody. This motion will be in effect for 90 days. Mr. Peabody, would you like to have the clerk schedule another hearing to discuss your own motions?"

"I'll have to confer with my client."

They whisper for a few seconds. Bill understands enough about the proceedings that he knows he's just been body-slammed. He slumps back in his chair with his arms crossed and his eyes narrowed into angry slits, glaring straight ahead across toward the empty jury box.

Peabody stands. "We're going to reserve our decision on that point, Your Honor. But there is that other matter you just mentioned—the criminal charges against my client."

Judge Riley slams his gavel. "Court is adjourned." He stands to leave.

"Your Honor, please! My client's other hearing, for interfering with a search warrant. It's set for 5:00 p.m. Can't we take care of it now? He needs to get home and tend to his campground business."

The judge stops halfway off the bench and glares at Peabody, his glasses slipping down further. "I don't see the county attorney in here. We'll see you two at 5:00 p.m. as scheduled."

He disappears into his chambers.

Joan approaches Peabody. "Just let us know what he needs out of the account for bail."

Peabody sneers. "You seem pretty sure the judge will order bail. You sleepin' with that old judge or what?"

"First time I've seen Riley. Yeah, he's cute for an old guy. I'd take him for a roll…except I roll the other way."

Sorting through Sally's things, Maureen almost feels like her sister has died. She is certain Sally won't come back for a long time—maybe never.

Maureen tells Sam the situation is similar to when Sally had left for Oregon years ago. She'd been pregnant that time, too, by a man she loved named Howard. He wasn't mean like Bill, but Sally discovered he had two kids already—with two different unmarried women, women he still slept with. Nobody else knew she was pregnant when she'd left that time. She miscarried somewhere in the middle of Montana.

It was three months before she called Maureen, who informed her that Howard had hanged himself in despair. He'd left a note stating that if only Sally had given him another chance, he would have changed.

Sam's palm stings all of a sudden. He's drawn to Bill's dresser. "Oh, Jesus."

Marcus and Maureen both ask, "What?"

Sam rubs his hand. He points to the top drawer, and says quietly, "The needle must be in there, the one I found in Dakota. What's Bill doing with it? Sally had it."

Marcus offers, "If you're sure it's Sally's, go ahead and take it."

Sam's hands tremble as he slides the drawer open. Yes, there's the broken needle…and what looks like a matching syringe.

"Oh fuck," Sam says. "It really *was* Bill…"

"What?" the deputy asks.

"Somebody tried to kill Sally's horse by jabbing a needle into its flank. It broke off inside Dakota. I pulled it out and gave it to Sally. I don't know who found the syringe or where."

"I can't advise you what to do," Marcus admits. "Take what you think is hers. All I can do is document it. They get a copy of this list. If they claim it's theirs and demand it back, they can ask the court for it. I don't really think they'll claim ownership of the needle and syringe, do you? But, after court this morning, who knows what they'll try to pull."

Sam goes about emptying Sally's closet shelf. A shoe box falls. Three swaths of wide, clear tape circle the box, holding the lid on. It's marked "LETTERS AND PHOTOS" with felt-tip pen.

"What's this?" he asks Maureen.

"I dunno. I've never seen it."

A smaller scribbling in Sally's handwriting reads, "*You're right, Mom. Dad didn't deserve to die on your account. I'll never forgive you, and pray I can forget you.*"

Speechless, Maureen turns toward the bedroom door, holding the box out in front of her. She heads for the living room, with Sam, Joan, and Marcus following. She never knew Sally had felt that way about their mother.

"Sam, do you have a knife?"

Maureen slides the blade between the cover and the box, her hands trembling as she slowly removes the lid.

Sitting on top is a photo of their mother.

"Holy cow!" Sam whispers. "Your mother was beautiful. Sally could be her twin."

Carefully, layer by layer, Maureen empties the box. Beneath the picture of their mother, the contents are in reverse chronological order. There are love letters to their mother, from a man named Al. The letters are dated the year before their father died. And a court document, a motion for a divorce. Their mother had filed for divorce two days before their father had died in the accident. An envelope with their mother's name written on the front. A note from their father to their mother—a suicide note. And a journal, written on a stenographer's pad, that their mother had written those years following their father's death. The years she was drinking and drugging herself to death.

Maureen picks up the photo of her father and notices writing on the back. It's dated two days before their mother had died from a sleeping pill and alcohol overdose.

"I killed him. He wasn't perfect. But he didn't deserve to die on my account. I cannot bear this guilt anymore."

Maureen picks up the shoe box lid and reads Sally's words again. Her eyes fill with tears and she rubs her forehead with the back of her wrist.

"Finally," Maureen whispers, "it makes sense, in a horribly skewed way, why Sally wouldn't leave Bill. She must have been afraid history would repeat itself. That she'd be no better than our mother. She gave him so many chances. She couldn't live with the blood of another man on her hands, no matter how terrible it was staying with him. It's like she picked Bill knowing exactly who he was, knowing that it could never work. He is her penance for Howard dying, and for our mother's sin. Bill is Sally's life sentence."

"And she left the shoe box right where she'd see it every time she opened the closet," Sam says, shaking his head. "I wonder how many times during the past couple months she's taken it down."

CHAPTER 6

A LIGHTNING ROD

Sam tells Laura the whole story—Pop dying, the funeral, smashing up the cousin's truck with a hammer, Sally leaving, and their time in court. Also about the shoe box. The litany takes up over half of his 50 minutes.

He apologizes for forgetting to call her to cancel his appointment the day of the funeral, and expresses concern about Sally taking on so much guilt.

"Yes, I've seen that syndrome before," Laura responds. "She might never get over it, although after Howard she did eventually return. It was like she gave herself a second chance, a do-over."

"If she does come back…eventually," Sam asks, "do you think she'll go back to Bill?"

"Unfortunately, that happens. Too often. So you should be prepared."

"Enough!" Sam growls as he holds his hand up. "I can live without her. I've already proven that. I pray she never comes back, because if Bill hurts her again—or worse—I'll kill 'im. And you can put that in your notes."

"Now what?" Laura closes her notebook and sets her pen aside.

"What, what?"

"What's next for Sam?"

"I s'pose back to life as usual. Rock jobs, drivin' the bus, canoein' the river. I do have my son's weddin' coming up on Labor Day weekend. We're gonna have it on the hill, at the fire ring, like Pop suggested. Hope it's a nice day. My son has invited my father to the wedding. I guess I think that's a good thing."

"Are you going to keep working on the sexual abuse issues, and the issues with your dad?"

"Well, my daughter understands now. We had a long talk. Keith and I are okay. Dad and I been talkin', too. Mostly just callin' a truce for now, agreein' to keep the lines open. I think he's truly sorry for his mistakes as a parent. And I have truly forgiven him. I've also asked both my kids to forgive me. Really, life is okay. We're all talkin'.

"Look, I didn't go crazy when Sally took off. Yes, I feel some guilt. Definitely a loss. But what you've helped me learn is that this works, just gettin' it out in the open. So thank you. I'm just not gonna go near anything or anyone like Sally again. Yes, I need some time to heal from what Sparky did to me. I don't want to be makin' any difficult decisions in the meantime."

Laura offers, "I'm not convinced you want to rule out such a relationship from your life. It isn't always necessary to crawl into a cave. Right now, my guess is that you're grieving the loss of Sally more than you admit. And you should. But life goes on—live it!"

Sam pauses in thought. "I'm doin' the math about Sally…"

"Things were movin' forward for the two of us, in a slightly weird way, for not quite a month—not counting the evenin' three weeks later when we slept together. I've been out of her life, at least as a potential partner, other than that night, for almost two months."

"That's twice you've mentioned that night in the past 15 seconds," Laura reminds him.

"Okay," Sam admits, "you busted me. But you don't understand. You never saw Sally ride. Or smile. You never talked with her, laughed with her, held her... Right now I feel like if I can't be with Sally, I'm never goin' there again. I feel like I'll never feel like that around another woman again. I'll never just have *sex* ever again. You can take me to the bank on that one. I feel like my memories of Sally will haunt me right to my grave. Another love like Sally, like Karen? What are the chances lightning'll strike me three times? My Walter Mitty world, without a woman in my life, isn't so bad anyway, I guess."

"Your chances are pretty good, I'd say, if you're a lightning rod!"

"A lightning rod?"

"Right. The intent, the willingness, to be a conduit, to attract what's out there."

"Let's say I agree I didn't have my grounding wire connected for those six years since Karen. So how did Sally show up?"

"Ever hear the phrase 'out of the blue'? That's whomever-is-in-charge's way of getting our attention when He's finally tired of waiting on us. The way I see it, you can wait another six years for another shot out of the blue, or you can be a lightning rod. You already are in many respects—delivering babies, driving your bus, making wine and sharing it, enjoying the woods and river. It's all connected."

Laura checks her appointment book. "I've got another hour if you want to keep talking."

Sam waves a hand. "No. No. Really, I'm okay. I think we've covered it all. Let's take some time off, okay? I've got a *very* busy month ahead of me anyway."

Sam is lying, sort of. There isn't that much left of the rock job. He only works it five or six hours a shift anyway. There isn't much else that he likes to do in the outdoors in August otherwise. Sure, he'll canoe the river once in a while. But no morels, and he doesn't know squat about the other mushrooms. Too hot to cut firewood or work on the trails. Raspberries all done. Fence fixed. Horse stalls already prepared. No wine making until September. Bow hunting not for a few weeks beyond that. God forbid he'd work on the inside of his house. And screw cleaning it.

Laura agrees. "You know how to find me if you want to chat."

"Umm, as long as you've got a few minutes, there is one more thing…" He stares at the floor and takes in a deep breath. "I went to see Sparky yesterday."

She picks up her notepad and pen and leans in. "Go on."

Sparky had built a new house on his grandparents' property across the road from Sam's family farmstead sometime shortly after Sam left the roost and married his first wife. It was off the road a ways, on a long, curved driveway. You couldn't see the house from the road.

When Sam drove in, there was only one vehicle in the driveway, a full-size passenger van with darkened windows. The backyard had a privacy fence around it. Sam could hear kids laughing, jumping into a swimming pool, splashing around. His hand trembled as he rang the bell. He could hear his heart beating in his ears.

Sparky's wife answered. She didn't recognize Sam until he told her who he was. They had never met, but she recalled him as a former neighbor from across the road. She grabbed both his hands tightly and invited him into the foyer, then cheerfully shouted at the patio door to Sparky, "Hey! Guess what? You got company! Sam Ryan!"

They hadn't been face-to-face for over 35 years. "Well, I'll be darned!" chirped Sparky as he stuck out his hand. That hand...Sam shook it, without looking at it. Sparky squeezed his hand harder than he thought necessary for two men who barely knew each other.

Sparky was wearing a baseball uniform with COACH across the back. He patted Sam's back.

"What brings you down here, Sammy? It's so good to see ya. Sorry we didn't get a chance to visit at Grandma Fox's funeral. Hey, come on outside and see my team!"

Sam followed him through the house. Sparky and his wife apparently never had kids of their own, but there were dozens of photos on the walls. Sparky and Boy Scouts, Sparky and 4-H kids, Sparky and kids' baseball teams, Sparky and confirmation classes.

Sam couldn't help but pause at one collage with half a dozen photographs. He wondered if there were any little Sammys among them.

Sparky noticed Sam was lagging and waved him over. "Come on out back and meet the team! They're my 15 years and younger team. I heard back then you were quite a ball player yourself! This is the same town team you played on all those years, the Blackbirds. I took it over when I moved out here, kept the town tradition going. I gotta introduce you!"

It was all too artificial, put on. Like nothing terrible had ever happened. Momentarily, Sam doubted himself, as if maybe it was all in his head—like most of his family believed. Sparky winked at Sam, just like when he'd asked his sister if she liked whipped cream. A wave of shame washed over Sam, and he flushed and felt light-headed as if he might faint. Obediently, like when he was little, he followed Sparky out the door into the backyard.

Out by the pool, sitting off in a corner, was a lad still wearing his baseball uniform while the other boys played. Sam could immediately sense that something was off. His slumping shoulders. His blank stare as he tossed a baseball into his glove over and over. The boy looked up at Sam and offered a weak "Hello." To Sam, what the boy was actually saying was "Help me!" It was like seeing his own reflection in a mirror 45 years ago.

The rest of the team barely acknowledged Sam. They just kept playing. The boy walked up to him slowly, shyly, and introduced himself, while watching Sparky out the corner of his eye, "My name is Jerry. Glad to meet you." The boy didn't offer Sam his hand. He just kept tossing the baseball into his mitt.

Sam answered, "Number 5, Jerry. That's my old number. What position do you play?"

"Second base."

"What a coincidence. That was my position, too."

Sam noticed Sparky was watching them from across the pool.

If Sam had harbored any inkling to retreat, it had evaporated. He was going to go through with it—to let Sparky know there was a big hole in his soul, thanks to him. Yes. He was going to make Sparky squirm, maybe even crack.

"You wanna go out in the driveway and throw me some fly balls?" Jerry asked.

Before Sam could answer, Sparky rushed over. "Umm, Jerry, Sam here has to leave, right Sam? It's a long drive, right Sam?"

Sam nodded reluctantly in agreement, and looked back at Jerry, already shuffling back to his chair with his head hung down, tossing the ball into his baseball glove.

"Sparky, we need to talk."

Instantly, Sparky narrowed his eyes. But then like a chameleon changes its color, Sparky put on a smile. He put an arm around Sam's shoulder and began walking him around the other side of the pool to the door in the privacy fence. Sam brushed Sparky's hand away and looked him in the eye with a steely glare. He paused to look back at Jerry, who was still sitting in his chair, still tossing the ball into his glove. It was like the kid had been sent back to death row, and his final appeal for freedom had been struck down.

Slowly Sam turned to Sparky, whose face had lost its energy, realizing that Sam had made the connection.

"I don't think Jerry's mom would want him playing catch with a stranger," Sparky lied. "A single mom, real protective. You know what's funny?" Sparky chortled.

"Jerry and his mom live in the rambler built on the lot next to your old farmhouse!"

Sparky laughed to himself. "Say, what did you wanna talk to me about, Sammy?" He pointed at Sam's old pickup truck and began walking toward it. "You sure that thing's gonna make it back up to the woods? Sammy, how about you let me cut you a heckuva deal on a nice used ride at my dealership? We're old friends, right? I've got a '99 F-150 four-wheel drive, loaded. Book on it is a little over 10 grand."

Sparky put his arm around Sam's shoulder and held it tightly. "I've got six into it. You can have it for three. Now there's a family and friends deal my sales manager's gonna think I'm crazy for approving!"

"Get your fuckin' hands off me," Sam whispered through clenched teeth as he pushed Sparky's arm off his shoulder.

Sparky stopped in his tracks and Sam faced him from a foot away.

"I'm not Little Sammy anymore. But you're still the same ol' Sparky. The lyin', controllin', connivin' abuser. Take your F-150 and stick it up your own ass and see how it feels. Maybe you better sell it for 10 grand. You're gonna need all the fuckin' money you can beg, borrow, or steal by the time I'm done."

"Wh—what are you talking about?" Sparky asked pleadingly.

"You know exactly what I'm talkin' about. I was thinkin' on the way down here this morning, maybe Sammy was a one-shot deal—a lone victim. And in that case, I was just gonna let you know what that did to me, how it so horribly affected my life. But I was gonna go easy on you."

"You're freakin' crazy!" Sparky spat angrily. "You went right along with it! You could've just walked home any time! Tell you what. I'll give you the damn F-150. I'll make a call and you drive over to get it. And I'll even have a guy tow your old truck home for you."

"I'm not shaking you down, Sparky. This isn't about you buying me off. If there's one thing you taught me, it's the ability to pick little Sammys out of a crowd. Jerry—he's one. I know it. How many others are there?"

"My final offer," Sparky begged as he pulled out his phone and began punching numbers. "A brand-new F-150, loaded."

Laura sits up straight in her chair, her mouth agape. "And then…?"

"Rather than rearrange his bridgework," Sam says, "I kicked him like a football in the nuts. I didn't want to mess up that evil face and not be able to see him suffer."

"I watched him in the rearview mirror lying there holding his crotch. Instead of taking a left to head home, I took a right—to the county attorney's office. Gave my statement to the Victim's Advocate. Not that it'll do anything for me, but she vowed (and I believe her) to start followin' the trail. She's an expert in childhood sexual abuse and predators. All she has to do is find one boy—grown-up or otherwise—who will tell his story."

"Looks like Sam is doing okay with this," Laura concludes. "How about Sammy?"

"Oh, it was his idea to kick Sparky in the nuts!"

It is 2:00 in the afternoon when he leaves Laura's office, too late to get anything done at the rock job before dark. He's thinking about a campfire and supper up at the fire ring. Just him and Deja. Take her to the river for a swim. A long walk to check for deer sign. Life as usual.

But first he drives to the dive bar a half block off the main drag in Walker.

If the bar has a theme, it's "every beer sign and poster imaginable", with a secondary theme of "pretty, skinny young women with huge, tan breasts hanging out". The poster of a young blond cowgirl reminds him of Sally a little.

The bartender walks over to greet him. Sam is her only customer. She's older, maybe 65, and skinny. Her hair is dyed bright orange, and the skin on her face and arms is desert-dry, wrinkled and brown from either too much sun or too many cigarettes. Or maybe her liver isn't hitting on all eight cylinders.

She asks hoarsely, "Waddya have?"

Sam looks up at the poster again.

"A glass of tap. Anything."

"I'm Dottie," she offers as she draws his beer.

As she sets a coaster under it, she comments, "Either you're a pervert, or your girlfriend who ran away looks like her."

"How did you know?" he demands, playing along.

"Which is it?"

"It's the second one. My girlfriend...ex-girlfriend."

Dottie turns out to be a good listener. It takes Sam two beers to get warmed up. And another three beers to tell her the whole story. Then he shares Laura's advice.

"That's a load of crap, if I ever heard one! Jesus! The love of your life gets PG by her degenerate husband, he beats her up because she's gonna get an abortion, she leaves for what might be forever to who knows where, and that hippie therapist wants you to go home and think about lightning rods? Christ! I'm surprised she didn't tell you to take up knitting! And they wonder why folks drink in the middle of the afternoon. I should advertise with a poster in her office."

Sam's feeling the beer. "So what do you think I should do, in your *professional* opinion?"

"That's easy. For starters, go kick hubby's ass from one enda the county to the other. Then tell 'im you had sex with his wife."

"Can't go there, either place. He says he's startin' the divorce right away. Don't want him to put it off and hang onto Sally just because he thinks he's keepin' her from me."

"Go look for her then. Got any idea where she went?"

"Not a clue."

"It's her move, then." Dottie wipes down the bar, shaking her head and frowning. "I hate to say this, but there's a chance she was just usin' you. You made her life bearable when she was with hubby, but now she's not with 'im…"

"I know. I realize that. It was a long shot right from the beginning." Sam pushes his change on the bar toward her for a tip.

"Where you goin' now?"

"To the Ben Franklin store," Sam says dryly. "To see if they got yarn on sale."

He smiles and slides off the bar stool. "Thanks, Dottie."

Deja and Sam canoe the river later that afternoon. Strangely, he finds himself giving Laura's lightning rod advice some serious thought as he drifts along.

What might it be like to allow myself the opportunity to start over, to invite another chance in? Just the opposite of how I've been for almost six years? Or should I be content to sit on my hands and wait for divine intervention? You know, that out-of-the-blue crap. Either way, what if the next woman is nuts like the last three I been with?

This exercise doesn't keep Sam from his diligence in scanning the river bottom and banks for junk. Even with his mind a million miles away, he possesses an unexplainable knack for recognizing items that don't belong in the river—cans, bottles, and even car parts. It's like he has radar, and the canoe has a guidance system, like those missiles the military shoots right down the smoke stacks of enemy factories and schools.

He'd once found a water pump off an old car engine, with just the nipple for the heater hose showing above the mud. And with just a corner of a bottle showing, not a square inch of it sticking out of the sand. It turned out to be close to 100 years old.

He googled it in the school library. "Seven Sutherland Sisters Hair Tonic. New York," it advertised on its clear, light-blue glass shell. Yup, circa 1900. Seven women with hair down to their ankles and their father, cohorts of P. T. Barnum.

Barnum had sold enough of that snake oil to build a fancy mansion on Long Island. It was anyone's guess what the hell this bottle was doing in a little river not much wider than a township road in northern Minnesota. Sam supposed it might have been discarded by one of the women "entrepreneurs" who followed the lonely immigrant loggers to the edge of the Smoky Hills Forest.

Sam isn't surprised when a stray breeze sets him off course and he sees two symmetrical bone processes, or outgrowths, about four inches apart, with a roundish hole maybe three-quarters of an inch in diameter between them. He's found other skulls in the river, from cows and deer.

The current at the lower end of the wild rice bed is substantial. He sticks his paddle in and thrusts it downstream, which causes the bow of the canoe to turn 180 degrees. A half dozen deep strokes, and he's over the skull again. The water is clear, and a good three to four feet deep.

Deja knows something is up. She peers over the edge of the canoe, causing ripples, so that her master can't see clearly. Sam noses Deja's end of the canoe into the swamp grass a foot, to steady it. His end of the canoe swings over the skull.

The ripples calm. Yup, some large mammal. Sam always thought that someday he'd find a human skull (or other parts of a hapless chap). Indians, trappers, drunks from the local watering holes, guys who were caught by big, jealous husbands. Sam had found a few cow and bison bones over the years down in the forested and shallow part of the river, stained almost black by the river, like the skull he is over now.

But as Sam's eyes adjust, more of it comes into focus. It's upside down, with two rows of upper molars just visible. He makes out the curve of a horn, half-buried in the mud, then another horn becomes visible. He mumbles, "A bison?"

Deja doesn't understand the words, but she picks up on Sam's excitement. Instantly she stands all four feet on the gunwale, like a cat preparing to leap. Instinctively, he lurches forward to grab her.

Most folks assume a canoe is easy to tip over. Actually, it isn't easy to tip over at all. But it's surprisingly easy to fall out of when it's tipped to the almost-taking-on-water point. Then without its former occupants, the canoe rights itself within a scant moment, sometimes without a drop of water taken on, as if the canoe's wondering, "Where did everybody go?"

Deja jumps to escapes Sam's grasp, and he rolls out of the canoe with a splash. The dog has propelled herself onto a clod of swamp grass. Unfortunately, it isn't growing from solid ground. It's only floating, and she immediately begins sinking.

Sam discovers that under the water is a good foot of loon shit, and under that is clay, which wants badly to keep both of his sandals. No sooner has he made those unfortunate discoveries then he has a frightened Lab puppy clawing at his face, frantically searching for high, solid ground.

And just that quickly, Deja is spread-eagled on top of his head like an octopus. He's facing upstream, her downstream. At first Sam isn't in a hurry to remove his puppy. He's busy getting a handle on the canoe, and barely gets his fingers around the rope dragging from the hole in the tip of the stern. Deja quits thrashing her legs, tipped with razor-sharp toenails, while he still has some skin left on his face.

Then he feels a substantial amount of water flowing down between his eyes. But the water is much warmer than the rest of the river water. And saltier.

Quickly, with his free hand, he plucks Deja from his head by the scruff of her neck and holds her at arm's length until she finishes her business. He pulls the canoe toward him with the rope and sets her on his seat.

"Stay, girl!" He pushes the front of the canoe a couple yards back into the swamp grass so it won't float away.

Unfortunately, he has lost both sandals to the clay. Now that his feet are free, he can swim, but he can barely hold his position against the strong current. He decides to stand on the mucky bottom as best he can and regroup his wits. His bare feet hit something solid on the river bottom, a log. He balances on it by leaning into the current. Not being sunk into a foot of muck, now the water's only chest-deep.

Sam reaches for the canoe with his left hand for an extra measure of balance. He looks down and notices the current has already washed away the silt he stirred up. He decides, as long as he can't get any wetter, he'll see if he can retrieve the skull.

Approximately four feet upstream from his watery, river bottom perch, not only is the skull in view, but so are what appear to be a shoulder blade, six inches wide and well over a foot long, a jumble of ribs, and two large leg bones.

Sam takes aim, closes his eyes, and dives. He's on target and can feel the roughness of one horn. It comes off the silty bottom as if almost weightless, and he finds the other horn with his free hand. The current quickly drags him backward. He starts to run out of breath, but doesn't want to drop the skull. Fortunately, his feet bump into the submerged log and he uses the current to help right himself.

He stands and sucks in a deep breath. Slowly lifting the skull out of the stream, he holds it up, face-to-face.

It's beautiful. The forehead and bridge of the nose are a marbling of charcoal-gray and deep umber. He swishes it in the water carefully to remove the mud and snail shells from the sinus cavities and cranium. The skull is perfectly intact. Even the thin bones of the nasal passages are in place.

He sidesteps to the shore-most end of the underwater log, and is able to reach the rope. As he pulls the canoe toward him, Deja watches her master intently. He shoos the puppy away and carefully places the skull on his canoe seat.

But the pup apparently has a short memory. Again, she is all fours up on the gunwale. This time, she leaps for the middle of the stream, thinking in her puppy brain that they're just swimming for fun like they often do.

Sam positions himself for another dive while she happily treads water in the middle of the stream. He comes up with a shoulder blade. It has a v-shaped chunk out of the top of it, about an inch wide and two inches long. It's heavy and solid, over a quarter-inch thick where the nick is. Considering the skull's in such perfect shape, he wonders what caused the fracture in the shoulder blade.

He decides to leave the rest of the bones where they lie for now, making a mental note of their location—a lone spindly skeleton of a white spruce, tipped 45 degrees in the bones' direction, inland about 75 feet.

Like Sam had told Sally, he'd only fallen out of his canoe once, and it was only two feet deep there. He hasn't a clue how to get back in the boat in this much water. So instead he floats alongside it, heading downstream, sidestroking with one arm and hanging onto the canoe with the other.

Deja thinks this is great fun. She swims over and slashes Sam's chest and swimming arm with her razor-sharp puppy claws while licking his face, as if to thank him for the great swim. He pushes her away. Her ears droop in sadness over the rejection.

Sam spots a pop bottle-size chunk of freshly debarked beaver wood floating along the shore, and swims five yards without the canoe to grab it. He tosses it downstream as far as he can while treading water, maybe 50 feet. Deja knows the drill well.

Sam catches the canoe, and resumes guiding it downstream while she retrieves the stick and paddles back to return it. It takes about half a dozen such retrieves to float the 300 yards downstream to the end of the rice bed, where Sam finds shallow water and solid ground underneath.

CHAPTER 7

FRIENDS WITH BENEFITS

The next day, Sam calls the school to see if anyone can help him make some sense of a buffalo skeleton ending up in the river.

The receptionist, Connie, says, "If you come in now, you might catch the new biology teacher, Abby Tucker. She's replacing Anderson, who just retired."

"Who?" Sam asks.

Connie, who considers herself the school *historian*, gives him some background. Abby had graduated from Stone Creek High School in 1977. She was valedictorian of her class of 24, and 7 months pregnant when she gave her graduation speech. She most likely would have been named to the all-state basketball and softball teams that year, as she had been the two years before, if not for her condition.

Abby had steadfastly refused to name the baby's father, but many suspected it was the first-year English teacher whose contract subsequently wasn't renewed. She gathered up her scholarship money and, with her four-week-old, Megan, went off to Fargo to attend college. She became a high school science teacher in three years and a semester. She never married.

About 26 years after she left, she moved back to Stone Creek to teach. She'd wanted to teach at Stone Creek right out of college, but back then the memory of Abby in her cap and gown with a belly like a beach ball had been too fresh in the school board's mind.

Sam pauses quietly at the classroom doorway. The new teacher busies herself in a file cabinet, her back toward him.

She's wearing a white sleeveless t-shirt and shiny, blue running shorts. Flip-flops, up on her toes, peering and reaching into the top drawer of the file cabinet. Her ample brown hair is in a spring-loaded tortoise shell clip, casually bunched up off her neck and shoulders. Sam feels embarrassed to be watching her without her knowing. He coughs self-consciously to get her attention.

She turns and smiles widely.

Sam had already done the math. She had to be around 43, 44. Really pretty from 30 feet. Could her eyes be hazel?

"You must be Sam the Jam. Hi, I'm Abby!" Apparently Connie filled in Abby about Sam.

She hurries around the desks to greet the dumbstruck bus driver. Prettier than he'd first imagined. Tan. Yup, hazel eyes, lively and friendly. She reaches out with both hands to shake his.

"A bison?" Abby asks, her brow furrowed. "Are you sure?"

"Pretty sure," Sam answers hesitantly, because Abby's still holding his hand. He knows damn well it's a bison.

He doesn't know where the sudden lack of confidence came from. He looks down at their hands. Embarrassed, Abby lets go. Her hands aren't particularly soft, but they are warm.

"Sorry. Do you have any idea when there were last bison in this part of the world? This could be significant!"

Abby's excitement is obvious. She turns toward her desk and computer.

"I already went online after Connie said you were coming in. Found some info from the University at Crookston."

She motions for him to pull up a chair close alongside hers. Abby turns the screen to face more toward him, and leans into his shoulder so she can point to the screen.

"Look. Over 120 years since bison were around here in any significant numbers. Last documented sighting of any free-roaming in Minnesota…says here, near Twin Valley in 1880."

Sam nods obediently at the history lesson. He's still dumbstruck over Abby. It's all happening so fast. Maybe, he thinks, it's her enthusiasm that catches him off guard. Anderson, the tottering old fart, probably would've fallen asleep on his desk by now.

He notices her tan legs are shaved smooth. How could he not notice? Her left one is touching his right one. And she smells nice. Suddenly a beer poster from Dottie's comes to mind. The tall, sweaty brunette dressed (barely) for a vigorous workout, which would apparently be topped off by a six-pack of low-carb beer she hoists in her hand with long, perfectly sculpted fingernails.

"Where did you find it?" Abby asks excitedly. "Where is it now?"

Sam shakes his head to clear it. He can't find a string of intelligible words to answer her.

"Yeah, pretty exciting, huh?" Abby misinterprets Sam's silence as awe over his discovery.

"Umm…Umm…It's in my truck, in the river."

"What's your truck doing in the river?" That smile of hers has a hint of devil in it that Sam likes.

But out of habit, he reminds himself that Abby's just another pretty young woman who thinks he's so darn old and harmless she doesn't have to pay any attention to what she's wearing around him, or how close she gets, or how good she smells.

"No, my truck's in the parking lot," Sam corrects, pointing with a limp wrist out the window. "The skull, and the scapula. And Deja, my puppy."

Flip-flop, flip-flop, flip-flop. Abby heads quickly for the door. Sam keeps staring at the computer screen.

"Come on," she waves impatiently for him to follow.

On the way to Sam's truck, she confesses, "I've always been in love with bison. Been fascinated by them and their connection with the Indians. My first day back in this school, and out of the blue…wow!"

"Yup. Some things happen that way."

Upon first sight, Abby readily agrees it is, in fact, a bison skull. By the scant wear of the molars and the medium size of the horns, she estimates the bison had been about two or three years old when it died.

"This chunk missing from the scapula," Abby says as she runs her finger over the sharp edge, "it doesn't appear to have been washed or eroded away, or chewed on. It was definitely broken out."

Sam offers, "A bullet or a musket ball would have left more of a fingerprint, so at least part of the hole would be the shape of such a projectile."

Abby nods in agreement and pats Sam on his shoulder. In her excitement she gives him a squeeze around his waist. "Wow! I wonder if a stone spear point could have done the damage? The spine is right above the notch. Maybe a Native hunter hit his quarry an inch or two too low? Or maybe it was a young bull who was taught a lesson by an older bull?"

"It looked to me like the whole skeleton was lying there on the river bottom pretty much in a heap. One reason I can think of is that the bison died right there where the river flows through the big swamp."

Abby is captivated, maybe even mesmerized. She keeps nodding, hanging on every word, her beautiful hazel eyes darting back and forth between his own.

"Bison are notorious for falling through ice. It might have been winter and it couldn't climb up out of the hole in the ice. Or maybe it wasn't winter? That would have been an awful spot for the band to fetch a dead bison from, even on a sunny summer day."

"I have to see this place!" Abby gushes. "How about tomorrow? Can you take me?"

"Sure," Sam acknowledges with a shrug and smile. "In fact, let's make a day of it. Float from the dam to the bridge by my place."

"Yup, I know the dam and the bridge…and your place, I think. What time?"

"Noonish. I'll pack some snacks. Do you like wild grape wine?"

———

Abby shows up at Sam's place right at noon, with a 16-foot jon boat lashed to the crossbars of her pickup truck's stake bed cariers. Under the boat is enough paraphernalia for a sizable garage sale—rakes, pitchforks, shovels, ropes, anchors, a small outboard motor and gas can, four or five sifting screens—and that's just a start. She must have gotten up before dawn to pack it all and tie it down with what looks like 200 feet of rope.

"Oh my," Sam says to himself. "*I was thinkin' we'd take my canoe and just look it over today...*"

He already has the canoe in the back of his truck, held in by two stout rubber bungee cords. Besides the paddles, Sam has packed his swimming goggles and two towels in a plastic bag, plus two bottles of wine, cheese, venison sausage, and crackers in his little cooler. The canoe is pretty much a fixture in the back of his truck, still there from the day before. His river gear had taken less than two minutes to gather and stow, and didn't require any rope.

Abby slides out of her truck, beaming with excitement over their grand adventure. She wears a long-sleeved khaki shirt with the buttons open and a swimsuit top underneath with a green camouflage pattern, which for all the world strikes Sam as an army-issue women's brassiere. And she's wearing those same silky, blue running shorts over the bottom half (Sam assumes) of the camo outfit.

Deja runs to her and jumps up, resting her paws on Abby's knees, begging for attention. She leans over to scratch Deja's ears, her breasts threatening to roll out of the swimsuit top. Sam makes sure he's looking at his truck when her eyes turn to him.

Sam's thinking they didn't make high school biology teachers like this back in the 60s.

When she looks up, Sam attempts to wipe the smile from his face. He'd never been a fan of what our leaders do with the military. Then again, if they're going to make swimsuits like this with the surplus material…heck, he'd even vote Republican next time.

"What's so funny?" Abby asks, looking herself over.

"I thought you were kidding," he says, pointing at the gigantic mound of equipment in her truck. "Hate to steal the line, but we're gonna need a bigger boat."

"But this might be HUGE! We should do this right."

"How about we just take our goggles and look it over for today? Maybe gather a few of the easy bones. The rest of 'em; nobody's gonna beat us to 'em. Hell, I prob'ly canoed over top of 'em 200 times without even realizing! Let's just leave your truck—and all that—in the yard. We'll walk back up here and get it to fetch my truck afterwards.

"Oh and I packed some wine. That okay?"

"What kind?" Abby asks. "And how big's the bottle? My dad's a winemaker."

"So am I. Wild grape. Only two 750s," Sam teases

Sensing Abby is waiting for more details, he continues. "It's a dryish medium-red, like a shiraz. Except I call it a petite. Doesn't coat your mouth, and it's fruitier—14% alcohol."

Abby nods in approval. "It's after noon, right? You sure two bottles will be enough?"

"Come on in. Might as well see if you like it first. Let's have a bump before we go."

He points out and explains about the winery on the way across the yard. Abby's quite interested and they detour to check it out. She names several types of rocks Sam has already cemented in the walls.

In the kitchen, he pours them each a glass. Abby swirls it and examines it carefully, like there might be a fly or a mouse turd floating in it. Sam has seen a few folks who consider themselves wine snobs do that. It always makes his gut tighten.

After peering carefully into the glass, almost going cross-eyed, they swirl it around endlessly in their mouth, and finally conclude his wine doesn't have enough "legs", or they ask why there isn't any hint of oak, or aroma of spice. He braces himself to give yet another explanation that wild grape wine isn't commercial vineyard grape wine. Wild grape wine is supposed to be friggin' different from that California swill!

Abby sips, pauses, and smiles. "Better than my dad's. A LOT better. You must be doing something different. Hurry up and get this shit into production. I think you're onto something!"

She gulps down the rest with one tilt of her head.

He's surprised to hear such language from a school teacher he just met, but not offended. Coming from Abby, it is obviously a compliment. He worries she's drinking too quickly, though.

Sam reaches for the bottle to pour some more for her anyway. But she grabs the bottle and shoves the cork back in.

"I can feel it already." Abby wipes the back of her hand across her forehead.

"How about a roadie?" Sam asks, plucking a couple of paper cups from a stack in the cupboard. "Wanna try the cranberry on the way?"

Unlike Sam and Sally's first river trip together, there's no concern about the adverse ramifications of falling out of the canoe, other than spilling their wine. With the buzzes Abby and Sam are feeling, that's a decent possibility.

The summer day is on its way to the high 80s, under a few puffy clouds that look like they might eventually billow into the quickly passing thunderstorms that do nothing more than make a little noise and a few muddy spots on your truck.

Together they carry the canoe off the bank into the water. At river's edge, the water is knee-deep. The middle of the river is gouged by the rushing water to chest-deep. The crystal clear water and the river bottom being gravel makes the landing an inviting place to swim. Abby decides she'd like to.

She shimmies her running shorts down and steps out of them before Sam can concur. Slowly wading, shuffling her way to the middle of the river, she leans over slightly to swirl the water with her hands.

Sam instinctively glances around to make sure no one's watching him watch her. She stands for a second, facing upstream with her eyes closed like she's saying a little prayer, leans facing into the current, then pushes herself gently forward into the rushing water. At first she swims barely under the surface, arms at her side, kicking with her feet. Her long, brown hair flows gracefully behind her. She angles deeper, her backside, legs, and feet following.

Sam slips off his shirt, tosses it onto the rear seat, and shoves the canoe up onto a log. He follows Abby's watery path. Entering the bath-warm, mid-summer water is effortless. He dives forward.

Where he surfaces upstream five yards, the water is up to his neck. Abby floats easily, letting the current carry her back toward him. She reaches him and hooks her arm around his shoulders to keep from drifting away. Her legs rise to the surface, and she floats on her back.

"We swam here a lot back when I was in school." Abby uses her free hand to wipe the water from her eyes. "And partied."

Sam isn't sure what to do or where to look, so he wipes his eyes, too.

She points to the far bank. "See that old timber bridge abutment?"

He nods, silently thanking God he has a logical somewhere else to look. He had never given the structure buried against the hillside a second thought before.

"Ever been over there, to take a close look at it?"

Sam shakes his head no.

"Initials. In the wood. A Stone Creek tradition: lose your virginity at the dam swimming hole, and go down in history. Those were the days."

Sam grins. "Are your initials over there?"

"Of course!" She suddenly lets loose, and kicks and strokes toward the shore. "Come on, I'll show you!"

Back at the canoe, laughing about the abutment full of initials, they towel off and pour wine.

Sam snickers, "That S. L. sure did a number on a lotta girls! His initials are up there with…what did we count, 15 others?"

"Yup. All those 'S. L.'s had been in the wood for a while before I got mine carved there. The tradition went way back. Doesn't look like anyone's using the swimming hole for anything but swimming and launching canoes these days. That's too bad.

"You know, I asked Connie about you before you came to the school yesterday. Actually she offered me a little more than I asked for. She told me you drive a school bus and do lots of other things for the school. She said some of the teachers think of you as a Renaissance man, a free spirit."

"That's a nice way to say that I'm odd," Sam says. "I'll take it, though. I'm curious, what else did she say about me?"

"She said you're different from the other bus drivers. In a nice way. That you've been volunteering to drive the kids in a van for their river studies three or four years already. That you put up a poster reading 'I love you all! Thanks for riding my bus!' for Valentine's Day with all the kids' names."

"I had to drive a basketball trip the next afternoon. The substitute driver couldn't stand it with the poster staring him in the face. A retired teacher, at that!" Sam chuckles. "I don't know what he did with it."

"He took the poster into the office. Connie showed it to me. He said nobody who would say such a thing to the students should be allowed to work with them."

"Lovin' the kids, just tryin' to keep from going stark raving mad. My own kids are grown and gone. My stepkids, too. I loved those years when our house was the gatherin' spot. Goin' to games. Maybe I should talk to my therapist about this chronic empty nest thing?

"Anyhow, come on." Sam stuffs his towel into a plastic bag. "The bones are just a half hour downstream."

After seeing the abutment up close for the first time, and Abby's initials carved in it, then watching her laugh at herself about those times, drifting along lazily with the current (and aided by the wine), Sam pursues the subject she seems more comfortable discussing: sex.

Her casual attitude reminds him of his old friend Patrick, who'd come of age in the early 70s (a few years before Abby had), when recreational sex and drugs were mainstream. In numerous duck blinds and fishing shanties, and on many road trips, Patrick claimed to have had sex with at least 50 girls before he got married at the age of 23—many whose names he never knew, and who he never saw again. Girls from other towns who showed up just to party and have sex. It certainly was free love.

Sam had been jealous of Patrick and those other 70s kids who were screwing their brains out. Not as a protest against the establishment and the war, or the church, or their parents, or because there might not be a tomorrow because of a nuclear bomb from Russia. But because, to them, sex was simply wonderful recreation.

Not that he had anything against that. He'd just been fully absorbed in raising a family and making a living at the time.

Sam admits, "I just never could personally wrap my brain around that concept. You know, that type of sex. Other than my very first intimate encounter in the back of my '55 Chevy, me and my paramours had at least pretended we were *making love*. And it was a promise of sorts, not just screwing our brains out."

"Nope. Making love was never part of the equation, and I never made anyone promise me anything—other than to use a condom," Abby replies matter-of-factly.

"How many *didn't* you make promise you anything?" Sam asks, fueled by the wild grape wine.

"You first!" Abby teases.

"That's easy. Six, if you count my first time. But that may have been like the five-second rule when you drop food on the floor—it probably doesn't count."

She giggles and carefully swivels around to face him. She holds her cup with two hands, her elbows resting on tan legs, like Sally had done on that first trip with him. Abby is gazing off into the sky and doing the math in her head.

"I don't know. That first time at the swimming hole Memorial weekend of my sophomore year was just to keep the Stone Creek tradition alive. Everyone was doing it, no big deal. I didn't have sex again until I got pregnant the fall I was a high school senior."

Sam knows the answer, but asks anyway. "You never married?"

"Too busy during college to make any kind of commitment. Had exactly three flings. Thought I was missing out on what everyone else was getting. You know, after the weekends, listening to the other girls' stories of wild parties. But all three guys got serious before the sheets were even dry. I'm not bragging, but I only had sex one time with each of 'em—during my last three years of college— and they were buying me rings. I wasn't in the market.

"I had *needs* after college. But I didn't need to get married. I dated, but never did that love thing. I even let myself get picked up by strangers a few times. Situations where I knew I'd never see them again, which was my choice. Over the years I had two long-term affairs with older married men, but they both ended up finding another woman to have on the side when they figured out I didn't need them, and that they could never own me or control me.

"I've never let myself get so close to any man that I'd call it 'love', at least not since my senior year in high school. I was too young to know what love was back then anyway. But I love to be friends…close friends…buddies. Even that has been a while. Anyway, I'd rather spend my spare time with my daughter and granddaughter. They'll be moving here with me as soon as she finds a job. If I wanted to seek out a truly romantic interest that wasn't everyone else's business, or even a discreet 'friend with benefits', trust me—I wouldn't have moved back to Stone Creek and invited the girls along!"

"A friend with what?"

"A friend with benefits. You know, someone you like and do fun things with, but don't plan on ever falling in love with—who you just have sex with once in a while."

"Gulp. That sounds kinda wham bam."

"No! You're forgetting the friends part! Someone safe, who you trust. You have to also be able to have a great time together NOT in bed. I admit, it's a fine line. Contrary to what they try to teach us as kids, sex is really more about liking someone than loving them."

Sam rolls his eyes. "You mean every woman I like is a potential sex partner? That covers a lotta territory folks don't normally visit this side of remote Appalachian villages."

"No, not really. It's chemistry—someone who causes your mind to click in that way. Sometimes it's a spur of the moment thing. It's riskier, which can make it sexier yet. Sometimes it's more long-term."

Sam chimes in, "Unless you're Sharon Johnson!"

"Oh geez. Guess who stopped by my place with a plate of cookies? All chatty about her most recent divorce being final. Said she's taking back her maiden name this time, hopes that changes her luck."

Sam has a hunch. "Hey, what's her maiden name?"

Abby shrugs. "I can't remember."

"Wouldn't be surprised if it begins with L."

They both crane their necks to look back upstream toward the swimming hole.

She says, "Now I remember. It's Lapinsky! Never occurred to us all those 'S. L.'s carved into the abutment were from a female. We even joked about what studly guy from which neighboring town did all those girls. Good grief. And I ate her cookies!"

"So did I," Sam admits. "But that was all."

Mystery solved.

Abby takes a contemplative sip of wine, then sucks in a breath. She looks right into Sam's eyes and asks, "Seriously, how many times out of the six did you think you were in love?"

"My first wife, for sure."

"Since then?"

He thinks for a moment. "Now you got me wonderin'."

"About who?"

"My second wife. We were way better friends than my first wife and I ever were. We were also way worse enemies. But the sex was unbelievable."

"There ya go!" Abby, suddenly animated, throws her hands in the air. "Fall in love with a great piece of ass, and everything else will be fine! That's strictly a male affliction. Women know better. Sure, sex is nice, maybe even necessary, but we never fall in love just because he's a good lay."

"So what happened that landed you back here? Who left who?"

"Same shit, different guy. Except this one was single. And rich. He was like you, equating sex with forever. Got tired of hearing me say 'No' to marriage. Couldn't understand how we could have sex—decent sex, and a lot of it—but then I wouldn't marry him. He found someone else who would play that game."

Abby swivels back around to face the front. "Not a big deal. Now where are those bison bones?"

Sam shoves the paddle in and digs hard on the left side. "Around this bend…almost to the end of the long straightaway, just this side of the beaver lodge. A dead white spruce pointed right at 'em."

Sam backs his end of the canoe into the reeds so Abby is directly over the bison bones.

"Hmm." Abby cups her hands around her face to blot out the glare of the sun. "Yup, that's quite a pile!"

"Get your goggles on. I'll kneel in the bottom and do my best to hold the canoe steady while you slip overboard."

Abby turns to fish her goggles out of the plastic bag. She tosses Sam his, then fixes hers on her forehead.

Sam backs the canoe as far into the floating swamp grass as he can, a third of the 17-foot length, by reaching back with his paddle and hooking the floating bog.

"I'll lean upstream," Sam directs. "You go over the other side. And hang on once you're in the water so I don't go overboard."

"How are you going to get *you* out?"

Sam laughs. "When I found the bones, I actually fell out! See that sunken log up there? You can hold the canoe steady for me from there."

Sam's around 200 pounds, Abby in the neighborhood of 120. Sitting on the canoe seat, slowly she turns while lifting her legs over the side. Then she inches her bottom toward the edge of the canoe. He watches her carefully, preparing for her to just let herself fall in. But Abby supports her weight with her arms while leaning back over the canoe, like a gymnast, and lowers herself gently into the water to her chest. The canoe barely makes a ripple.

"Nice job," he offers. "I wish you had shown me that before I was here last time."

Abby finds the log with her feet and holds the canoe rock-steady as Sam scrambles forward to the center of the canoe. The boat doesn't tip when he slips over the side. Again he is surprised that Abby is much stronger than her feminine soft-in-all-the-right-places figure suggests. He also finds the submerged log with his feet and pushes the canoe safely back into the floating swamp grass, arm's length away.

The strong current pushes against them and Sam holds onto Abby's waist while she fixes her goggles in place. Yup, he thinks, soft in all the right places. She returns the favor.

"Let's just take a look first," he suggests.

Abby holds his elbow. She grins behind her goggles, like a kid at a birthday party. Then she slides an arm around Sam's waist and squeezes him. He puts his arm around her to help steady her.

The bones are only four feet out in front of them, and under a mere four feet of water, which is running clear, as if it's pouring out of a gigantic tap. They each take a breath. Arm in arm, they lean so their faces break the surface of the water.

It's like looking into a huge aquarium. The bones come into clear view. The marl has been washed away around the bones, down to the lumpy-smooth, blue-ish clay. There are sticks among the bones, clam shells, and a school of small sucker minnows. A tangle of rib bones is immediately obvious, as is the other scapula under them. Many other bones are visible, all within two yards of each other, some of them partially buried in the clay.

Sam runs out of air first and lifts his face out of the stream. Abby follows suit.

She shoves her goggles onto her forehead and stammers, "You are right! OH MY GOD! The whole skeleton's here!"

She scans around the wide, swampy valley. Recalling Sam's theory, Abby concurs. "That's gotta be what happened to this one. Injured in winter. It was trapped. It had to have been wounded. But not by another bison. The rut is in the summer. It was chased out here. Solid ice over the swamp. But when it got onto the thin ice over the current…"

"Shall we gather what we can today?" Sam suggests.

"Why not?"

She takes a deep breath and plunges down over the bones. Sam watches her fight the current for about 10 seconds then rise to the surface, where he catches her around the waist when the current washes her to him. She holds up two bones.

"Ribs!"

In her other hand is a vertebra, which she hands to Sam.

"That's got to be thoracic two or three! There's a whole bunch more vertebrae right there under the ribs!"

The vertebra's the same color as the skull, nearly black with blotches of dark umber.

They spend two hours diving, taking turns and helping each other fight the current to stay over the bones, sometimes using each other's legs as anchors. Each search of the river bottom stirs up a cloud of silt, which quickly flows away downstream.

Once they've recovered all the bones from the surface of the clay, they dig deeper. Sometimes Sam feels something within the river bottom with his feet. He stands there up to his neck, and Abby follows his legs down, and wrap hers around his, to dig with her hands. Digging for the bones becomes a game, a challenge, like an Easter egg hunt.

Sam and Abby are surprised the lower leg bones are stuck upright completely within the clay, as if the bison had died standing. Abby names all the bones as they put them into the canoe: mandible, hyoid, humerus, tarsal, atlas and axis, cervical, metapodial, radius, ulna, femur, sacrum, and many more.

Abby takes a mental inventory of their find. Strangely, the pelvis—a sizable bone—is missing, even though they have the sacrum and both femurs. They recover only one set each of the hoof and phalanx bones, which are located directly above the hoof. They are certain the others are buried deeper in the clay. All total, they find around 90% of the bones above the creature's ankles and forward of the tail.

Like on that day with Deja, getting back into the canoe in deep water is an issue, compounded by the fact that they don't want to risk tipping it and spilling the bones. Sam suggests it will be a simple and pleasant enough solution to let the current drift them to the solid ground downstream 300 yards.

One on each side of the bow, each hanging onto the top edge of the canoe, they float on their backs alongside each other, arm in arm when they aren't paddling with them, occasionally kicking with their legs to keep on course.

"So now what?" Abby wonders, as they drift along and she gazes skyward. "What are you going to do with the bones?"

"You know," Sam admits, "I haven't given that any thought, other than I hope the state or some agency doesn't own them. I don't know how public we should go with this."

"Technically, the state does own everything in and under its waterways. But folks have been finding bison bones in the Red River, the Red Lake River, and others pretty regularly. The state has never stepped in, as far as I know."

Sam points back upstream toward the dam. "When my neighbor wanted to build a house above the dam, he found some Native artifacts—arrowheads, chunks of pottery, grinding and scraping tools. Some agency swooped in and put the whole project on hold for months while they sifted through the soil. A big deal, in the newspapers."

"That's different. Ancient sites with evidence of humans are the responsibility of the state to investigate for historical significance, or in case the site is a burial ground. I've worked on several of those myself."

"Monetarily speaking, are the skull and the bones worth anything? Did I just find the golden egg to finish building my winery?"

Abby laughs. "Oh, if they were that valuable, you'd definitely have the state on your butt! And they'd sell the bones to the highest bidder!"

"Hmm."

"They'd make a nice attraction in your winery, though."

"Or," Sam suggests, "at school."

He smiles and looks over at Abby, who stares back with wide eyes and open mouth.

"Then again, that would take someone at school who knows something about bison, to put the skeleton together and preserve it."

"You would really give the bison to the school?"

"As a matter of fact, I have a friend, an elder from the tribe. The reservation school has bison bones on display. A few times a year, they have a sacred ceremony to feed the bison spirits. I think that would be a great experience for our kids, to have the elders visit and do that."

Sam bites his lip; he can feel his eyes moistening. It feels like when he was at the births of those babies. Or when Sally won the rodeo, while he was right there in the arena tending the third barrel. It's like destiny's being fulfilled and something is very right with his world.

At that moment, directly above them, a jagged bolt of lightning streaks and crackles from one billowing cloud to another. Before the lightning bolt has disappeared, the thunder booms. Instantly, rain drops as big as bison tears begin falling all around them.

Sam smiles at Abby, who's biting her lip. Her eyes are wet, but not from the rain.

He jokes as he points to the sky, "I'll take that as a sign."

She whispers as she runs her hand up and down his neck, "You dear man…"

Sam Ryan likes Abby Tucker, a lot. It was an immediate attraction he hoped she felt, too. He knew as soon as she'd grabbed his hand in the classroom. His attraction to her wasn't only that of some horny, old fart lusting after a nicely put-together package 10 years younger. That was only part of it (well, about two-thirds, he'd say).

Sam's always the river tour guide. He admits he doesn't possess much technical knowledge about the flora and fauna. To his neophyte canoe occupants, he's more of an orator-type than one to recite snappy Latin names.

"That's the log I floated within 50 feet of when a bobcat was sunnin' itself during a January thaw, sittin' on its haunches just like a house cat on the kitchen windowsill, its eyes just sleepy slits."

Or "Get here in the first or second week of June. There will be a thousand wild iris blooms on this bank, a genuine purple haze."

Or "One time I lay in the bottom of the canoe for half an hour—letting it drift and bump along as the boat, breeze, and the current wished—with my eyes closed. When I finally rose to my elbows, and peered over the edge, not 15 feet away there was a beautiful ten-point buck in the river up to its belly, antlers still covered with velvet, staring at me."

Abby rattles off scientific names of all different kinds of trees, plants, and flowers and adds in the common names, like a baseball savant recites MVPs and World Series winners. Sam learns that the common name for the wild iris growing at water's edge in June is Southern Blue Flag. He asks Abby why a flower from the northernmost part of the lower 48 has "southern" in its name. Abby, with the wine kicking in, suggests that someone from Canada must have named it.

They climb the high sandbank, hauling along their snacks, wine, and towels. They eat and drink their fill, then lie alongside each other in the shade, like they'd been taking such jaunts and naps together for years.

Sam has never liked being around women who assume that just because they possess Part A and he has the complementing Part B and they're horny, that he's automatically going to obediently drop his trousers upon their command. He doesn't think Abby has been flaunting her sexuality today, or yesterday either, to tease or to actually get something going. She just seems perfectly comfortable in her skin, although he admits he finds her feminine charms considerably distracting.

The Karen comparison haunts him again. Abby reminds him of Karen, who was a few years younger than Abby when they'd met, and who was also seemingly oblivious to how physically desirable she was. With Karen, it was the whole package. He loved her mind, her heart, her soul, in addition to being physical with her.

But they became friends first, which—except for his first time ever in the '55 Chevy (which might not count anyway), and one time drunk in a hot tub with the neighbor lady—was the way he operated when it came to having sex. The physical part with Karen didn't happen until after he'd fallen in love with the rest of her.

Sam props himself up on one elbow, facing Abby. She's so close he can see every hair on her stomach. Sand is stuck under the elastic of her swimsuit top. She feels him stir.

"What's up?" she asks, her eyes still closed. A small smile plays on her lips.

"Um…you've got, um…sand in your swimsuit top."

Sam knows for sure his comment is the result of the wine. He'd never said anything remotely like that to any woman he'd just met the day before. Except, he did with Sally the evening they'd met at the quarry bottom, with the crack about her carpet not matching her curtains. He wonders if maybe he's turning into a dirty old man. He's always entertained such R-rated thoughts. But now they flow out of his mouth like wild grape wine from the bottle.

"Hmm?" Abby smiles with her eyes closed. "I bet you've got some sand stuck, too…somewhere."

She stands up, smiles devilishly, and begins side-stepping down the steep sandbank to the water. Turning away to pull off her swimsuit top, she shakes her hair so it hangs evenly down her back, then wades into the water to her waist. She shimmies her swimsuit bottom down and steps out of it.

"Come on," Abby beckons. "Help me with this sand and I'll help you with yours…"

They laugh like a couple of silly, drunk hippies at Woodstock, harmlessly skinny dipping in broad daylight. They put their freshly rinsed swimsuits back on their perfectly cleaned and inspected bodies, laughing about how sand gets into everything no matter what, so doing the deed back up on the high sandbank on their towels might be painful, and is therefore out of the question.

They spend another hour floating and discussing their views on sex and relationships, making it all the way down to the birch clump hanging over the river.

Sam noses the canoe onto a sandbar. "This is where I bring my kids for their river experiments." He points to a path that heads downstream, parallel to the river. "An easy walk from the bridge, five minutes. You're certainly welcome to use this place, too."

Abby gets out of the front of the canoe and takes her towel. The riverbank is only a foot high, the ground is moss-covered and soft. With her back to Sam she pulls her swimsuit top off over her head.

She turns to Sam. "We've talked enough…"

She saunters seductively back to the canoe, beckoning with her finger. She takes off her bottoms, too, and drops her suit onto the canoe seat. Helping Sam pull off his swimsuit, she leads him up onto the bank to a particularly soft-looking spot. She throws down their towels and hands him a condom. He hasn't a clue where she got it from.

It's a good old-fashioned groping-biting-sweating-hollering and finally flopping-onto-their-backs-exhausted romp.

Neither of them had noticed that the canoe had drifted away—with their swimsuits in it.

"Oh shit!" Sam exclaims. "Oh God, I wonder how long it's been gone?"

"Could be at least 20 minutes," Abby teases with a grin. "Nice job, Sam!"

"Here's what we'll do," he suggests frantically. "You walk down the river. It's all sand and gravel, knee-deep at the most. If you find it, holler. I'll take the trail. Hopefully

I'll beat it to the bridge, or at least it'll be hung up on the pilings. If it made it through the bridge, oh shit—then we'll be walkin' to my place in our towels."

Sam wraps his towel around his waist and awkwardly hurries down the trail, hunched over, as quickly as he possibly can. He looks like a guy who's just jumped out of a bedroom window, an angry husband crawling out after him.

Abby tosses her towel over her shoulder and walks into the river in the all-together, proceeding nonchalantly, like she's window shopping at the mall.

When Sam reaches the barb-wire fence by the bridge, he is relieved to find that the canoe is there. But it's lodged precariously and about to catch the rushing water and head downstream. He ducks through the fence and a barb catches his towel. The canoe swings free.

He streaks across the ditch. The canoe is loose under the bridge and moving away rapidly. Bare-naked Sam dives headlong between the pilings and takes several frantic strokes. He barely reaches the rope that trails the canoe. He's under the bridge, and the canoe is in the stream beyond the bridge, in full view of an approaching vehicle he can hear. Quickly, Sam pulls the canoe toward him. The vehicle stops and he hears a door slam.

"Sam!" Maureen hollers. "You down there?"

He pulls his swimsuit on in a hurry, not realizing it's on backward.

"Yup, Maureen," he hollers back. He hurries to hide Abby's suit, tossing it into the cooler. He can hear Maureen making her way down the hill. "Canoe got away from me, ha ha. Be there in a sec…"

He sloshes between the pilings and comes out the upstream side, forcing a happy grin for his friend who is waiting for him.

"Hey, Sam! Whew, that's a pile of bones!" Maureen exclaims, pointing to the canoe. "Whose truck is that at your place with all the junk in it?"

"The new science teacher's. She helped me gather the bones. A bison skeleton. Found it yesterday up in the rice bed."

"Oh! Where is she?"

"Umm," he points downstream. "Takin' care of business. You know."

"Oh yeah? I'd love to meet her."

"Uhh…she said it might be a while."

"Why didn't she just wait 'til you guys walked to your house?"

"Heh heh. Well, sometimes you just can't wait, and… well, you've seen my bathroom."

Sam adds, "If she found some special plant or something, could be a while. She's really into that shit."

"Alright then. I gotta get home anyway," Maureen says. "I'm sure we'll meet some other time."

"Yup. Sounds good. Some other time. Bye-bye now!"

She turns to climb back up to the road, and Sam sucks in a breath of relief.

"One more thing. I didn't know men's swimsuits had the tie string in the back."

Sam feels back there. "Yup. Yup. A new style. From France."

He reaches behind his back with both hands, gives each end of the strings a pull, and ties them tightly. There already isn't enough room for his nuts.

"Damn French!" Sam curses, shaking his fist toward Europe. "That's the last time I'll ever try to be a fashionista!"

Maureen laughs and shakes her head, hopping into her truck and driving away.

When the car is out of sight, Abby appears with a shit-eating grin, naked except for the towel around her neck, the ends hanging down just covering her breasts. She shakes her fist toward the sky, shouting loudly and proudly, "Damn French!"

CHAPTER 8

TURD IN A PUNCH BOWL

Wednesday August 13, 2003

Laura eyes Sam suspiciously. He looks too upbeat.

"How's it going?" She peers over the top of her reading glasses, holding her pen ready in one hand, and thumbing her temple with the other. "To what do we owe this appointment?"

"I'm fine. Just fine." Sam avoids his therapist's gaze by looking out the window, a hint of a smile crossing his face.

"In my professional opinion, and pardon me for sounding unprofessional," Laura offers, "You look like a man who just got, you know...*a girlfriend*."

Sam smiles devilishly. "Five or six times since my last visit, is all. Who's countin' anyway? Out of the blue!" He thrusts his arms up and apart.

He points at Laura. "You know, you should have your own weekly spot on Oprah for handing out such great advice! Out of the blue! That's what she said, too!"

"Who said that?"

He tells her the story of the bison bones he'd found the very day he left her office last. About meeting Abby, the biology teacher/bison expert not 24 hours after he'd found the bones. About their dive effort not 24 hours after then, including the detours to the high sandbank and the birch clump. Abby's friends with benefits theory. About how they'd been seeing each other just about every day (or night) since then. And about how he's going to invite her to accompany him to his son's wedding.

Laura comments, "Friends with benefits, huh? Are you sure? No offense or judgment. Maybe that's what it is for Abby. But that's not the Sam I know."

"That's what it is. I think the problem is keeping Abby from falling in love with ME!"

"Sounds like you definitely stepped outside your comfort zone when it comes to sex and intimacy. You allowed Abby to make the move, to have sex with you, even though you barely know each other."

"Yup. There was always guilt associated with uncommitted sex that I viewed as one-sided, her-sided. I'm pretty sure I'm over that now."

Sam smiles and does a quick cobweb-clearing head shake. "It didn't feel anything like Sparky coercing me. It was just fun. A whole lotta fun."

"Lord knows the timing seems divinely inspired," Laura agrees. "I hate to bring this up when things are going so well, but what about Sally?"

"What about Sally? She's history. Ran off."

"Pardon me, but I'm trained to interpret an answer like you just gave. There's still a lot of emotion there, maybe even anger?"

"You're the one who said to open myself to the possibilities."

"That I did. And that's still good advice. I'm glad you're happy with your new friend, Abby. I'm not questioning the timing. Nor am I questioning your intentions or motivations. I only need you to decide if you still want to work on your losses. Do you agree it took an awful long time for you to think about anyone but Karen?"

Sam nods.

"And do you agree that Karen dogged you and Sally? There were all of those comparisons, expectations, and pain. Not just about losing Karen, but the pain of being with her?"

He sighs and blows out a deep breath.

"It's up to you. You're not necessarily your history. We've talked about this. It's your perspective of that history that defines who you are now, and where you're likely headed. I'm glad Sparky isn't shadowing this intimate relationship."

Sam admits, "This thing with Abby, it's not that big of a deal. I s'pose, in a strangely hedonistic way, that's where I needed to go—guilt-free."

"But I wonder if you're getting wrapped up in this, even though it's only two weeks along. Having expectations. What if she declines to attend your son's wedding with you?" Laura cautions.

"Okay. Okay. I get it."

"Friends with benefits can be a good thing…once you've known each other long enough to really become friends. I think even Abby might not put you two in that category yet, if she gave it serious thought. She might have gotten caught up in this, too, for her own reasons.

You wouldn't be the first two rebounding folks on Earth to quickly fall into each other's arms and find it pretty darn good stuff."

Sam rests his hand on his chin. "So now what?" Then he smiles. "Excuse me, but didn't I see you in a punch bowl once?"

"No." Laura responds. "That was a Baby Ruth."

"Have all the fun you can stand. But without Karen or Sally, or Sparky, looking over your shoulder. Like they say, three's a crowd."

Sam hadn't spoken with Maureen about Sally, but she let him know that Bill had filed for divorce right away, and she still hadn't heard from her sister.

Maureen had been served with Sally's divorce papers on August 8th. There was a preliminary hearing the next Friday. Joan represented Sally and Maureen. Peabody had no luck convincing Judge Riley to give his client the entirety of the joint assets. Riley set the ground rules. If Sally didn't surface within the next six months, Peabody could proceed with the required published notices, and the court would grant the divorce. But the property settlement would have to wait for Sally.

They also had a preliminary hearing on Pop's estate that day. Joan had drawn up Pop's new will for him shortly after Sally and Bill married. Maureen was named the executor and would be paid 3.33% of each beneficiary's take. Sally was willed a full third of Pop's estate, as were each of his sons.

So of course Peabody feigned disbelief that such an obviously tainted will should be enforced. (Everyone in the courtroom figured Peabody knew all about tainted wills because he'd drawn up so many of them on behalf of his crooked clients.) Riley set ground rules for the estate, too. Unless Bill could prove some sort of hardship, and Peabody could prove Pop wasn't of sound mind when he signed the will, they weren't going to do a darn thing without Sally. Period.

The subject of Roy and Elvis came up as well, with Bill demanding they be seized and returned to him and Robert. The horses that Sam, with the help of his runaway wife, had "hoodwinked" Pop out of. Joan produced a bill of sale for the team, the wagon, and all the gear that Pop (wisely) had drawn up. The judge sternly advised Peabody and Bill that the team of horses would be neither the subject of the estate nor the divorce.

Bill and Robert hadn't a clue that cases like theirs were like the proverbial goose that lays golden eggs for a crooked attorney like Peabody. If history was to repeat itself, and it likely would, there wouldn't be much left, if anything, of their share of Pop's estate for them after the trial was over.

The boys didn't know a valid legal motion from cow flop. Whatever scheme Peabody suggested, the brothers eagerly lapped up. All Peabody had to do was bring up any of those four names—Sally, Maureen, Joan, or Sam—and Bill and Robert would automatically salivate with revenge. And the legal fee meter would keep ticking. Peabody even talked them into suing Sam for the horses. One time, Bill did ask what it was all going to cost, but Peabody blew him off, said they'd settle up after they won, assuring his client there'd be plenty for everybody.

Normally the opposing attorney attempts to nip such frivolous issues and wasted court time in the bud, by asking the judge to award attorney's fees to be paid by the other side. Joan, was providing her legal services for free, and Riley could see what Peabody was up to in his fleecing of the brothers, but neither was the least bit inclined to put a stop to it.

August 27, evening

Maureen doesn't recognize the number on her caller ID.

She answers tentatively, hoping it's Sally.

"Where are you? It says Mesa, Arizona. I'm coming right down to get you!"

"No, I'm not in Mesa," Sally replies. "Not anywhere close to there. I'm using a calling card."

"Please, please…let me help you!"

"I can't come home." Sally sobs into the phone.

"Why not?"

"Bill will kill me! He tried to kill Dakota. He shot Sheba. He shot my trailer as I was driving away."

"We can get him put away. We have the needle and syringe."

"I found the syringe in the barn. But then he found out. I don't know how many times I saw him or Robert looking in the barn for it. A kitten had taken it."

"Sally, we can get Bill put away for a long time. All the assaults. Trying to kill Dakota…Sheba. And now threatening your life with a gun. But we need your help!"

"None of that will stand up. Nobody saw him stick the needle into Dakota. I never let the cops do anything about the beatings. He'll claim self-defense with Sheba. The bullet hole in my trailer doesn't prove anything."

"He filed for divorce."

After no response from her sister, Maureen continues, "He wants everything. Claims you ran out on him and told him you don't want a thing."

"I didn't tell him that, but he's right. I don't want anything."

"That's crazy! I know Pop set it up for you to get your share and get the hell out! Honey, are you gonna deny Pop his wish to help you, to thank you?"

"I can't think about any of it right now."

"There's already been a hearin' about the divorce and Pop's will. The judge put everything on hold until you show up…or are found. Joan's doin' the legal work. I'm the court-appointed trustee for all your things in the meantime. There's no hurry, we got six months before the judge will act."

Again, no response from Sally.

Maureen asks, "Are you gonna tell me where you are?"

Sally simply sighs and asks tentatively, "How's Sam?"

"He's doin' okay. That night after you left, he went to the farm and got Sheba. Bill had dragged that poor dog out to the pasture and just let her lie there. Sam buried her at his place. Why don't you call him?"

"Has he been askin' about me?"

"Well…no."

Sally cries softly.

"He helped Joan and me and the deputy pack your things, get 'em off the farm."

"Tell him thanks for buryin' Sheba."

"I will."

Maureen asks, "Hey, did you ever hear the real story about what happened to Bill's cousin's pickup truck?"

"What?"

"Rumor has it Bill and the cousin tried to hijack the team and wagon after the funeral. To say Sam put the fear of God in 'em would be a gross understatement."

"Good for him. But they'll still try to get even."

"Sally, you gotta tell me where you are. I care about you and I worry so much it hurts."

"I'm at a ranch in the Black Hills. But you can't say a word to anyone. And don't come out here, okay?"

"I promise. And you promise to stay in touch, okay?"

"I'm fine now. My nose was broke. Had to get it set. Doc and his wife, Maria, took me in."

"What're you doin' for money? Are you workin'? Want me to send you some? I can get whatever you need from Pop's estate."

"Helpin' out here. They got a herd of grandkids. I'm teaching them to barrel race. I'm takin' care of the horse stock, and keepin' house for Doc and Maria. I'm fine, really, sis. I get room and board for me and for Sparky and Dakota, plus a little cash. I told 'em the whole story. About Sam, too."

"So are you gonna call him?"

"No. I've done enough damage. If you want, tell him I'm okay, but not where I'm at or what I'm doin', okay? I still don't have it all sorted out."

Sally gives Maureen her address and phone number.

"One last thing," Maureen says. "How'd it go at the women's clinic in Fargo? Their number was on your phone."

"I can't talk about it. Forget I ever went there."

With a small, damp paint brush, Sam smooths the mortar joints between the rocks he'd laid up on the winery. He usually put rocks up in the morning, but he'd had company overnight again. And he'd worked with Abby on the bison skeleton at the school until after lunch.

Deja is playing with a mouse she has cornered in the winery when Maureen drives in.

"Lookin' good," she says. "Got time to pour a glass of wine for your neighbor?"

Sam nods, smiles and points to a rock. "Last one. Just a sec…"

He gives the mortar joint two more careful brushes, then swishes the brush clean in a bucket of water.

Deja, proud as punch, brings her master the mouse, whose wiggling hind feet hang out the side of the puppy's mouth.

"Drop it," Sam orders firmly.

The gangly puppy opens her mouth and lets the mouse fall out.

"Stay!"

Deja watches intently, ears alert and tongue panting, as the mouse scurries into the rock pile.

"Those two! They can do that all day. I swear the mouse is playin' along willingly. Come here, girl."

Deja obeys long enough to get her ears jostled. Then she dashes along the mouse's trail and sniffs furiously around the rock pile.

Sam jokes, "Who needs a damn cat, huh?"

He invites Maureen to follow him into the house for wine. She sits at the table. Sam plucks two wine glasses from the dish drainer and examines them against the kitchen sink light.

"What's up?" he asks, as he pulls the reusable cork from a bottle.

"Saw your picture in the paper! With that new biology teacher, Abby Tucker. The bison bones. That's pretty nice of you, givin' 'em to the school. And she's an expert. What are the chances?"

"Well, the school and I are sharin' 'em, actually," Sam corrects. "The superintendent wouldn't let the school take ownership. He's worried about gettin' in trouble with the state, and the tribe, and the Department of the Interior…maybe even the Pope. Once I get the winery up and goin', I'll have 'em here during the summer. Don't think I want the entire skeleton—it'd take up too much room. The skull, a few other bones—a small display.

"Abby, umm, Ms. Tucker and I took two of her students who scuba dive to recover what we didn't on our first attempt. Maybe we'll put some photos of the dive in the winery. The newspaper articles, some history of bison 'round these parts."

"Yeah, you're pretty famous," Maureen teases.

"All the way from Park Rapids to Detroit Lakes! Heh heh. So, what's really up?"

She hesitates and lifts her eyes to watch his expression. "Sally called."

Sam faces away. He stops pouring their wine and sighs.

"She's fine. But she's not comin' home, at least not for a while."

He hands her the glass and slides into a chair. "Why not?"

"She didn't exactly say. But she did say Bill threatened to kill her if she came back. How's that for irony, when all along Sally's been worried about *him*."

He shakes his head. "Where is she?"

"I'm not s'posed to tell anyone. And I won't. She said to thank you for buryin' Sheba, though."

There's nothing left for Sam to say, so he only nods.

"I'm sorry. You really loved her, didn't you?" Maureen reaches out to touch his arm.

"Not sure what to call what it was..."

"That's awfully past tense."

"Yup, sure is."

CHAPTER 9

QUESTIONS AND ANSWERS

The first Thursday afternoon of the new school year, Sam sits in a school van out front, waiting to take one group from the biology class to the river for their monitoring and experiments. He will escort them upstream to the overhanging birches like he had previous years.

Abby's wearing jeans and a sweatshirt, a pair of hip boots draped over one arm. Her brown hair is pushed back by sunglasses so she looks right out of an Eddie Bauer catalog. She waves and heads for the second van, which she'll be driving.

They had decided not to go public. But one student, Stephanie, sees them exchange what might be interpreted as a fond glance.

She approaches Sam's van and asks, "You got to know Ms. Tucker pretty well finding that bison skeleton, huh?"

"Sure, a little."

"How well?" Stephanie quizzes, eyes squinting and hands on hips. "Drove by your place Saturday and saw a ton of cars, including Ms. Tucker's."

"Hosting my son's wedding. She pitched in a little."

"And her truck was still there in the morning…"

Sam is caught off guard but quickly thinks up a plausible lie. He shrugs. "Truck wouldn't start. Dead battery."

They park the vans at the canoe landing next to the bridge.

Abby comments, "The kids said you usually take them upstream and the other group works near the bridge."

Sam nods.

"The bridge sounds boring. Got any suggestions? Anyplace interesting?" She points upstream, smiling.

"Yeah, Anderson never got too far from the van."

He points to the fence on the upstream side of the bridge. "A deer trail along the north bank. Follow it about an eighth of a mile. Remember where we floated past the birch clump that's tipped almost into the water? A nice shallow spot. I remember a hard bottom there. Umm… you know, I mean solid ground," Sam stammers.

Abby turns with a sly smile.

"Thanks, I think I remember the place. See you in an hour. Hey, what's that?" She points to the fence. "Looks like a beach towel. Somebody must have forgotten it there."

"I'll take my crew downstream," Sam offers.

Sam catches himself watching Abby walk away. And Stephanie catches Sam watching Abby walk away.

"Dead battery, my butt," Stephanie says as she rolls her eyes.

Friday, September 5th

Maureen knocks on Sam's screen door. It's noon and she's lucky to find him home, because he'd been hauling rocks for the winery during midday lately. He subbed on a regular bus route in the morning, and is scheduled to drive the varsity football team to their away game at 1:30 this afternoon.

"Sam! You in here?"

"Yup," he hollers back. "Come on in. I'm in the spare bedroom."

Maureen walks down the hall to find Sam stirring the wine must. The walls are lined with large, plastic vats.

She inhales deeply. "Ahh, I love that aroma, fruit and yeast workin'. Whew, you got a good start!"

He stirs the must with a stick of oak molding about four feet long. He'd had that stirrer since he'd moved into his house. Halfway up, the molding is permanently stained a beautiful burgundy.

"Yeah, 10 vats. About 75 gallons."

"Where'd you get all these grapes? They're not ready up here yet, are they?"

"Matt usually helps me pick south of here, where I lived with Karen, on Labor Day weekend. The wedding took priority this year. But, unbeknownst to me, the kids and their friends picked near the Rum River north of Anoka—enough for three vats—and brought 'em up. So we made the wine making part of the wedding festivities. They insisted. All the guests took a turn with the crank on the crusher and helped with the mixing. Very symbolic. I s'pose that's how me and the kids will celebrate their anniversary every year now.

"Here's the best part: Dad got all caught up in it, takin' the measurements and readings, makin' notes. The mad scientist us kids grew up with has returned! So Labor Day he and Jill and I and…a friend went down to Villard to pick.

"Matt and Marsha followed us there on their way home. Dad spent most of his time sittin' in the shade, drinkin' beer, and tellin' us when we missed a cluster, reminding us to pick off the bad fruit. It's a bumper crop down there. That's where the other seven vats came from. Jill and Dad stayed an extra day to get 'em crushed and into the vats."

"That's great news. Your dad, huh?"

"That's not even the half of it! Soon as Matt and Marsha get that baby on the ground and dried off, they're movin' to Walla Walla for two years. Going to enology and viticulture school. Looks like I got partners for my winery!

"Oh! Almost forgot. My daughter, Keith, and the boys will be movin' back to Minnesota next summer! Can hardly wait to get those boys on the river."

"Wow! Sounds like it's all comin' together. That's wonderful."

"So, anyhow, what brings you over here?"

"Got a letter for ya. From Sally." Maureen watches for his reaction.

"Oh," he says, his gut turning into a knot.

Sam pulls a paper towel from his back pocket and runs it down the stirring stick to clean off the juice and crushed berries. He quickly looks around for a place to set the damp stick. Distracted, he dunks the stick back into the vat he'd been stirring and stirs it again.

His back to Maureen, he attempts to seem uninterested. "Um, just put it on the bed, please."

Sam pulls the stirring stick out, and lets it drip off a couple of seconds. He quickly moves the stick into the next vat, never looking back at Maureen.

"Gotta get over to Detroit Lakes," Maureen says. "If you're gonna write back, bring it over and I'll send it."

He doesn't look up from his task. "Yup. Yup. See you. Thanks."

He continues on to the next vat and stirs it with gentle, circular strokes until the crushed berries sink into the must. The screen door slaps the frame, then he hears it creak open again.

"Lettin' Deja in!" Maureen hollers.

Sam finishes stirring the final vat, wipes the stick dry with the paper towel, and covers all 10 vats with bath towels. As he starts to leave, he glances at the envelope, the knot in his gut tightening further.

It's plump, at least three or four sheets of paper. Reminds him of the letter he'd received from his father the year after Karen died, when he was wandering around the countryside, living in a camper, and losing what was left of his sanity. He'd written to his father that winter. Spilled his guts. Not angrily, he thought, but just informing him what it had been like as his son.

Sam had considered it a plea for help, for forgiveness. Told his dad the good stuff, too. After no reply, he had written again a month later, just about current events. And another a couple of months later. In the meantime, Sam had given Jill a copy of his story. His dad finally wrote back after the third letter.

Sam wasn't his son anymore. Disowned.

Sam hadn't been ready for that. And he's not ready for this letter, either. He has no idea what, if anything, he wants to hear from her. Maureen had already about covered it anyway.

He grabs a half-drunken soda from the fridge then fetches the letter. Deja declines to ride with him in the golf cart. Instead, she runs ahead down the trail. Sam drives slowly toward the fire ring.

Another red oak is growing a fresh bright orange and lemony yellow chicken-of-the-woods fungus on its trunk. Abby had given them all a lesson about the delicacy after the wedding ceremony. She even sautéed up a huge pan for them to try. It was delicious.

The grass around the fire ring is still flattened from all the wedding traffic. Sam sits on the west rock and takes a sip of soda before he slices open the envelope with his pocketknife. It occurs to him that there are matches in a jar on the stump in case he wants to start a fire with the letter.

Dear Sam,   Monday, September 1, 2003

Maureen and I talked. Things are going so well for you. Your dreams are coming true! I understand why you're counting me out of your life. But I'm not going to apologize for anything.

I've thought long and hard about you and me. Sometimes people like you show up in a life to help others like me make changes, seemingly getting nothing out of it for themselves. Sometimes people like me show up in a life for the same reason, but the purpose isn't so obvious.

I know I received plenty from you. I really needed your friendship to realize the true state of my marriage. I needed you to show me there was another way to live. Maybe I needed to show you the same, huh?

I'd like to stay in touch with you. But if you don't write back, I'll understand. And I won't bother you again.

I'm going to make it easy for you. I know this is grape season and you're getting ready for bow hunting. You probably won't have time to write a real letter. So if you want to, just fill in the blanks and give this back to Maureen to send to me.

Sally

Sam reads through the questions. He decides to write back *only* to show her how it could have been with him if she'd had the courage to leave her asshole of a pinhead husband.

He carves a chicken-of-the-woods off the oak tree on the way home. Like Abby had showed him, he cuts off the fronds and outer edges and checks for wormholes. There are none. It's a perfectly fresh specimen—firm and brilliant blaze orange on top, with the underside bright lemony yellow to lime green.

He calls Abby at school, informing her proudly of his find, and invites her to a late dinner. And to after-dinner, after he returns from the football game. She declines, says she's spending the weekend in Moorhead with girlfriends.

Sam still doesn't know Abby that well yet, but there's something about her voice that makes him wonder if those really are her plans. She doesn't apologize for not being able to make it that evening, even though they've barely been out of each other's sight for over a month. Maybe Laura is right. Are his expectations beyond what they should be? Is he already pinning his needs to Abby's actions?

Finally, he asks himself, *Is Abby right about what men fall really in love with—a great piece of ass?*

Hell, in her defense, they'd really never even cuddled and talked. The only time the term "love" had come up was about food, drink, the kids at school, the natural world. Although there was that time she said, "I love when you do that."

Sam has to get to the bus garage. He'd answer Sally's letter that evening, after his bus trip.

How is the grape crop, on a scale of 1 to 10? Highlight of the season so far?

It's a 9.5. My dad came up to help out. We mended a lot of our personal fence. My son and his wife are going to winemaking school in Walla Walla in a year. Looks like I got partners in this venture.

How's your daughter and the boys?

The boys are still CLFs (Cute Little Fellas). They're moving back to Minnesota next summer.

Is the big buck still out there? If so, will you shoot him if you have the chance? What if he attacks you?

Yes. No. Then I guess I'll be having a pair of fawns in the spring.

What kind of ducks did we see on the river that day, after you found me naked in the woods with all your morels already picked?

Wood ducks (Was that you?)

What was I wearing at the rodeo the day you helped, and Dakota and I won?

The same outfit you wore when Bill helped, the night Dakota tried to kill him by the third barrel. By the way, I was there that night.

Forgive me for tossing in one of Pop's favorite jokes. George W. Bush's presidential library was destroyed by a flood when his toilet overflowed. What kind of books were they? And how many?

Coloring books, 2. God bless him (Pop, that is)

How are Elvis and Roy doing?

Fine. The senior class has dibs on them and the wagon (and me) for their homecoming float.

And Deja?

Growing like a weed. Taught her to fetch my slippers. She's going to be a helluva grouse dog. Already caught a young one all by herself. I might even take her duck hunting on the river. Haven't hunted ducks since my last Lab died.

How was the wedding? Highlights?

Pop was right. The fire ring was a wonderful place for a ceremony. Highlights include my ex tripping over fresh horseshit in her $150 open-toed sandals and her present husband drinking too much *homemade wine and comparing her butt to Elvis's. (She hit him over the head with a can of Pringles.) Actually, it was a wonderful celebration. I don't know if I've ever seen a couple so suited for and committed to each other as Matt and Marsha.*

When will you find out if your son and his wife are having a boy or a girl? Do you have a preference?

Late Oct. Marsha will be 20 weeks on the 29th. A boy to carry on the family name would be nice. But if my son fails with that, I told him I'll make a family name-bearer myself. Really, I'm just happy to be a grandpa again so soon. They're talking about having Maureen be the midwife and having the baby here at my place.

Maureen told me about the bison bones. Congratulations! See anything else interesting on/in the river lately?

Now that I think about it, after the two dives to recover the rest of the skeleton, I canoed it again shortly after the second dive (alone) to offer tobacco and thanks for the bison. And I apologized for not doing that first, before disturbing him. Otherwise I've been working a lot—finished a fireplace, and made some progress on the winery.

Why did you stick with me so long? Why does it feel like I've known you my entire life?

That's why I read weird books, to try to make some sense out of relationships. There's no logical reason we hit it off like we did. So I'm blaming it on past lives or karma or the way the planets lined us up.

Do you miss me?

Of course I miss the connection we had. But not the part that kept drawing you back to Bill or the part that made you go away and stay away.

Can you understand and accept that I need to be on my own for a while? At least until Bill and I are officially through and everything's settled? Me being around would make it worse to get it over with. Maureen and Joan are taking care of everything just fine. Plus, I need this time for myself. I can't ask you to be a shoulder to lean on. Lord knows I've already used you to the point you probably don't want to hear from me ever again.

A month or so ago I accepted that I might never see or hear from you again. That was a huge step for me. I just have to keep you, or anyone else who comes along and turns my head, in perspective. I'm not chasing after any more rainbows. It has to be real...it has to be possible...we have to be on the same page.

I know about your mother and father, how they died. And your boyfriend who killed himself. Maybe those were good reasons for you to be so reluctant to leave Bill. Maybe having a baby with him could have healed things for you guys. But I can also see why you went to Fargo for the abortion. Why you finally had to make a choice. Why you couldn't share a child with him after all. No doubt, Bill would make your life and the child's a living hell forever.

I've already heard all I'm ever going to listen to about Bill. You see, I'm not putting my life on hold while you straighten out your shit. I loved you, but you used him to keep from loving me back. And continue to do so.

If I write again, will you write back?

No, I don't think writing would be a good idea. This isn't a threat or some sort of trick to get you back here. Yes, maybe someday we will both be in the right place at the same time. But that might never happen. For now, I'm putting myself first. I need to take care of myself and all the things in my life I love that are real.

I'm sorry.

Sam

September 17, 2003

"Not that I have a thing against this arrangement with Abby," Sam informs Laura. "Even though there's no romance to any of it…to us. We really are just friends with benefits. She's never gone out of her way for me or anything I like to do that isn't already about her. You know, she loves helpin' with the wine, mushroomin', and havin' sex. Sometimes she's not even much of a friend back. Occasionally cancels an outing and disappears without offerin' an explanation."

"What do the folks and school kids think about you two? Do you wonder about that?"

"Honestly, we don't act like a couple around others. We have gone out, like we did for drinks with the other teachers after the ball game Friday evening, but as separate parts in a big group. Abby didn't even sit next to me in the bar. It was weird when I left the gang fairly early because I had a big day of pickin' grapes ahead of me Saturday.

"When I said goodbye to everyone, the teachers looked at me then at Abby, waitin' for one of us to make a move for a more formal goodbye. I mean, everybody knows we been seein' each other. She only said she'd see me about 8:00 the next morning, to help if I wanted."

"Did she show up?"

"Yeah, at about 6:00. You get the picture."

"So, now what?"

"It is what it is." Sam shrugs. "I'm not gonna over-analyze it, don't even wanna talk about it."

"What do you want to talk about?"

"Sally."

"Do you miss her?"

"Of course. But that is what it is, too. Which is nothing. When I answered her letter, I left no doubt about that."

"Why do you *not* want to talk to her? Do you wish you'd left the door open a tiny crack?"

"When it comes to relationships, I'm not forcin' that issue ever again. Either we have that mutual connection and we both pursue it, or we both don't. I really liked Sally—even loved her—and wanted to be with her. But she didn't want to be with me…at least on the level I wanted us to be. I consider Abby and me just a plain and simple friendship, because there isn't that…ethereal connection, real or imagined, by either of us. It's rather refreshingly honest, actually. No offense, but being with Abby is like therapy."

"What was different about Karen? You said you weren't intimate with her for a while after you met. That you became friends first."

"Funny you should ask. I was thinkin' about that the other day. What I was missin' in the tail end of my first marriage was romance. Validation."

"Any idea what Karen was looking for?"

"Same thing."

"So what kept you two going—and out of bed—during that time?"

"We were both good listeners. And fairly good complainers."

"Had to be more to it than that."

"We did like the same things—the outdoors, campfires in winter, bein' with our kids, music, partyin' with friends. All things that our previous partners didn't share with us. We validated each other nicely. And it was so easy. I think we both sensed that sex was gonna be the dessert, not the main course."

"What do you really think happened? The troubles with her family? Is that what drove you apart?" Laura asks.

"Maybe that was the straw that broke the camel's back. But honestly, no. I was really out to prove a point—*for richer or poorer, for better or worse*—that'd caused me to leave my first wife. Emotionally, physically, she'd abandoned me when things got tough for us. Same thing happened with Karen, with her family's help. At least, that was my final perception.

"I think right from the beginning with Karen, I was waitin' for disaster to strike me, or us. To make sure she shared my ideal about love. And disaster did strike—my undiagnosed Lyme disease, then goin' broke. But I already knew if somethin' terrible happened to her, I'd be there to take care of her forever. 'Course I didn't get a chance to prove that to her, compliments of you-know-who."

Sam nonchalantly gives God the finger as he tilts his head and looks skyward.

"This godly intervention crap aside, hardly anyone's comfortable in their own skin these days. Like me, they demand validation from the outside. Hell yes, when you first meet someone you like, and vice versa, you both heap it on plenty high. And it feels great, like a drug! But when it slows down, you nag or beg for it and wonder loudly and often what the other person has changed into, and whether they're just being the self they always were, but you were too blinded by your infatuation to see. And by then you're already headed down the toilet. Ever try to stop a toilet mid-flush?"

Laura smiles. "So what's all this got to do with Sally?"

Sam thinks for a moment. "You're right that I hadn't done my work about Karen...about Sparky. Had Sally stuck around, I no doubt would've found a way to put her to my old test. Found a way to blame her for not takin' good enough care of Sammy. But now I'm glad she went away before I put her through that. And I wonder if my response to her letter—before I figured all this out the other day at the fire ring—was a way of tellin' her I'm angry she dropped out of school even before the first test. That wasn't fair of me."

"What if she contacts you again?"

"You know...this isn't a judgment, but she's not so darn healthy in the relationship department either. Good grief. Married to that idiot—even wantin' to have a baby with him—'cause she was afraid she'd repeat her mother's history."

"And what about Abby?"

"Besides sharin' some much-appreciated sack time together, she provides a plain and simple reality check 'bout how I get wrapped up in expectations of others. I mean this in a positive way: If I don't take Abby for exactly who she is, and in the dosage she offers, she's gonna quickly make herself part of my life's history. No games about her. Honestly, there's no real soul or heart connection. Someday I still want to be in love with the person I'm intimate with. I know Abby never wants that."

Laura asks, "In the meantime, are you leaving yourself open to being in love?"

"Honestly, not right now. I'm pretty busy with my fall jobs. Abby's a great wine helper. And she never goes anywhere without her special condoms. It's like she's the magician at a kid's birthday party who finds quarters behind kids ears. Whenever we need a condom, there it is! She even had one with her on the river that first canoe trip we took. Must be a special compartment in her swimsuit?

"Except one night at my house we had to use one of mine because (I'm not bragging, I swear) she didn't bring enough. Hell, far be it for the likes of me to question the good Lord's judgment in sending me loveless, safe sex. Sure beats the hell outta Prozac and cold showers!"

Laura checks the clock and puts her notebook down. "So, one more thing before you go. How did it go with your dad at the wedding? You've been talking for several weeks now, but that was the first time you've seen him in all these years, right?"

A small smile creases Sam's face. "We still haven't gotten to the nuts and bolts, but he brought me a present.

Actually a couple of 'em. Somehow he found my ol' teacher, 'PMS'. Long since retired, but she remembered the whole ordeal. Told Dad if there was one thing in her teaching career she would change, it was that F I ended up with that cost me graduating with honors."

Sam shakes his head at the painful memory of PMS penalizing him 50 points, which put him at the bottom of the class. And his folks going along with it—a measure to force Sam to abandon the rebel that was building inside him—all for forgetting to spit out his gum after lunch.

"Well, together they went back to my old high school. The principal (actually a girl from my class, Mary Clark, who I often competed with for head of the class) let them fix my report card! And she re-figured my grade point average all the way through. Mary awarded me a framed plaque reading: *Samuel Ryan, National Honor Society Member*. Dad gave me the plaque and the special tassel with a gold NHS emblem pinned to it."

"I'd call that progress," Laura says. "*Excellent* progress."

CHAPTER 10

UP IN A TREE, THINKING

September 27, 2003

After the crushing, the wine must spend 7 to 10 days in the primary fermenters, which for Sam are simply 10-gallon plastic garbage cans with bath towels over them to keep the fruit flies and those damn Asian beetles out.

First, he eliminates the skins, stems, and seeds by ladling the must through a fine mesh bag in old Italian oaken press. Then the wine—which at that point has worked itself to around 8 or 9% alcohol (on its way to 13.5 or 14%)—is poured into the secondary fermenters, glass carboys of five and six gallons. On the tops, Sam sticks an airlock, which is shaped like a tiny toilet trap. It lets the carbon dioxide escape without allowing air to enter, which would ruin the wine, oxidizing it.

He lets it work the rest of the way in the carboys, which takes another three weeks or so. After it has quit bubbling and the sediment has settled to the bottom, Sam carefully siphons (or "racks") the clear wine into another carboy, and rinses away the sediment. Racking gets done a couple more times over the next few months.

Eventually, Sam kills the remaining yeast with a sulfite (so after bottling they don't explode, and the live yeast won't ruin the wine), puts it in the barn for 10 days or so, keeping it from 25 to 35 degrees so the acid crystalizes out (which really mellows the wine). Then it's ready for bottling at Sam's leisure.

God willing with the grape crop (and so far He is quite willing), if Sam wants to this year, he can get into a third picking and crushing, after his vats are freed up from the second harvest. Sam had purchased four more vats for the first harvest, and easily refilled them all with the second harvest, bringing him to 210 gallons of raw wine, which would reduce to 200 after racking. More than enough, Sam had teased Abby, for a couple good buzzes.

His house overrun with wine, Sam has begun wishing Abby wasn't such a ready and willing wine helper. He'd been making wine alone (except for the Labor Day weekend batch with his son and Marsha) for many years. Abby pushes and pushes him, like it's some kind of a contest to keep his vats full. She's not much of a follower.

One year when the grape crop was sparse and he'd only found enough grapes for a mere 70 gallons, he'd joked to his son, "Uh oh, think I'm gonna run outta wine by the end of February. Then what am I gonna do?"

Matt answered glibly, "Check into rehab, Dad."

But now, on the weekend of September 27th, after pressing the second batch, Sam's more than content with the take. Besides, they're two weeks into bow hunting season for deer, and Sam hasn't been in a tree yet, which is his plan for the weekend. But Abby insists they don't stop making wine 'til every damn grape within 100 miles is on its way to a wine bottle.

"Make you a deal," Sam offers, as they lie in bed waiting for the sun to rise on Saturday morning, when he should be climbing up into a tree. "Whatever we pick today will be *your* wine. I need to save room in my carboys for the cranberry. Hell, I actually have to buy carboys to hold the cranberry wine. And I want to get into bow huntin'."

Sam suggests they set up an operation at her place for these last grapes. He offers to buy her the vats and carboys she'll need, as thanks for her helping so much. But Abby says she'll just borrow the equipment from her dad, that Sam doesn't owe her a thing, except a case or two so she can compare the wines from the different batches.

Abby says her dad will be thrilled she's making wine, but maybe not so thrilled that hers will be a lot better than his ever was. By this time, she's figured out what makes Sam's wine different. Her dad leaves the must in his vats even after it's done fermenting, forgets about it for a couple of weeks so it oxidizes. Then he adds cheap vodka, which cuts the burned, bitter oxidized taste a little, and makes his wine into a not-so-reasonable facsimile of a very bad port.

Sam had tried some. It certainly wasn't the stuff you can sit down and enjoy while making supper, eating, and watching *Wheel of Fortune* afterwards.

They're heading to Moorhead in Abby's truck, a half dozen pails and two ladders in the back. There hasn't been much conversation this morning, mostly music louder than Sam prefers. As they cruise down Highway 10 near a town called Hawley, Abby reaches over to turn the radio down.

"Sam," she begins, staring straight ahead. "I want to make sure you and I are on the same page."

"Which book?" he asks.

"The friends with benefits book," Abby answers evenly.

"Okay, which chapter?"

"Expectations." She finally glances over at him, her eyes narrowed.

"Not sure what you mean."

"Well, we've been having more fun, both in bed and out, than any two consenting adults should be allowed."

Sam nods and grins.

"That concerns me."

"Why?"

"I just want to make sure you aren't falling in love with me."

"What makes you think I'm fallin' in love with you?"

"Well, for one thing, since that first day on the river, we haven't talked at all about our pasts. But I remember you've been divorced—twice."

Sam lets that error go without correction. He had successfully made it a strict point not to talk about old loves with Abby.

"And you've been single for quite a few years. In the canoe that day, I could tell you wished things hadn't gone wrong with your second wife. That you were very good friends—and totally in love. I'm guessin' you did the things together that you and I do. Do you realize you've called me 'Karen' three times?"

That revelation, or accusation, or whatever the hell Abby's statement could be classified as, flabbergasts Sam.

He sits straight up and answers while looking down the highway, "I'll try to be more careful. Sorry."

"That's it?"

He turns and looks at her, his brow furrowed in exasperation and hands outstretched. "What do you want from me?"

"It's more about what I *don't* want!" Abby squeezes the steering wheel with both hands and leans forward in her seat. "I don't want you to be in love with me! I can't see you anymore if you're in love with me!"

Sam puts a hand over his eyes, but can't stop the giggles from bubbling over.

"What? What's so damn funny?"

"You mean…" Sam starts laughing. "If I wanna keep sleepin' with you, I have to tell you I don't love you?"

He disconnects his seat belt, slides tight next to Abby, and composes himself long enough to whisper into her ear, "I mean this from the bottom of the pit where my stone of a cold, cold heart used to reside: I don't love you, and I never will!"

"Me neither!" Abby shouts, slapping her hand on the dashboard and her eyes lighting up like she just got a new pony for her birthday.

She slams on the brakes and careens the truck onto a gravel road to the right. The grape buckets and ladders crash against the truck bed walls.

Sam grabs the dash with both hands to avoid ending up in her lap. "Where we goin'?"

"The first abandoned farmstead I can find, so I can screw your brains out!"

She is still serious.

And she does.

After grape season, Sam spends much of the autumn up in a tree, thinking and being philosophical. One sidebar of his friendship with Abby: It's much easier to think when he's been having sex regularly (with another person, that is). Here's what Sam came up with, 13 feet in the air.

Seems to him, most of those who feel blessed believe God is part of the recipe. For some (such as the Christian Coalition politicians), He's definitely a partner or even a Benevolent Benefactor (like for those cowboys on the Pro Bull Riding Circuit, kneeling in the arena and giving public thanks).

Others swear to God that He's the damn butthead traveling down the road just out of sight in front of them, testing their belief by tossing out kegs of nails and busting beer bottles on the pavement, suggesting that a hit to the wallet (of Biblical proportions) to replace your ruined brand-new tires will make you a much better tenant when you arrive in heaven.

Sam most definitely used to think of himself as the perpetual target of extra testing until the auspicious timing of Laura's "out of the blue" speech followed by that very day discovering the bison skeleton, then meeting Abby, and carrying on with her in a manner he'd never thought he was capable of.

In dissecting his life, Sam certainly admits his blessings. But, in all honesty, not any kind of decent run of them—like if he could just drive to the tire store and have them install a set of nice, new shiny tires, and still have enough coin left over for a large bottle of Gentleman Jack.

Am I on a roll now? he asks himself. *Lots has gone perfectly since 'out of the blue'. Do I need to do anything else to stay on this roll?*

Which brings to mind his old Sufi friend and poet, Rumi, who says, "WE ARE God! At the very least, we are equal partners in this venture called life. We (God and Us, as One) create our lives. Every last festering pimple on our butt and unbelievably beautiful tropical orchid of them!

Well hell, if that's the case, who's to blame when things go horribly haywire? And who do we thank when we win the lottery—or get laid?

Nobody (which includes Us).

And everybody (which includes Us).

Yes, Sam has a very good late summer and early fall going. But he's still not convinced it's quite this simple.

Because…there's Sally. She hasn't completely gone away. Sam wonders if he might still be in love with her. And her with him.

Saturday, October 18

Maureen had noticed Abby's green pickup truck parked at Sam's at least a time or two a week. Sometimes it was even there early in the morning on her way to the clinic, covered with frost. It's there again this afternoon. Maureen hears loud music playing as she approaches the front door. And laughter—a woman's laugh.

She knocks. Deja barks.

Finally, Sam answers the door. "Maureen! Come in!"

He turns down the music. Abby's at the sink cleaning something. She looks over her shoulder and smiles at Maureen.

"Have you two met?" Sam asks.

Abby grabs a towel and wipes her hands dry, and Maureen shakes her head.

"Well then...Abby, this is my neighbor Maureen Novotny, from the other end of the trail. You remember her place beyond the gravel pit, don't ya?"

She nods, smiles, and sticks out a hand. "Yes, yes. A real pretty place."

"Maureen, this is Abby Tucker."

"Glad to meet you," Maureen says. "Saw your picture in the paper a couple times. You and Sam with the bison bones. And you and Sam on the homecoming float."

"Nice to meet you," Abby replies. "Heard a lot about you and your work from Sam. Turned him into a regular midwife, didja?"

"Oh, stop. I'm retired."

"Glass of wine?" Sam asks Maureen.

Maureen waves him off. "Nope, I'm on call."

"How's yours, Abby?" She indicates with a nod that hers is getting low.

Sam says, "Abby's cleanin' some fall mushrooms we found today. We popped two grouse, too. Makin' a stir fry. Wanna stay and join us?"

Maureen is surprised Sam seems to be having a helluva grand time with this woman. She can maybe chalk up some of the fun to the wine. Not that she doesn't want her friend and neighbor to move on if Sally's never coming back.

"I don't want to intrude," Maureen says.

"Not at all!" Abby holds up the colander full of shiny, yellow mushrooms, some a good five inches across. "Lord knows we got plenty."

"Well, okay. If they're not poisonous…"

"Tricholoma…flavovirens?" Sam says hesitantly.

"Very good!" Abby is impressed with his memory and correct pronunciation. She slides her arm around his waist and gives him a little squeeze.

"I still think that name sounds like a bad disease of a certain body part not normally exposed to the light."

Sam leans his butt against the kitchen counter where he can watch Abby's careful scrubbing of the mushrooms with a vegetable brush. He is clearly relaxed, and stands closer to her than necessary. The back of Abby's jeans and sweatshirt are dirty, like she'd been lying on the ground. So are the knees of Sam's jeans and the forearms of his flannel shirt.

He asks Maureen, "What brings you to this side of the woods?"

"Um, a letter for you came to my place by mistake. I'll just…put it on the mantel."

Sam barely shows any interest, only offers a nonchalant, "Thanks."

"You know," Maureen says, "I s'pose I should get home after all. No offense to your mushrooms. I got a baby on the way. And I need to get supper started for Joan, so…"

Abby turns away from the sink. She stands alongside Sam, their hips touching, and smiles warmly. "Really nice meeting you."

"You, too." Maureen nods and walks quickly out the door.

Dear Sam,   Tuesday, October 14, 2003

I've spent the last month trying NOT to respond to your letter in a way that is unbecoming of a lady. Here's the best I could tone it down for an opening line: QUIT YOUR GODDAMN WHINING ABOUT Bill!

Have you any idea what it was like to live in the shadow of "Saint" Karen's memory? Sure, technically, legally, you were more available than I was. But emotionally you were not one bit more ready than I was to move into a healthy relationship. So don't blame the fact that I didn't jump right into your arms totally on me...or on Bill!

As far as what I need to do for myself, I'm not gonna discuss it with you or anyone back home, nor am I going to ask you or anyone to put their lives on hold for me. Not that I don't care about you. It's not that at all. I just can't make any guarantees where I'll be after this—emotionally. Or where I'll spend the next years of my life. Not that I think you should wait for me. Who knows where you might want to be, or might already have gone?

Speaking of things that are REAL (your words), that night was so very real, as were all our other times together. Although that night was also magic, it didn't change me like magic. It was a big step. And so necessary. I will never diminish our night together, and I'll certainly never forget it. You were right about what it's like with someone you really care about.

On to other things. Maureen told me you shot the big buck. Congratulations! I mean it. We don't always act or react exactly as we think we will when the time comes. None of that is wrong. I know you well enough that you did right by the buck.

I'm anxious to hear what Matt and Marsha are having. And your grandsons are coming home next summer! I hope it all works out so the baby can be born at your place. Could there be a better way for a new life to come into a family, into this world? I don't think so.

I'm not going to get into the divorce and everything else, only that I've asked Joan to put it all on hold until after the holidays at least, if she can. She said if that's the case, the earliest the trial will be scheduled is sometime in March. That works for me.

Joan told me you all know about the shoe box. I'm working on that.

So, I'm sorry about the tirade at the beginning of this letter. But you deserved it! And I deserved what you said to me last time. Hope you can consider us even now.

Believe it or not, I've never had a friend like you. I miss you. But I'll understand if you don't write back.

Love,

Sally

October 22, 2003

Laura invites Sam back into her office. "It's good to see you again. To what or to whom do we owe this visit?"

Sam settles into his usual chair. "Sally wrote me. Again."

"How does that make you feel?"

"Really, I got so much on my plate. Things are goin' good," he assures her, although he isn't convinced himself.

"So what are you concerned about?"

"It's been nice to have her as just an occasional memory. Since this second letter, got my wheels turnin' again, too much of the time. But I'm still seein' Abby. I'm just not sure what I want anymore. But it's not because of what Sally wrote. This Abby thing...whew." He fake-wipes his forehead with the back of his hand.

"Does Abby know about Sally?"

"I've never brought her up, at least not as an ex. I've told Abby about Pop and that she's Maureen's sister, about the team and the funeral. That Sally left her husband and moved away. But more like it was gossip I heard in a bar."

"Why didn't you tell Abby the truth?"

"Honestly, I don't know what the truth was...or is. Sometimes I think I made up the whole thing in my head. Doesn't seem like it was ever real. Besides, I told Sally way too much about Karen, and that bit me in the butt."

"You sound angry toward Sally."

"I guess I am, in a way. I'm just gettin' on with my life, makin' pretty darn good progress with the abuse thing, then she comes waltzin' back with this letter. Has the nerve to give me hell, then on the other hand tells me all these touching things. I mean, which is it? Don't I have a right to know where I stand?"

"Does it truly matter? It's over, right?"

"I wish it really was. I run through my mind over and over what I'm gonna tell Sally if I ever see her again. Half the time I'm pissed at her; the other half I wonder if I still love her. I mean, what is there to love? How long will this shit last? I ask myself every time I get that ache in my guts. Feels the same in my gut either way."

Laura clasps her hands under her chin. "So, let me see if I've got this right. You put yourself out there, and Sally used you to get from Point A (which was Bill) to

Point B (which we're not sure of). Would it be safe to say that Abby has put herself out there, and you're using her to get from Point A (which is Sally) to Point B in kind of the same way?"

Sam protests, "It's not like that with Abby and me. We're both single and on the same page about who we are to each other. No strings attached. It's totally open and honest."

"I wonder then, Sam, why Sally's letter affected you so strongly."

Sam stands to leave. "Umm, excuse me. I think I need some time 13 feet up a tree. I'll get back to you on that one."

CHAPTER 11

BABY BOY RYAN

Dear Baby Boy Ryan,   October 29, 2003

I heard the happy news yesterday afternoon. You're about 20 weeks along, and a boy! According to the ultrasound, everything about you is perfect. I always joked with your dad that if he didn't produce a family namesake, I would take on that task myself, even with me being 50-something. But that would involve bringing a young and willing second person into the equation—a woman. I suppose when you're old enough to understand this, and I've been pushing up daisies for a while, they'll tell you about Grandpa R's trials and tribulations in the women department. (Please don't believe everything you hear!)

Anyway, as has been my custom with your two cousins, I am writing to you long before you're born. I truly believe you are with us, watching us—a complete and beautiful soul already. Why not begin getting to know us right now? Here's an evening in your grandpa's life, from a couple weeks ago...

His antlers weren't as expansive as they were the previous year. An additional gnarly brow tine protruded from each side. The base of the antler was wider, although not as polished as it should have been. The big whitetail buck was over the hill, so to speak.

That evening, just before sunset, he stepped carefully out of the dense poplars, heading for acorns with two other bucks—one bigger and one smaller in the lead—walking in a line down the deer trail. They passed eight yards from the tree I was bow hunting from. The second buck looked healthy and vibrant, tight and strong, with a sleek coat. A monster buck by anyone's account. I let him go by.

The buck I knew, the one whose shed antlers will be displayed in the winery, brought up the rear. His back sagged and, compared to the other two bucks, he appeared gaunt. Not exactly unhealthy for October, but he hadn't put on the summer fat to get him through the rut and the winter. It's old bucks like him who still have the desire, but are a year or two past prime. Who lose the battles, run themselves skinny, then become raven and coyote food during the first bitter cold spell of January.

I picked a spot behind his shoulder blade, low on his chest, not taking my eyes off that spot as I slowly raised my bow and silently drew the string back. I took him, even though I'd told my friend Sally I wouldn't. But one second he was sauntering down the trail behind his two pals, the next he was wherever deer go when they die. Wope la—that's Sioux for "Thanks to the Creator"—for providing the animal and helping my shot be true.

Sometimes I truly believe a deer presents itself as a gift. Giving up its life to feed me (or the coyotes and ravens) so that we may live on. The deer's body providing us lifeblood. Or maybe I felt sorry for him? A mercy killing of sorts.

At first, I felt bad about even considering having him mounted. But then, he was a gift. If I wasn't really willing to share him with others, I shouldn't have shot him in the first place. Now I'm glad I did. Someday after they've scattered my ashes in these woods and over the river, his progeny will nip browse and grind acorns and wash them down with river water, partially thanks to me. And that makes me happy. And maybe you will take deer, too, compliments of your old grandad. The circle of life goes on.

The deer rut's kicking in now. I'm not allowed to shoot another buck this year. But all the deer in the woods are moving, the bucks chasing. The does who aren't quite ready are avoiding them. I'll try to take a doe with my bow before the gun season begins. If I'm not that fortunate, I'll hunt with the rifle my Grandpa Ryan gave me, one that'll be yours someday.

All the wine has been pressed, including the batch we made the weekend of your parents' wedding, and the wine your Great-Grandpa Ryan helped with. It's fermenting along nicely in the jugs, 210 gallons total. Next year, when you're here, I'm hoping the wild grapevines I transplanted three years ago will produce enough fruit to make a batch all of its own.

As if I don't have enough bad habits, a science teacher (Abby) in Stone Creek has taught me about fall mushrooms. I had never picked anything but morels. I suppose you'll be the first to know if I die from eating the wrong ones. We'll meet in the cosmos—me on my way back up there (hopefully that's the direction I'll go), you on your journey down here.

One more thing. The geese have been using the river to rest. I know where I can sneak up on them and pop a couple, then have Deja fetch them. You're gonna love my puppy. And there's no doubt in my mind she'll love you. Canada goose—on the plate, it rates right up there with venison chops, fresh morels, and wild turkey. If I'm lucky enough to connect, I'll eat one fresh and save the other for Thanksgiving.

Anyway, thanks for volunteering to make the trip into this family. We'll look forward to meeting you in person mid-March. See if you can time it so your folks can make it up here for your arrival. I'm sure it will be quite a party.

Love,

Grandpa R

November 1, 2003

Abby hasn't stayed overnight at Sam's all that often lately. For certain she doesn't on school nights, and she's often away on weekends. Sam wishes she hadn't invited herself over the Friday night before gun season for deer.

He has an opening day ritual from way back when he and his dad used to hunt together. A good night's sleep, up at 4:30 a.m. A lumberjack breakfast, thermos of coffee (or hot chocolate when he was a kid), and a lunch (packed the night before) to take along for an all-day sit. Layers of clothing laid out, with the required blaze orange (it was red back then). The aroma of Hoppe's Number 5 gun-cleaning solvent wafting toward him as he unzips the gun case. A slow walk under the inky blue-black sky to his gun stand, accompanied by Orion the Hunter high in the sky. Steady, slow enough to avoid overheating and being chilled from sweat in the 10-degree air.

Sipping a hot drink in the dark quiet, while the eastern sky's glow gradually brightens into enough light to shoot, if the opportunity presents itself. More often than not, at least since Sam had bought his place and selected a gun stand site at the other end of his field, that opportunity arrives in the first hour of legal shooting. Before it's fully light out, as the deer drift back to their daytime bedding haunts in the swamp.

But on this opening morning, it's dawn when Sam's suddenly awakened by a rifle shot across the road. It's already legal shooting light! He has overslept by at least two hours.

"Shit!" He tosses off the covers, startling Abby awake.

She must have shut off the alarm clock.

Abby pulls the covers back over herself, rolls over away from Sam and growls, "What's the big deal? You already got a deer. Try to be quiet, will ya?"

He hurriedly turns on the coffee, letting it drip while he dresses quickly in his hunting clothes. He'd NEVER overslept deer opener in the 47 years since he'd begun tagging along with his dad! At least his lunch was packed and his gun and hunting pack are ready.

It's a windless morning that would have been perfect for deer hunting. No snow, but leaves frozen so it sounds like the deer are walking on potato chips. If a hunter could sit quietly, he'd be able to hear deer approaching and ready himself long before they'd come into sight.

As Sam hurries down his trail, a staccato of gunfire issues from across the countryside. He alternates between jogging and walking as fast as he can without becoming airborne between footfalls, working up a helluva sweat. Rather than being a ghost in the woods, he is the runaway eight-team stagecoach.

He isn't just angry with himself; he's angry with Abby. That took a lotta nerve to invite herself over, unannounced, on the eve of such an important day. Then to hijack his alarm clock…GRRR.

Despite all that racket, when Sam tops a small hill, a lone doe stands broadside 50 yards away, as if mesmerized by the sight of him hurrying through the woods at such a late hour. A big doe with no fawns tagging along—exactly what he wants for his freezer. She allows him time to raise his rifle and lean against a tree to steady his aim. But the instant he begins to press the trigger, he knows the pull doesn't feel right.

His rifle isn't cocked. He'd forgotten to load his gun. Another first. The doe bounds out of sight.

Sam curses and resigns himself to the fact that his opening day of gun season ritual is a complete disaster. He unzips his coat and opens his wool shirt to his belt to release the steam from his overtaxed body. He turns and trudges slowly back toward his house, releasing a huge sigh and shaking his head. A coyote howls and yips from near his deer stand. The Trickster, the Indians call it, having a good laugh at Sam. He decides not to even bother loading his gun.

As he begins descending the last hill before his farmstead, he is relieved to see Abby's truck taking a left out of his driveway. That took a lotta nerve for her to be pissed-off because he was getting out of bed early on opening day of deer season. He isn't sure what he would have said to her anyway. But with her gone, he decides to make his lumberjack breakfast. Might as well cool his jets and let his clothes dry until the evening hunt, when the deer will surely drift back out of the swamp and past his stand. He makes a mental note to load his gun this time.

CHAPTER 12

FEELING CHEAP AND USED

November 19, 2003

"Laura, please keep a straight face, because I'm serious. This Abby thing. I'm beginning to feel cheap. And used."

Sam looks right into her eyes for any kind of expression. There is none. So far, so good.

"She even called me another guy's name one night. Julio. When I asked this morning who Julio was, she looked at me like I was from outer space.

"That evening, she called and accused me of checkin' up on her, like some stalker. Hell, when she disappears, I haven't a clue where she goes. I've never called her cell, unless she's told me to. What's up with this?"

"Are you assuming that Abby has only been seeing you?"

"At first, yes, I was hoping for a monogamous thing—both ways. But about a month ago, I began not givin' a shit one way or the other. For the past two weeks, I just wish she'd go away. When she stops by in the middle of the week now, sometimes she doesn't even undress all the way. Just has her way with me and away she goes! And leaves the living room light on, on her way out. I need to change the locks. No, wait, I don't even have locks."

"Do you want this to end?"

"Well, I been havin' a lotta tree time lately. Thinking. Heard about a syndrome once—nymphomaniacs. Somethin' wrong with their pituitary glands. Or was it brain tumors? At any rate, sex doesn't seem to be as much fun with Abby anymore. It's like a compulsion for her. It's angry. I'm afraid if I cut her off, she'll cut ME off, if ya know what I mean."

Laura smiles and places a hand over her face. "Sam, just how high have you been climbing? Have you fallen out of any trees? You been watching daytime talk shows?"

She laughs but stops when she notices Sam's not joining her. "Sorry. So did you come up with a plan? I mean, now that you've apparently ruled out being direct?"

"Yup. I'm gonna start callin' her Karen, right in the middle of it. And skip washin' my sheets the next full moon. Not gonna clean the toilet or the shower every month, either."

Sam has three deer in his freezer. He'd taken a doe with his gun that first evening, then another the following Sunday. The limit is five deer this year, and he's been *allegedly* bow hunting since the gun season ended, although it's really just an excuse to sit in a tree and think. Otherwise there is no need to sit in any more trees until dark; he has plenty of venison.

Besides, it starts getting dark by 5:00 p.m. The high school basketball games won't start until the second week of December. So on the drive home from Walker, he decides to postpone his plan to rid himself of Abby. Really not much to do in the evenings otherwise, so what the hell? He washes his sheets and cleans the toilet and shower—ahead of schedule.

After two more weeks of Abby's visits—a particularly interesting two weeks, after she'd had been to one of those parties where women buy special underthings and various potions and lotions and contraptions—Sam's not sure if he can handle going cold turkey with the sex thing. So he devises a Plan B to implement before Plan A, to ease her and himself out of each other's pants.

His new plan is to turn her down the next time she calls to say she's on her way over (that is, if she calls first). He's confident he can handle cutting back from the four or five times a week they're at now to twice or so.

He's never turned Abby down before, so he has no idea how badly she might take this.

Finally, it's the night of the first girls' home basketball game. Sure enough, just as Sam is getting supper ready, Abby calls. Says she's on her way over, saying that they'll have time before the varsity game begins around 7:00 p.m. And of course, they'll arrive at school for the game separately and at slightly different times.

"Thing is, I'm frying venison chops. They are extremely delicate and should be cooked just right and eaten right out of the pan—not reheated," Sam instructs cheerfully. "Only have time to cook 'em and get a bellyful if I'm going to catch the second half of the junior varsity game. Sorry, I only have enough thawed for myself."

"I wasn't coming over to eat," Abby snarls just before she hangs up on him.

Sam still doesn't think anyone at school has figured out what he and Abby had been doing all fall (and how often), although a lot of folks had suggested that the two of them should hook up because they'd make a cute couple. Little did they know.

All along, Abby had made it a point to act very uncouple-like around him—other than being innocently and mutually interested in the bison and river trips with the students. There has never been any touching or a look that might suggest they were sleeping together. Which is all fine by Sam anyway.

However, the homecoming photo in the newspaper looked as if they were a little cozy. Abby was one of the advisors for the senior class, so she was sitting with Sam on the wagon. They had their arms tightly around each other and were laughing, but only because one of the kids had spooked Roy and Elvis into a couple of quick steps, and they almost fell into the back of the wagon. It was a lucky shot by the photographer.

But this evening at the game, everyone notices (including Sam) how Abby and a teacher named Jensen are practically joined at the hip during the first half of the game. They sit up in the far corner of the bleachers—no one within 30 feet of them—whispering like two eighth graders, as if everyone else were invisible.

She even lets him buy her popcorn, which they share quite publicly.

Sam has a gut feeling that he'll never hear from her again, except maybe about the bison. He thinks (not meaning to bastardize the phrase by the great Martin Luther King, Jr.) *Thank God, (I hope) I'm free at last.*

Sam returns home after the game, has a big glass of wine and a small plate of cheddar cheese and crackers—comfort food and drink. Just in case, he jams a kitchen chair under the front doorknob before he crawls into bed.

Still, he has a hard time getting to sleep, so he resorts to a mind trick that always puts him out within 10 minutes. He imagines himself launching his canoe at the dam on a warm summer day. He guides himself down the river, peacefully around each bend and smoothly down every run. The hairpin turn where a blue heron is usually fishing for minnows; the first eagle tree at the head of the rice bed; the Mary, Mother of Christ stump. He rarely makes it all the way to the solid ground beyond the rice bed before drifting off.

When Sam awakens, he wonders what Sally had been doing in his canoe that night. And who was the angel—halo, wings, cherubic smile and all—escorting them?

Sam subs a bus route in the morning. In this little town, in this small school, rumors travel at the speed of light.

After his kids have unloaded, Sam walks into the school to use the faculty restroom. Marvin, the day janitor, motions him and two male teachers into a storage room, closing the door. Marvin gushes with excitement and can hardly wait to tell his story.

He whispers, "Jack was emptyin' wastebaskets in the classrooms during the second half of the game last night. He hears gruntin' noises and a pile of books hittin' the floor in Jensen's classroom. So Jack unlocks and opens the door, turns on the lights.

"There's Abby Tucker, slidin' off Jensen's desk with only one leg in her jeans and panties and her blouse half off. She screams at Jack to go away and shut the damn lights off. Jensen's already turned away and has his pants most of the way up. He's wearin' one of those string underwears that look like they hurt.

"Jack is dumbstruck. Before he can do anything, Abby turns away from him and bends over to put the other leg in her jeans, her naked butt stickin' right at him not 15 feet away! While feelin' back for the light switch, Jack sees Abby's got a tattoo of an insect, like it's crawlin' outta her…you know…butt crack!"

Not an insect. Sam thinks to himself. *A spider, one that I'm very familiar with.*

Lactrodectus mactans. The Black Widow.

December 10, 2003

"Maureen," Sally speaks into the phone through gritted teeth. "Why did you send me this photo of Sam at the homecoming parade?"

"God, I hate gettin' in the middle of this. But when we talk, you act like Sam's just too busy to write."

"Yeah, it's fall. He's huntin', makin' wine, drivin' the bus…"

"He's busy, alright. With all those things and then some."

Sally pauses, then asks tentatively, "The woman in the photo…?"

"For almost two months, I been tryin' to figure a way to break it to you. Sam's moved on. He hasn't asked about you at all. Abby, the woman in the photo, they been seein' each other since he found the bison skeleton last summer."

After a beat of silence, Maureen asks, "Sally? You okay?"

She hears her sister suck in a long, deep breath. "Whew. Not sure why I'm surprised."

"I talked to Joan. Thought maybe we could move the trial up, get this all cleared up and you can come home—keep it from gettin' ugly."

"What? What do mean?"

"It's not what they want out of you, it's what they want outta Sam. They claim they can prove Pop was coerced—a conspiracy between you and Sam to get the Perch team from him."

"Does Sam know about this?" Sally asks.

"No, I just found out from Joan today that they're gonna subpoena Sam for the divorce. Joan doesn't think the judge will disallow his testimony if they come at it from the direction of a conspiracy to bilk the brothers. And even if the judge eventually disallows that testimony in the divorce, there will still be the perception of a connection or conspiracy between you and Sam. They'll file a civil suit against the two of you and try to get the team that way."

"Shit. I need to talk to Sam. I think I know what's goin' on. You better fill him in right away. Ask him if I can call him."

"What're you talkin' about? What's out there that would pin that on you guys?"

"Hopefully nothing. But I need to talk to Sam."

"Those fucking goddamn bastards!" Sam smacks his kitchen counter so hard a wine glass bounces from the dish drainer and crashes onto the floor.

Maureen winces.

"No! No way in hell they're gettin' those horses!" he vows through clenched teeth. "What in the hell do they think they're doin'? I mean besides that crooked Peabody stealin' those two idiots blind?"

Maureen's brow is furrowed and she holds her hands apart. "Sally said she thinks she knows what's goin' on, but didn't say what. She wants to talk to you."

"I just wanted to stay outta this mess and move on with my life. And now this…" He throws one hand in the air then takes a long swig of wine. "They can't hurt me. Don't know how they think they can get to Sally this way, but I'm sure as hell not gonna let 'em."

"Sam, it's Sally. I'm sorry to call you…"

He cuts her off. "Don't apologize, not for anything. I'm sorry, too."

"Listen, when Maureen and I talked this afternoon, somethin' popped into my mind that gave me the chills."

"What's that?"

"That night we…made love, Deja growled at the window. Just like Sheba used to growl when Robert was prowlin' around. Then the next mornin' when I went into my trailer for fresh clothes, my clean panties were missin', and the drawer looked like someone had been in it. I know Robert's messed with my things before, at the farmhouse. One time I found a pair of my panties by the bathroom window outside. They were stained, like Robert… had…had…you know…into them.…"

"You ain't kiddin', are ya? Deja was playin' with a rag or something that morning, came from behind the house with it. That musta been them. Shit. I'll kill that son of a bitch…both of 'em."

"Doesn't matter if Robert watchin' us is illegal. That's a small price for them to pay to get their hands on Elvis and Roy."

"Fuck 'em," Sam growls. "They can have the horses. I won't let 'em drag you through this. We'll just say it didn't happen."

"What if they have proof? What if Robert took pictures?" she asks.

"What?!! He's not that bright. Don't give him that kinda credit."

"He's got a dark room! Who knows who he's got photos of? I know what they really want. Sam, they want the horses so they can kill 'em. That's their best revenge against you."

"How are we gonna fight this?"

"I don't know." Sally cries into the phone. "Those horses don't belong anywhere but with you at the winery. That was Pop's wish."

"Do Maureen and Joan know about…you know… that night?"

"I didn't tell 'em. Doesn't sound like Peabody told 'em either…yet. But I'm sure he knows."

"Let's call their bluff. Let 'em call me to the stand. I've gotta lot to say."

"From what Joan's told me about Peabody, if you don't play ball with him, he'll do anything he can to ruin anybody who gets in his way."

"Sally," Sam speaks softly. "I'm not afraid of that asshole Peabody. When the truth about everything comes out, not even Judge Friday'll give Elvis and Roy to those idiots. If you're okay with callin' their bluff, so am I." He tears up over the thought of Sally getting dragged through this.

"What about your girlfriend? The photo from the newspaper. Maureen told me about her."

"My ex-girlfriend," Sam corrects. "No, she wasn't really even that. A good teacher, though. Not just biology at school, but she inadvertently taught me a lot about my perspective on relationships. She's moved on.

"Sally…I'm sorry I was such a jerk in my letter last fall. I wouldn't have missed our time together for the world either. In fact, you and I—and you aren't gonna believe this—you and I and an angel went down the river together just last night."

"What? Really?"

"Can we keep in touch?"

"I'd like that. I'll call Saturday. Will that work?"

"Any time will work. Even the middle of the night, if you can't sleep."

The next night, Sam's lying awake thinking about her. He's not surprised when the phone rings at 11:00 p.m. Sally asks if he'll take her and the angel down the river again tonight. And he does.

Through the rice bed in his mind awake, and through the forest in his dream.

As usual, Sam attends the high school basketball game on Friday night. Parents who normally encourage their kids to give him a hug seem to shepherd them away. The teachers he usually visits during halftime turn away from him as he approaches. Folks seem to avoid eye contact when they walk past him up the bleachers. Even though he's being treated like a turd in a punch bowl and hasn't a clue why, he really doesn't give it much thought. His mind is elsewhere.

Sally and Sam talk on the phone both days this weekend, for an hour each time.

"Just trust that I'm safe and loved here," Sally says. "I'm so sorry I can't say where I am. It's all part of my healin' process—the battered women's group and my individual counseling."

"Wherever you are, I thank God you're okay," Sam says, sniffling. "And I'm thrilled you're workin' with horses, and with kids. And I'm sure they're thrilled, too." He tells her he can see her in his mind—the horses and the kids all focused on her, as if mesmerized by her wisdom and love, like last summer.

"I've been workin' on my stuff, too" Sam offers. "Karen, family relationships, the other abuse I never told you about. Laura's been wonderful helpin' me sort out those emotional breakdowns. I'm still afraid they'll come back. I never wanna put anyone I love through that again. Or myself."

It seems they're both being cautious. And that's just fine with Sally Hunter and Sam Ryan. They're becoming friends, real friends. Sam doesn't think they'd ever really been friends before. There was too much in the way.

Sam receives a peculiar phone call Sunday evening, from his bus boss. Irv, who normally wouldn't say horseradish if he had a mouthful, does all the talking then quickly hangs up. It's like his house is on fire and he has to escape in a hurry.

"I decided to put Dave on Dick's route in the morning. You know, it's nice to have a coupla subs who know all the routes. Won't be needin' you for the junior high girls' basketball trip Tuesday either. Gotta go."

Sam receives a second weird call Monday morning, from Marjorie, a reporter from the *Record,* who's also the town gossip. He had driven her kids to many school events and was even invited to their graduation parties.

"You gotta know what's goin' on. I don't believe a word of it. Meet me…oh geez…somewhere we won't be seen."

"What the heck *is* going on, Marjorie?"

"Your place," she suggests. "Is there somewhere I can park so nobody sees me? I'll get fired if they find out. Half an hour."

Sam pours the breathless Marjorie a cup of coffee. She's a slightly built woman in her forties with dark hair and eyes. She always appears a bit unkempt, her hair never brushed all the way and her pants and blouse wrinkled. She is always on the move. Marjorie's jittery, glancing out the kitchen window toward the road every few seconds, even though her car is safely out of sight in the barn alley. She'd even made him close the barn doors.

"You know Angie Wilson? Her kid rides Bus 3, I think?" Marjorie leans toward Sam like someone might overhear them.

"Yeah," he answers, confused. "That's Dick's route, last stop way out toward Halfway. Little Missy, a second grader."

"Well, Angie went to the superintendent Friday. Claims Missy said you gave her more than a hug goodbye. Then Angie came to the newspaper right after, demanding the *Record* expose you as a pedophile. Sounded to me like she'd been put up to it. Gosh, if they find out at the paper I told you this…" Marjorie shakes her head and bites at a fingernail.

"Okay. Isn't Angie Wilson the one whose trailer house got raided about a month ago? She and her boyfriend got charged with making and selling meth among other things, didn't they?"

"Yup, that's her. I covered the story!"

"All the way to court?"

"Yup."

"Do you remember who her attorney is?"

"Lemme think," Marjorie massages her temples. "That big bald, guy with the bushy beard, from the next county. The judge had to keep tellin' him to sit down and shut up. Oh gosh…umm umm…his name is like a vegetable?"

"Peabody."

"That's it! Why?"

"Oh, just a lucky guess."

He glances out the window as a car drives by. Marjorie ducks.

"I'm outta here. You never seen me." She bolts out the door and runs to the barn, ducking as she crosses the yard.

Sam hollers across the yard, "It's our secret…and thanks."

Before her car has disappeared down the road, Sam's calling Joan's office.

"You gonna fight it?" Joan asks Sam. "That's the kinda lie that could ruin not just your career (like it apparently already has), but your whole darn life if you leave it out there dangling. Unfortunately, that's also the kind of crap Peabody puts to frequent use and has slithered out of scot-free about 20 times."

"He's not even waitin' to see if I'll just give the boys those goddamn horses. He's not even worried about exposing his Peeping Tom client. I won't let them kill Pop's horses," Sam vows.

"Yeah, Peabody doesn't give a darn about either of those boys. What do you mean, his Peeping Tom client?"

"Forget I said that."

"No! What the hell's really goin' on here?" Joan demands.

"You mean, other than the fact that I stole Pop's horses, ruined Bill's cousin's truck with a big goddamn hammer, and slept with Bill's wife?"

"We need to get Sally on the phone right now!" Joan says.

"We already talked. Last week. And twice over the weekend. Listen, those horses are as good as dead. Shit, if you can look into people's bedrooms and take pictures and shoot someone's dog and shoot at your wife after you've beaten the shit out of her…what's so wrong with sleeping with some asshole's wife?"

Sam appears as if he's a thousand miles away, slowly looking around Joan's office, but not actually seeing anything.

As Joan dials the phone, she asks, "Sam, you okay?"

He doesn't answer, but seems to be in deep thought.

Sally answers.

"Oh, thank God. Listen, Sam's here in my office. We're on speakerphone. He says Bill and Peabody know you two…um…slept together."

Sally gives a heavy sigh. "Yeah, I'm guessin' they do. It was the night Sam saved Dakota's life, after Bill tried to kill her."

The sound of her voice brings Sam back.

She continues, "I'm pretty sure Robert saw us, might've even taken pictures. Sam can give you the details. I can't talk about it. Every time I think about Robert, I wanna vomit."

Joan replies, "Yup, that's Peabody's smokin' gun to prove his conspiracy theory. It won't affect the divorce itself, even if Judge Friday gets back on the bench. But who knows how it'll play in a civil suit. I don't even wanna think about trying that case in front of Friday. My guess is, Peabody's sending him get well cards as we speak."

Joan's assistant knocks lightly on the door. "Sorry to interrupt, but Maureen's here. And so is a deputy sheriff, with some papers to serve. Also, I just talked to court administration. Friday'll be back on the bench first of the year."

Joan sighs and covers her face.

The deputy follows Maureen into the office. He serves her the lawsuit papers, alleging the conspiracy over Pop giving Sam his two horses.

"That didn't take long," Joan mumbles.

"I s'pose you got some for me, too, huh?" Sam asks.

He again appears numb, as he signs for his papers and is given a copy of a temporary court order.

The deputy mumbles, "Sorry, Sam," as he turns to leave.

Maureen and Joan begin reading their copy together, both shaking their heads. Sam reads his copy, his face expressionless.

Sally asks over the speakerphone, "What does the court order say?"

"Just what we figured," Joan replies.

Sam adds without emotion, "In the meantime, Elvis and Roy will be kept at a ranch the other side of Park Rapids. Neither side is allowed to go near them."

Joan sighs. "This is so ridiculous. We're goin' attorney fees on this one?"

"You're hired," Sam says as he gets up to leave. He stops at the doorway of Joan's office, and turns to look back. All eyes are on him. It takes him a few seconds to speak.

Finally, his voice cracking, he says, "Sally?"

"Yeah, Sam," she answers quietly.

"I gotta take care of some business. You know I love you."

"I love you, too, Sam."

Maureen is shaken by his strange demeanor. "You gonna be okay, Sam?"

"Gotta get home to say goodbye to Elvis and Roy… and handle some other things."

He walks out without answering Maureen's question.

"What should we do?" Joan asks.

Sally thinks for a few seconds. "Trust him. I got a feelin' he'll be alright. He's got a guardian angel on his side. But just in case, you'd better give his therapist, Laura, a call. I'm afraid it might be happenin' again…"

CHAPTER 13

THE BACK WAY TO STREETER

On the drive home from Joan's office, Sam's mind fills with all sorts of bad things from his past, like before when he'd had an attack. He doesn't pay notice to the inch of snow that has already fallen or the leaden sky that promises many more inches. A mile from home, when he turns onto the gravel road to his place, he spots vehicle tracks that have been snowed on only lightly. The tracks turn in to his yard.

A dually pickup truck with a gooseneck horse trailer is backed up to the pasture gate, with a sheriff's squad car parked next to it. Two men wearing matching sheriff's mounted patrol overcoats have Roy and Elvis on lead ropes. The horses aren't cooperating—they pull back and rear. Elvis breaks off a fence post with his butt. Roy screeches and charges the man who has his lead rope. Deja barks furiously and lunges at the two men.

Just as Sam slides to a stop alongside the deputy's car, the deputy sprays Deja in the face with mace. Blinded, she runs yipping and stumbling toward the barn.

"Son of a bitch!" Sam yells at the deputy, as he charges toward him.

The deputy points the spray at Sam, places his other hand on his weapon, and warns, "Don't take another step."

Elvis and Roy settle down in Sam's presence.

"You couldn't even wait 'til I got home!" Sam snarls.

He runs to Deja. The pup is curled up in the straw. She growls at Sam, still blinded by the spray.

"It's okay, girl…"

He sits down slowly next to her. Deja sniffs cautiously, then crawls onto his lap. Tears flow from Sam like a river running high in springtime. Together they huddle in the stall.

Finally, he hears the truck and squad car leave. He and Deja stay in the barn another hour, curled up in the straw.

It is dusk when they leave the barn. What of the landscape hat isn't white with the fresh snow is shades of gray, even the pine trees. Sam doesn't feel the sting of the snow or the bite of the wind. The deputies' tire tracks have already filled in with snow. He peers through swirling flakes toward the gate, which the sheriff's men had left open. The pasture is dead and lifeless without Roy and Elvis.

Sam paces in the house like a madman until complete darkness falls. He doesn't know what he should do next, so he trudges out into his snowy yard, stumbling like a drunk, and screams at God again and again at the top of his voice. He thrusts both middle fingers as high into the air as he can.

"You motherfucker! You son of a bitch! Fuckin' me in the ass again! Just when things were turnin' around…"

He trudges all around his yard in the foot of new snow, screaming more sacrilegious epithets. The wind howls and the snow pelts Sam. Soon he's soaked with sweat on the inside and melted snow on the outside. Deja pushes her way out through the front door and comes to him. Her ears are down. She's afraid of the man who looks like her master but is somebody else tonight. She butts him with her nose, then jumps up to put her front feet on his belly, as if begging him to come indoors and dry off.

Sam seethes as he changes clothes. Deja watches from a distance, unsure. He hasn't noticed the light blinking on his answering machine.

Had he played the messages, he would have heard Sally's voice thanking him and telling him she loves him, asking him to call her right away.

He also would have heard a concerned Laura leaving her home and cell numbers, explaining that Maureen had called her. Laura said if he didn't call back by suppertime, she'd call the emergency contact on his chart, his son.

Sam would have heard Maureen apologizing that she had to go back to the rez and couldn't be with him.

And Joan, asking for his help after she'd slid her car off the road in the storm.

Instead, Sam finds the rifle in his closet—the one his grandfather had given him when he was 12—a gun over 100 years old, which he'd taken at least 30 deer with. Sam could hit a Copenhagen can with it at 90 yards. It was rare he didn't hit a deer in the heart and drop it in its tracks. His hands tremble as he reaches into a drawer for the box of cartridges.

He takes the rifle and ammunition to the kitchen table, and fumbles with the ammunition box. Finally, he jerks the plastic cartridge container out. It's upside down, spilling half the cartridges. He gathers a handful and stuffs them into a front shirt pocket, leaving the box and the rest of the cartridges scattered on the table along with the canvas rifle case.

Methodically, like his battery's going dead, he pulls on his winter boots, an overcoat, and a wool stocking cap. He grabs Deja's half full bag of food from the pantry. He sets it back on the floor, then stuffs a bottle of wine in each side pocket of his coat.

Into the blizzard, Sam carries the dog food in one hand, the rifle tucked under the opposite arm. Deja follows him to the barn, into the stall. He kneels in the straw with her and begins crying again. She licks Sam's face.

"Okay, girl. Enough food here for a while. You know where the horse waterer is."

She follows him to his truck.

"No! Goddamn it! NO!"

Deja slinks back. The interior light of Sam's truck shows her brown eyes pleading, her ears hanging in fear.

She runs alongside the truck to the end of the driveway. Sam brings the truck to a sliding stop. He barrels out of the driver's seat.

"NO!" he screams at her through the blizzard.

Deja sits in the snow two yards away, her head drooping.

Sam charges at her and screams again, "Get the hell back to the barn!"

Deja doesn't move. Sam kicks her in the side of the chest, knocking her over sideways. She yips, then limps toward the barn, her tail tight to her butt.

Sam knows the back way to Streeter on county and township roads. The same 20-mile route he'd taken home in the rain with Elvis and Roy the day of Pop's funeral. He isn't in a hurry, but is determined to make his destination no matter how long it takes. In the open areas along farm fields and swamps, he inches along in the near zero visibility of the horizontal snow. In the protected areas, he has to drive hard to keep momentum in the deep snow. There hasn't been another soul on those back roads to break a trail.

He figures Bill's working his job in Grand Forks. Sam doesn't know where Robert's house in town is. He knows Robert's old car though, and doubts the dummy would have enough sense to park it in a garage, if he even had one. Streeter isn't that big of a town. He'll find Robert's place.

A ramshackle house on the edge of town, backed up to the swamp. Tire tracks in the deep snow. No car. A mailbox that reads *Hunter*. The house is dark inside. Sam figures Robert had gotten orders from Bill to go do something at the campground.

Sam doesn't try the doorknob, he just kicks the door in. The house stinks of garbage, cat shit, and rotting food. If Sam didn't have a bottle of wine in him, he'd be gagging. He finds the light switch by the door. Three scraggly cats are curled up on the couch. They look too emaciated to move. Only one of the cats seems to notice him. Half a dozen splotches of runny cat shit stain the carpet in front of the couch. A couple dozen pornographic magazines are scattered about, most of them old and worn. The covers indicate all sorts of deviant behavior.

Sam guesses correctly which door leads to the basement. He leans the rifle against the wall and feels inside the stairway for the light switch. Three more cats lumber up the stairs past him.

The darkroom, which takes up half the tiny basement, has a padlock on it. Sam finds a hammer and knocks the lock and hasp off in one swing. He flips the light switch inside the door and the room glows pinkish-red.

A workbench displays various tubs of liquid. Four strings span above the bench, between the right and left walls. Photographs and negatives are hung with clothespins. Sam notices a small chain hanging from a light fixture. He pulls the chain and a regular incandescent bulb fills the room with white light.

There, right in front of his face, is a grainy photograph of Sally—taken through his bedroom window. Sally, naked, atop him, leaning forward and cradling his face with her hands.

Sam quickly scans some of the other dozens of photos. The ones on the front string are of Sally. One batch of photos was taken through a window, of Sally and Bill in their bedroom having sex. And more of Sam and Sally—photos taken through the kitchen window—Sally helping Sam with his belt, undressing herself, facing him. Photos through the steam on the bathroom window of Sally stepping out of Sam's shower and toweling off. And blurry photos taken through various other windows of women Sam doesn't know.

Sam is eerily calm. He notices a cardboard box sitting on a chair at the end of the workbench. It contains dozens of beige file folders. The first file he checks has pictures of two very young girls—less than 10 years old, he guesses—obviously posed. He assumes they were Robert's stepdaughters.

Suddenly, Sam hears boots shuffling behind him. He turns slowly—and finds himself staring right into the barrel of his own rifle. Robert has his finger on the trigger, smirking and nodding.

"You just made it so easy," Robert warns, as he jabs the barrel into Sam's chest.

"No," Sam answers sternly. "*You* did."

Sam slowly places his hand around the gun barrel, and squeezes it firmly, the barrel still stuck against his chest.

"I'll shoot. I'll shoot ya, goddamnit!"

"Pull the fuckin' trigger then," Sam challenges.

"I mean it!" Robert threatens, his eyes wide and voice trembling.

Robert's shaking hands poke at Sam with the gun barrel again. Sam places his other hand around the barrel. Robert steps one leg back, bracing himself for the high-powered rifle's recoil.

Sam directs the end of the barrel to his own forehead.

Robert gapes, wide-eyed. "You crazy motherfucker!"

"You got any balls, Robert? I mean, besides for little girls and spyin' on women at night?"

"You're makin' me do this!" Robert stammers. "You broke in here! It's self-defense! I had to kill you with your own gun!"

Robert can't control his shaking. He closes his eyes and squeezes the trigger.

Click.

Sam snatches the rifle from the bewildered Robert and kicks him hard in the groin. Robert drops to the floor in a fetal position, holding himself and moaning.

"That's from Sammy."

Sam works the bolt and feeds a live round into the chamber. He points the barrel at Roberts hands, which are protecting his crotch.

"Never bring a gun into the house with a cartridge in the chamber. Somebody could get hurt."

Robert rolls away, and Sam kicks him in the ass. Robert crawls under the stairs and huddles like a frightened mongrel, his whole body shaking uncontrollably.

Sam pulls the strings of photos and negatives from the walls then stuffs them into the file box.

"Whatcha…whatcha gonna do with that stuff?" Robert whines from under the stairs.

"Robert, I'm gonna do you a big favor."

"Yeah, right. What kinda favor would you do for me, besides turn that stuff over to the cops?"

"I'm not gonna tell a soul I was ever here. And neither are you."

The snow and wind have let up by the time Sam leaves Robert's house; the worst of the blizzard has passed. It's just past midnight.

Sam stops his truck in the middle of the trackless road by the cemetery. He finds Pop's grave in the dark and takes a big pull of wine while standing over it. He pours about two fingers' worth into the snow in tribute.

The roads still haven't been plowed and are nearly impassable. In some places, the snow has drifted up as high as his bumper.

Sam plods on, as if guided by a guardian angel, returning home just before 2:00 a.m. He parks in the barn alley. The headlights shine on Deja, who stretches and yawns herself awake.

Deja has either forgotten or has forgiven him. She wiggles up and stands on her hind legs with her feet on

Sam's belly. He jostles her ears and gives his puppy a kiss on the nose.

"We got a job to do, girl."

Sam installs the tire chains on the little Ford tractor. He loads nine bales of straw into the trailer, plus a tarp and a snow shovel. He covers the box of Robert's pictures and negatives with a sleeping bag so nothing will blow out. Deja leads the way, happily loping in the deep snow ahead of the tractor, up the trail to the fire ring.

It's 10 degrees below zero when they arrive, and going on 4:00 a.m. The clouds have cleared quickly on the back side of the blizzard. The Milky Way glows softly in the inky, blue-black winter sky. A lone coyote howls from the flatland to the south.

Sam builds a roaring fire, then shovels the snow away from his and Deja's nest for what little remains of the night. He stacks two piles of straw bales at a right angle for a windbreak, four bales high. He drapes the tarp over the two stacks to trap the fire's warmth. Opening the last bale and spreading it around under the tarp, he snuggles Deja deep inside the sleeping bag, carefully settling her onto the soft bed of straw.

A handful at a time, Sam drops the photos, negatives, and folders into the fire. He doesn't look at any of them, but tends the fire with a branch from the big jack pine he'd felled to make sure every scrap burns completely. Finally, as the eastern sky glows faintly, Sam burns the box.

He adds another few logs to the fire and unzips the sleeping bag. He draws his puppy tight to his chest and pulls the bag over them. No, he doesn't think he'll sleep—that's the way the attacks ago. But it's different this time. He feels calm, satisfied. The fire flickers in his eyes. He thinks of Sally, and his eyes moisten.

Man and dog fall peacefully to sleep.

Deja's growling wakes Sam. The sun is up and shining. He estimates it's just past mid-morning, maybe 10:00 a.m. He hears voices coming from up the trail, calling his name. Deja recognizes one before Sam does. She relaxes and prances off toward them.

"Dad! Dad!" Matt calls.

"Sam!" shouts Maureen.

"Son!" yells Sam's dad. "Are you okay?"

Sam stands up, still getting his bearings.

"Up here. Yeah, I'm fine."

The three of them shuffle quickly through the snow up to Sam's camp. The fire has been reduced to coals, barely smoking.

Matt grabs Sam by the shoulders, then hugs his father tight. "You scared the crap out of us. Why didn't you call?"

"Call?" Sam wonders aloud as he shakes his head.

"Jesus, son. There's a dozen messages…"

"I been gone. Didn't occur to me to check when I got back."

"Where'd you go?" Maureen asks anxiously. "What was the rifle for?"

They all stare at Sam, waiting for an explanation.

"It's complicated," he offers as he rubs his forehead. "After they took Elvis and Roy, I went drivin' around. Then came up here last night."

"Laura called me," Matt says. "What's this post-traumatic thing all about? She said she can't discuss it with me. That I'd have to ask you directly."

"Son, whatever it takes, I'll do, I'll help."

"It's not just about what happened when I was little. It's complicated. I'm not sure if we want to go all the way there, Dad…"

His dad assures, "Yes, we do need to go there. I wanna hear it all."

Sam's dad gets the coffee going, while Sam takes a long, hot shower. Matt plays the answering machine, taking down messages and phone numbers.

When Sam emerges from his bedroom with fresh clothes on, Matt informs him, "Sally called, too. I didn't call her back. Maureen told us about her—why and how she left. Are you going to call her back?"

Sam nods. "I'll call from the bedroom."

"I still can't come home," Sally apologizes. "But I love you. I'm asking you to wait for me…if you can."

"However long it takes. I love you, too. I'll be here."

"Your dad and Matt gonna stay for a while?"

"Yeah, I s'pose—at least overnight. We're gonna talk."

"I hate to pry open this coffin any more than we already have," Sam admits, looking into his coffee. "But we're all here. Let's get it open once and for all—the Ryan family crypt—then lock it for good."

Sam looks at Matt and says softly, "It's gonna be up to you to break the mold."

He looks at his father through glistening eyes. "You gotta believe two things before I start. I am thankful to be your son, and I love you."

"I love you, too, Son."

"I look at Sally's husband and her brother-in-law. Bill's a wife-beater and a womanizer who can't see beyond his pants zipper. He tried to kill Sally's horse. He shot Sally's dog right in front of her, then shot at her. Robert abuses children and takes pictures of unsuspecting women. He didn't even help save his father's life, when he was only feet away, hiding. I'm no better than them in some ways. But somehow I turned out better, in other ways. I owe both parts to my parents."

Dad and Matt sit silently, cupping their coffees, staring into them.

Sam continues, "As far back as I remember, Dad, I was—and still am—deathly afraid of you. You're not a monster, I know that. I understand how hard it was raisin' a big family then. You workin' so hard to make ends meet, to give us wonderful Christmases, decent clothes, and plenty of food on the table. There wasn't much room for any of us kids to mess up. Punishment was swift and severe. You had to keep order, in order to provide.

"My perception is that I bore the brunt of your anger, of your fear, of your lack of rest and need for security. I feel like I got beaten often only because of your frustrations. I was an easy target—curious about the world, precocious, and with too much energy to be livin' in a cramped little farm house with eight others."

Sam's dad sighs. His eyes are welling up. Matt is expressionless, slowly looking in Sam's direction, then his grandfather's.

"That's all we knew," Dad replies. "I mean, that's the way it was back then. It didn't occur to your mother and me you'd be scarred by that. Really, I wanted the best for you. I wanted you to be able to get along in a world that demanded doing good, being good."

Sam continues calmly. "I was so convinced everything was my fault, those feelings of guilt still haunt me. That I was the cause of everything bad that happened to me. That when Sparky did those things to me, I was sure I'd get beaten if I told you. I didn't dare come to you or Mom for help."

Dad asks tearfully, "Those things you wrote about?"

"More than I put in the story I wrote…"

Matt sobs quietly into his hands.

"Bill and Robert did try to tell their grandma what an uncle was doing to them. She threw them both in the shower, naked, and ran the cold water on them for who knows how long, standing guard with a belt, whipping them when they tried to escape. Their dad came to the house to get them after work and found that going on. Pop, we called him—the man who gave me the team of horses. I knew him only as a very good and generous man, although you have to wonder why he didn't confront his mother… or the boys' uncle.

"Pop never chastised his boys for their faults. I always wondered if Pop felt responsible, felt it was too late.

"On the other hand, I really think I turned out okay in many respects. I do owe that to you and Mom. As tired and frustrated as you were, there was a lotta love. There was forgiveness. You saw the good in everyone, and taught us kids by your example not to judge. You always did whatever you could for anyone in need. I think I was able to separate out how your hurtin' me wasn't from the same father who did all that good. In fact, when I'm workin' with kids, or just bein' a friend, I often ask myself, 'What would Mom and Dad do?'

"But when I failed you, I felt like I'd failed myself. Your wrath would come out. I'd actually feel like I would leave my body and watch what was happenin' from a ways away. I loved that little Sammy dearly. But as I grew older, I hated the older Sam—for not protecting the little guy. When I got older and felt someone was attacking the Sammy in me—that innocent little kid who was doin' the best he could—I'd go into a rage, or I'd drink.

"These past six or seven years, when either Sam or Sammy felt unfairly attacked and helpless, I'd sob and beg, then I'd run away, staying awake and keeping moving for two or three days—my mind a blur, until I dropped from exhaustion. And then life would go on—until the next attack."

"Is that what happened to you yesterday?" Sam's dad asks. "Maureen told me all that's been goin' on lately—the crooked lawyer, the crap at school, those assholes takin' the team of horses."

"It sure felt like a PTSD attack at first. But I came out of it. It just occurred to me I came out of it—not even half a day of that blur and mania. Shit, it was only a few hours, and then I got down to business."

"Up in the woods?" Matt asks.

"No, I was fine. I was rational. I went up there because I wanted to. You know, I sleep up there every once in a while, any time of the year. The old attacks...like I said, you wouldn't have seen me for two days, maybe three."

"What do you think was different this time?" his dad asks.

Sam thinks, sighs, and sips his coffee.

"I finally told someone—my therapist, Laura—what happened. Not just Sparky, but the other bad stuff I was convinced I deserved. Then Dad, you came up and helped with the wine. You wanted to mend some fences, like I wanted to. I sensed you were showin' me I was okay in your eyes, even though we didn't talk about that stuff. I didn't hear a word of the old crap, like 'When you gonna get your shit together?' Instead, you said things like, 'Those kids on the bus, they're goddamn lucky to have you.'"

Sam slides out of his chair and goes to the pantry. He brings out a decanter of cranberry cordial he'd made two years ago. He sets it in front of his dad, then goes to the cupboard and selects three snifters, pouring an inch of cordial into each one.

"Okay, Matt," Sam announces proudly, sliding him a snifter. "Let's see if you learned anything. You're gonna be a father in a couple months!"

Sam's dad looks at his drink and swirls it. "Matt, what's the first thing that should come to your mind if your kid busts a delicate, expensive, family heirloom Christmas tree ornament with his pop gun?"

Dad takes a sly sideways glance at Sam and raises his eyebrows—obviously remembering when Sam had done that very thing.

Matt thinks for a second. "Umm…say, 'Nice shot, son!'"

"Bingo!" Sam's dad raises his glass to clink.

"My turn." Sam asks, "And what would you do if your son 'borrowed' your Playboy magazine with the Vanna White spread in it?"

"Get him a box of tissues and a little time to himself?"

"Bingo again!" Sam shouts and they all three clink glasses.

Matt pours another round.

The rest of the day, with the hardest work done, the three generations of Ryans laugh and tell fatherhood stories. They cook a beef burgundy supper Matt had seen on the food channel (with venison instead, totally destroying Sam's kitchen in the process), and they make and draw plans for the winery, well into the night.

The next morning, Sam's head feels like a big, rotting pumpkin. He hears his tractor running and wanders to the front door. His dad, dressed in Sam's coveralls two sizes too big, is teaching Matt to run the tractor and bucket to clear the yard. Deja prances around excitedly, throwing snow with her nose and chasing her tail.

Suddenly, Sally comes to mind. Sam has to call her. The phone rings before he can pick it up to dial.

"Hello?"

"I love you," Sally says softly. "I'm gonna tell you I love you every day the rest of our lives—so don't you dare leave the phone off the hook! And you, ya Jackpine Savage, might think about gettin' a cell phone so I can tell you I love you wherever you are."

CHAPTER 14

CANOES IN WINTER

December 17, 2003

"You had us all pretty scared," Laura says. "But I think you're right. This episode was different. Rather than being uncontrollably sad, you were mad as hell. And in control—in an out of control sort of way. Giving God the finger doesn't make you crazy. Not that you didn't have the right to be angry, with them taking the horses away, and what they did to poor Deja. Give Him all the hell you want. He can handle it."

Sam replies, "Please don't put anything in your notes about what I did at Robert's, or what I did with the photos and negatives up at the fire ring. Maybe I shoulda turned that stuff over to the cops. It was just so disgusting…the whole lot of it. I don't know the law. Maybe my goin' into Robert's house uninvited woulda made those things inadmissible as evidence. I was also tryin' to cover my own ass."

"I think you were doing what you had to do to protect Sally. Sounds like you were perfectly lucid. You remember every detail. So that's good."

He smiles at the mention of Sally.

"So how are you with her staying away and not telling you where she is?"

"I admit, it's difficult. I can't explain it. But it's a good kind of yearning. It's a *patient* kind of yearning I had no idea I was capable of."

"Any idea how long before she'll come back?"

"Don't know. Probably not until after the divorce. March, maybe?"

"Can you wait that long?"

"To be honest, I don't know the answer to that question either. The whole thing still doesn't seem quite real. I'll defer to God's timing. Found the bison bones the very day we had that talk about openin' myself to the possibilities, and along came Abby the next day. Then the day after I finally get rid of Abby for good, Sally and I finally talk after five long months. I'm not sure why the Big Guy's takin' his darn time actually gettin' Sally and me together under one roof. Maybe we still got some work to do."

"Speaking of that," Laura says as she opens her appointment book. "The next two Wednesdays are Christmas Eve and New Year's Eve. How about we meet the week after?"

Sam nods.

"Ahh, the holidays. Hasn't been a good time of year for you in the past. Any thoughts about this year? Got any plans?"

"Ya know, I haven't even thought about it. Hmm. Might be the year to go stay with Dad for a couple days. See Matt and Marsha, my sibs."

"Even Mac?"

"Naw, he won't come to Minnesota for the holidays anyway. He's still the biggest asshole on Earth. I'm sure he'll be on some tropical island with his fat cat buddies. I hope he gets some bad ice cubes in his $100 Scotch."

He thinks for a second. "But Sally…I don't wanna miss her calls. Maybe I'll just stay home."

"Why don't you get a cell phone so she can reach you anywhere?"

"You know, you're the second person who suggested that in the last 24 hours."

He slaps his hands on his thighs, then stands up to leave, suddenly in a hurry.

"I know just the Christmas tree to cut from my woods. Need decorations, a stand—everything. Got ridda all that stuff, seems like a lifetime ago. I need to go shopping! I don't know what to get for Sally. Oh God, what about my kids! Good thing I don't have a job to slow me down!" Sam jokes.

"Sounds like I'd better not keep you any longer," Laura says, obviously satisfied with her patient's progress. "See you after the holidays. Merry Christmas."

Sam is happily deep into his mental list making as he opens the door to leave. "Yup. You, too. It IS gonna be a Merry Christmas."

Sam stops for a beer at the dive bar on his way home. As he slides onto the bar stool, Dottie asks with that leathery, wrinkled twinkle, "How's the knittin' going?"

"You remember me?" Sam asks, surprised.

"Course I do," Dottie answers. "Only had about three customers since you came in last summer. You been to see that hippie therapist again, I presume?"

"Yup. Been comin' over pretty regular. But things are gettin' a lot better. Windin' down, comin' together. But actually, I stopped in today for *your* advice…and a beer. Just occurred to me Christmas is only a week away!"

Dottie looks at Sam with her eyebrows raised. "Well, that's progress."

Sam laughs. "No, no. I need some womanly advice. Remember the woman I was all upset over? The one who ran off last July? Well, I'm in love with her. But I haven't seen her since."

Dottie furrows her brow and purses her lips as she pulls on the tap.

"I haven't a clue what to buy her for Christmas. Or where to send it."

She stops pouring halfway, puts her hands on her skinny hip bones and asks, "Thought you said you were gettin' better?"

"Long story…"

"If all else fails, buy her jewelry. Easy for her to pawn if she don't like it. That's what I always did with it."

There are two jewelry stores in downtown Park Rapids, which is on the way home. Sam stops at the first one, closest to the highway. He has no idea what type of jewelry to buy for Sally and is panicking in a big way. Only five business days before Christmas, including Christmas Eve. He has no idea how far Maureen will have to ship the gift. Nothing in the first store resonates with him.

The second store has a display of crystal angels in the big front window—knick-knacky things you'd put in a lighted cupboard along with your fancy wine glasses, or on a coffee table where you'd have to dust them at least once a week. None of them seem right.

But angels, again—they're always popping up.

He asks the woman behind the counter if she has any angel jewelry. Sure enough, she has a display of angels in two trays. Pendants on necklaces and brooches, all in small velvety boxes lined with shiny satin. When she sets the first tray in front of him, the light catches on a necklace, making the angel's wings sparkle a rainbow of colors. Sam's hand is drawn to it. He's not even seeing the rest of the display.

The angel is white gold, about three-fourths of an inch in diameter, on a white gold chain. Not a cherub, like in his dream about the river, but a genuine guardian angel—worldly and wise. It's standing rather than flying sideways as cherubs usually are. The edges of the outstretched wings are lined with tiny diamonds. The angel has its hands cupped out front, holding a slightly bigger light-blue stone.

Sam can't take his eyes off the pendant. "What stone is this?"

"An aquamarine, the March birthstone," the clerk says.

"Do you have another angel just like this one, holding an emerald instead, my birthstone?"

"I'm sorry. We're all out."

"How about a June birthstone? I have no idea what kind of rock that is."

She looks over the tray carefully. "That would be a pearl. Nope, out of them, too."

In fact, the aquamarine pendant is the only guardian angel birthstone necklace she has left.

Sam doesn't know why he's compelled to buy it for Sally, but he does. The blue of the aquamarine is pretty close to the color of her eyes anyway.

He has the jewelry lady gift wrap it. She also gives him a bigger box that Maureen can use to mail it and reminds him to insure it.

Next, he hurries around the corner to the cell phone store. Within 15 minutes, they have him signed up for a year, and hand over his new working cell phone.

He tests it from inside the store. He can't remember Sally's number, so he calls Maureen.

"I just bought a darn cell phone (though I swore I'd never own one) so Sally can call me over the holidays whenever she wants to, because me and Deja are going to the cities. Can you call me right back so I can see if the thing really works?"

Maureen hesitates. "I'll be busy for a few minutes, but I promise to get back to you before you get home."

Sam is across the prairie and into the hills, a good 15 minutes toward home, before his new phone rings. The sound surprises him, even though he'd barely taken his eyes off the thing sitting in his cup holder. He remembers the instructions from the lady. All you have to do is flip it open, then press any number button to answer.

He steers with his knees because it takes him both hands to figure out which end opens. Once opened, he holds the phone alongside his head. It isn't very big. For sure it doesn't go all the way from his ear to his mouth like a real phone. Sam opts to make sure he can at least hear, placing that end of the phone right over his ear, and hopes Maureen will be able to hear him, without him having to move the phone from his ear to his mouth as they take turns talking.

Hesitantly, he answers, "Umm, hello?"

"I love you," says a woman's voice.

"Oh shit. Excuse me! I just got this damn phone, and the first call I get is a wrong number. Sorry…"

"Sam! It's not a wrong number! I love you!"

"Sally? SALLY?"

"Pull over, ya big goof! If I know you, your eyes are leakin', and you can't see where you're goin'. You're probably steerin' with your knees."

"Just a sec…and I love you, too!"

Sam pulls off the highway into the wayside rest.

That Maureen…

It's Tuesday, December 23rd, right after supper. By the light of only candles and Christmas tree bulbs, Sam's bodily fluids are being nicely replenished by homemade wild grape wine, which he'd spiced and heated. He sits on his living room floor wrapping gifts for his trip to the cities in the morning. He has left the string of Christmas lights on along his porch roof so he can gaze out the front window and watch the snow fall. It is Christmas movie snow—large, gentle flakes that float down slowly and land softly.

A car pulls into his driveway. Through the front window, he sees it is Maureen.

Sam hurries to fetch a mug of spiced wine, which he hands to her as she enters.

"Hope you're not on call," he says. "Pop said I should give folks sleigh rides and serve 'em spiced wine. First batch I ever made. You wanna be my guinea pig?"

She smiles and hands him a grocery bag, then takes the wine and inhales deeply. Sam sees a wrapped present in the bag.

"My pleasure," she says as she takes a sip.

She hands the mug back to Sam while she stomps her boots and takes her coat off.

"What's this?" Sam asks, holding the bag out in front of him.

"Came for you today. At least the card and this square package did. The rest of it has been going back and forth in the mail for a week. Just needed an elf, namely ME, to put it together. Go ahead, open 'em."

"Oh, wow. Shall we call her?" Sam asks.

"Good idea."

He heads for the kitchen phone. It rings when his hand gets within a foot of it. He somehow knows it's Sally.

"Talk about perfect timing! Maureen just brought me somethin' from you. We were gonna call you while I open it. I'll put us on speaker. Maureen, come on, bring your wine to the kitchen. Don't worry about your boots."

"And I got something in the mail today as well," Sally replies.

Maureen bites her lip, holding back tears, as she comes around the corner. "Hi, little sister. Now tell Sam that I didn't tell you to call right this moment. This wasn't a setup."

"Not a setup…at least not by anyone we know. Been happenin' a lot lately."

"Sam, you go first."

"Okay." He opens the card. "The card, it's beautiful—the Christmas angel. Angels everywhere these days!"

"Now open your gifts," Sally urges impatiently.

"Which one first?"

"The flat one. It was originally gonna be for Pop. He'd want you to have it. I hope you don't think I'm being presumptuous."

Sam can tell by feel that it's a picture or something in a frame, even before he slips a finger under the wrapping.

He is dumbstruck. A photo of Sally on Dakota, turning a barrel so tight and so low that the stirrup is only an inch from the ground. Dakota's mouth is agape, nostrils flaring, ears pinned back, the soil of the arena a cloud under her hooves. Sleek and fluid, strong and so beautiful—like a mythical horse-god.

And Sally atop her horse, a snapshot of perfect grace, leaning forward and twisting her body with Dakota's. A perfect profile of her beautiful, determined face, her blonde hair flying behind her.

On the back, she has written: *To Sam, All of My Love, Forever. Sally*

Okay, so Sam's eyes are leaking. That's a lot—a gift from Sally and Pop.

Sally asks, "Do you like it? Sam?"

He tries to find the right words, and a way to get them out intelligibly.

Maureen speaks up first. "I hope that thing's waterproof. Sam here has developed quite a leak." She dabs at her eyes. "Well, he's not the only one…"

Sally says, "Sam, a company takes these pictures at the rodeos and sells 'em afterwards. That was the rodeo Dakota won, when you were right there in the arena with us! The photo—that's the second barrel. Look closely, up in the right corner. That's you!"

"I don't know what to say. Other than thank you. Oh God, you are so beautiful."

"Hey," Sally asks. "Is it my turn now? Which one?"

Maureen suggests, "I have a great idea. Why don't you both open your little square boxes at the same time? After all, they're about the same size…"

"Maauureeeen?" Sally questions.

Sam tosses his little gift about the size of a small tissue box in the air a couple of inches. It's fairly hefty for its size.

"I think I know what this is," Sally says.

"Me, too," Sam concurs.

Maureen apologizes. "I'm sorry, Sam. I told Sally about your old coffee cup."

"I really needed to get rid of that old one anyway." Sam pulls it out of the box and unwraps the tissue.

"Holy shit," he exclaims under his breath.

"Ditto," Sally says softly and begins to sob. "It says 'Sweeten my coffee with a morning kiss.' I will, Sam. I promise…someday, you'll see…"

Sam shows his mug to Maureen. "So does mine." He wipes at his eyes. "Holy shit again. I'll sweeten your coffee, too, Sally…right before I shave your legs!"

"Too much information!" Maureen shouts as she holds her hands over her ears.

Sam laughs, takes a deep breath and bucks up. He announces to the sisters, "We're not done yet! Sally, the card next, if you will."

"Opening the card," Sally informs. "So darn cute! It's a wintry farm scene…the animals. Looks like your place, Sam! The rail fence, a yellow Lab just like an adult Deja, sitting posed…a horse behind, bunnies, chickadees… makes me excited to get home. Won't be too long, I hope."

"Now the present," Sam urges. "Hope you like it."

Maureen waits with her spiced wine an inch from her mouth.

After seconds of silence except for the wrapping paper rustling, Sally cries softly, "Oh my God! An angel! It's beautiful. Are those real diamonds?"

"Yup," Sam answers.

"And the gem the angel's holding?" Sally asks. "Is that an aquamarine? The March birthstone?"

"Sorry, I liked the angel so much. I was so drawn to it. They didn't have your birthstone. Or mine. But it's Aquamarine…just like your eyes, right?"

"My hands are shaking," Sally confesses, crying. "I can't get the clasp open. I want to put it on right now. Just a minute…"

Maureen and Sam hear a door open, then happy, hurried voices from another room. It sounds like an older woman shouting, "It's perfect, a sign from God!"

Sally's breathless when she returns to the phone. "You dear man. I can hardly wait to thank you in person for this. It's so perfect. More perfect than you know."

Sunday, January 11, 2004

In these hills that Sam calls home, it is 35 degrees on Friday. Clear blue, sunny, and 40 degrees Saturday, the day the river began to open up at the bridge—just a sluiceway in the middle, at noon. By dusk, the river was as open as it would be until the real spring thaw in two months; the middle two-thirds ran ice-free. The water had dropped three feet. The ice shelves, two feet thick, cantilever out over the water from the banks almost 10 feet, the water running underneath them a foot.

Sunday is the third day in a row the temperature has risen above freezing. Sam can tell today is the final day of the warm spell, by the mare's tail clouds streaking in from the west. It didn't freeze overnight. The south wind promises the temperature will rise to the mid-40s in the afternoon, maybe higher if the clouds don't thicken too soon. Today will be Sam's last opportunity to canoe the river for a while, for on the warm spell's heels is another cold snap.

The river has been Sam's friend and confidant for over six years now. He never makes an important decision or takes any kind of leap without checking with his friend, the river. Sometimes he desires a simple, quiet time with her before what he knows will be a hard day ahead. If he's going away for a while, he stops to say goodbye. Sometimes Sam will ask for her help. Or fill her in on what's going on in his life. Sometimes he complains.

Doesn't matter what time of year. If she's frozen, he sits near her, making a small fire. If the deerflies are out in hordes, he wears a couple layers they can't bite through— even if it's 90 degrees. (He takes plenty of beer for those days.)

The river, she is a great friend and ally.

Sam delivers his canoe and gear to the landing below the dam. Driving his truck to the bridge, he ties a rope to an alder brush and tosses the other end to the edge of the ice shelf, so he'll be able to haul himself and his canoe back up onto the shore at the end of the trip.

Maureen picks him up at the bridge and drops him off back up to the dam at noon.

Before Sam shoves off, he calls Sally to tell her that he loves her and to promise he'll call her when he gets home. He expects she'll advise him to be extra careful.

"I'm not worried," she tells him. "There's a guardian angel watching over you. Say hello to the river for me. Both of you."

"Dear River, we've got a lot to talk about," he says aloud as he pushes away from the bank. "I'll be quiet now, but you'll still hear me. You always do."

Sally first. I miss the hell outta her. I can barely remember what she looks like. How she feels in my arms. I so want her home with me. It's not my call, I know. I won't push her. I say silent prayers for her to begin her journey home. I do trust she's headed home. Right?

I thank you—God, the spirits, and my friend the river. I imagine Sally is with me again, drifting lazily through this rice bed. And she'd smile and take in a deep breath and hold it over this pair of trumpeter swans, who take noisy flight downstream. Running on top of the water to gain speed, then gracefully they lift off, trumpeting all the way until they're out of earshot. And then she'd turn to me with that incredible smile…

Please forgive me as I think back to Abby right here at the bison site. Her memory will last to where the river runs to the high ground, for another 10 minutes. Pardon me if I do some naughty grinnin'. Who wouldn't? I can't believe I didn't think of Abby where I launched the canoe, near the old bridge abutment with her initials and all the others carved into it.

Dad. Down the first set of decent riffles. A happy place. Where Deja learned to dive, that rascal! The keel of the canoe clanks noisily against a rock, the Deja rock. Shit— sideways in the river. Rocking the canoe to loosen myself. Won't be seein' any deer for a while after this lapse in navigation. The ice shelves never form up here. The river drops too quickly, and the water doesn't back up.

I laugh over Dad's antics—picking grapes and making wine with us. The otter den has muddy footprints around it. Their slide by the basswood clump has been played upon recently. I wonder how Dad got so mellow. What would I do without him right now? I have no job, and the spare socks in the dresser drawer are empty.

The tiny creeklet flows into the river. A mink hunts along the bank. It stands on its hind legs to stare at me, displaying the white chevron of its chest fur. The mink disappears into the creek and swims underneath a thin ice shelf.

A check for $1000 came in the mail yesterday—from Dad. And a note: Thank you for being my son. And my teacher. Love, Dad.

The ancient Indian campsite. The river is narrow here. Hills on both sides. Rocks piled across the river, except for a fast chute near the north bank—a crude man-made dam. I heard once there was a mill here, in the old days, used to grind the settlers' wheat. Now it's a great place to spear suckers and swim. Sometimes man-made stuff does turn out okay.

Court tomorrow. Sally and I are being sued! For Roy and Elvis. Good grief. The Big Conspiracy! I trust, dear River, there's no evidence of such immoral shenanigans by the likes of a law-abiding citizen such as Yours Truly or my Sally. Can't believe even Peabody and Tweedledee and

Tweedledum are still bringing this thing to court—with no evidence! Wonder what they're up to?

What's that, dear River? Don't worry, you say? Did I hear you, River Lady, tell me to just sit back and enjoy the show tomorrow? I know, I know, popcorn is appropriate when clowns are performing. But no, it says right on the courtroom door: No Food or Beverages. *Yes, I agree, what kind of circus is that where you can't stuff your face and drink your fill? We'll find out at 1:00 p.m.!*

Yes, the ice shelves begin on the long straightaway above the double hairpin turn. I'm not disappointed one bit, dear River. Pretty, how they protrude from the tops of the low banks, enveloping the trees at water's edge and anchoring themselves on shore, where the river flooded during the cold spell. They're dripping steadily underneath. I can see under them all the way to shore. Next to the shore, they're almost as thick as the bank is high, two feet or so. They thin and taper to a dull, lacy tip out over the water, sometimes 15 feet. The water running gently underneath reflects the ice shelves' undersides, worn to smoothness but gently undulating. The ice is milky, full of air bubbles, layered like whitish agates.

A large tree root in the middle of the river, a foot in diameter, sticking up three feet above the water. It wears a hat of ice a foot thick, pointing upstream a yard like a giant bicycle helmet.

School, Ms. River. I miss the kids so much. The ones I've run into say they miss me, too. Eric told me he was gonna grab 20 rebounds for me during one game. He got 23. I hope my staying away from the games during the investigation hasn't made me appear guilty.

Joan says we should hear tomorrow if the state's gonna press charges. That goddamn Peabody. Grrrr. My saving grace here, besides the fact that I didn't do that or anything to Missy, is that kids are honest. Pardon me for usin' such language in front of a lady, Ms. River, but it doesn't get any lower than what that fuckin' slimeball Peabody put Angie Wilson up to, and what they're puttin' Missy through.

Buck Island also wears a hat, a much bigger one, at least 75 feet long. Well, because of the brush on the island, the ice looks more like a starched collar.

The bonsai tree on the inside of the next bend, growing from the top of a stump out in the stream. The one-foot tall balsam took root there on top of the stump who knows how long ago. It hasn't grown two inches in the six years I've been drifting past it. I wonder if I'm the only person on Earth who knows such wonders exist within a couple hundred miles of a few million people.

Yup, yup. I understand, friend River. I'll only tell a few folks about you. And first make sure they care about you. Yes, yes, I hear you—they must care deeply about you before I share you with them.

But I refuse to live off my dad 'til I can round up a rock job, hopefully in the spring. The check is wonderful, but I'm gonna tell him that's it. What's that, dear River? Why not let Dad help? I don't know why not. Maybe I can round up an inside job or two this winter of fake rock.

Yes, Ms. River, I realize that sometimes even the best artists have to prostitute themselves just to eat gooey white bread and buy 80-grit toilet paper. Or maybe an indoor real rock job will come along. Got a helluva pile of 'em under the snow next to the winery, thanks to too much time on my hands tryin' to forget Sally last summer. I'll leave it up to you, friend River.

Sailing on past the high sandbank, you notice dear friend I'm barely crackin' a grin. I've convinced myself my smile is only for Sally anyway—you remember, the morels we found up there. And now I feel a nap coming on…

Thanks for the perfect weather to snooze. Less cloudy than I thought it would be. At least 50 degrees.

Sam backs the canoe into a dead water pool, where the river bottom is shallow and muddy-dark and the river insects and crustaceans dart around the sun-warmed shallows. He is facing south, out of the breeze, and slides his legs under the crossbars to sit on the floor of the canoe. Using the seat as a backrest, one boat cushion under his butt, and the other for a pillow, he closes his eyes. He knows there's not room for both of them, but still he imagines Sally lying next to him in the sunlight, snuggled into his chest.

"You will fall asleep in each other's arms soon," Sam's friend, the River, whispers.

I believe you, dear River.

After about half an hour the clouds have moved in and the chill wakes Sam up. Another half hour to the bridge. The sun is quickly losing its strength. He paddles hard the rest of the way to stay warm.

CHAPTER 15

GREAT TO HAVE YOU BACK!

Monday, January 12, 2004

The clerk announces, "All rise! Court is in session, the Honorable Judge Friday presiding."

While pulling his chair back and peering at the pile of folders on his desk, Friday instructs, "Please take your seats."

Peabody remains standing and pipes up, "It's great to have you back on the bench, Your Honor!"

Judge Friday glares at Peabody over his reading glasses. Friday seems annoyed, for a change, to be having his butt kissed so publicly.

"We got a lot going here, a schedule to keep," Friday says as he picks up the top file and pushes the others aside.

As he settles into his chair, Peabody steals a glance at Joan and winks at her.

Turning to the clerk, Friday asks politely, "Have we got Ms. Hunter on the speakerphone?"

The clerk nods.

"Please identify yourself, Ms. Hunter."

Sally does.

Peabody winces. He had never heard Friday call any woman "Ms." Even during divorce trials, Friday always called the women "Mrs." and used their husbands' first names, to boot.

"Mr. Peabody, you have brought both of these actions: a civil suit against Ms. Hunter and Mr. Ryan and the marriage dissolution of Mr. and Ms. Hunter. Today we're just scheduling for them both. Let's talk about the civil suit first."

Judge Friday looks to the gallery.

"Mr. Ryan, would you take a seat next to your attorney and Ms. Hunter's sister? Robert Hunter, come to the table with Mr. Peabody and William Hunter."

"How much time are you going to need for discovery, Mr. Peabody?"

"Your Honor, we don't need anything from the defendants, other than an opportunity to depose them both."

"Miss Adair?"

"All we need is a look at the unspecified evidence Mr. Peabody claims will prove his coercion theory. Depending on what that evidence is, I may or may not depose the Hunter brothers."

"Sounds simple enough," Friday says. "Mr. Peabody, when can you have that evidence to Ms. Adair?"

Sam looks at Robert, who's fidgeting. Apparently they are the only two people who know that no such evidence is in the Hunter brothers' hands anymore.

"Anytime she wants," Peabody answers, smirking. He points to Robert, the only one of the three at that table not acting smug. "I'll have my client make copies for her and deliver them to her office." He continues condescendingly, "Will Friday be soon enough, Ms. Adair?"

Joan raises her eyes and nods at the theater going on. "Yes, that'll be fine."

Peabody's so caught up in himself, he doesn't notice Robert motioning to him urgently.

Judge Friday interrupts, "Um, Mr. Peabody, it appears that your client wants a word with you."

"Excuse me, Your Honor," Peabody requests.

Peabody and the brothers confer in animated whispers. Finally Peabody says, "Excuse me, Your Honor. I'm afraid Friday will not work. Robert says he can't have the copies ready by then."

Sam whispers something to Joan. She looks confused, but responds, "We're okay with just reviewing whatever they have on Friday. We won't require copies until later, let's say the following Friday."

"Done," Friday orders.

"One more thing," Joan says, her finger raised. "Your Honor, we will be countersuing for attorney's fees and deposition costs, and will be asking the Court to have the plaintiffs pay the costs for the horses' care and transportation, alleging the parties have knowingly filed a frivolous lawsuit. I'll be filing the papers after Court. I'm asking that Mr. Peabody wait for his service."

Peabody jumps up. "Your Honor, I take great offense at such an accusation!"

"I'm sure you do. Now sit down, Mr. Peabody!" Judge Friday orders.

"Clerk—schedule a pretrial for a month out, and the trial in two months?"

After consulting the calendar, she responds, "Yes, Your Honor. An hour on February 12th, at 9:00 a.m. Half a day March 22nd, also at 9:00 a.m."

"Good. Thank you."

Friday checks the clock on the back wall and nods.

"How's that?" he whispers to the clerk.

She smiles her approval and gives him a thumbs-up.

"Let's move on," Judge Friday says, setting aside that file and opening the next one. "Mr. Ryan and Robert Hunter, you're done for now." He motions for them to leave the tables.

Sam holds the swinging gate open for Robert, who walks through quickly, darting his eyes nervously, then hurries to the courtroom exit.

"Excuse me, Your Honor," Peabody pleads with his hands spread apart. "I need to catch my client. I didn't know he was going to exit the courtroom!"

Peabody quickly pushes his chair back and rushes through the gate. He holds his hands around his mouth and shouts at the closed door, "Robert! Wait a minute!!"

Joan and Maureen both raise their eyebrows at Sam.

Friday rolls his eyes and frowns, drumming his fingers loudly.

"Bailiff, please go find Mr. Peabody. Tell him if he's not back here within two minutes, he'll be conducting the rest of his business with this Court today over a speakerphone from next door's holding cell."

Friday glances at the clerk again for her approval. The bailiff returns in less than a minute and informs Bill his attorney wants to see him in the foyer. Friday again rolls his eyes skyward, crosses his arms on his chest and sighs.

Peabody is pale and sweat is glistening on his forehead when he returns 10 minutes later. Bill follows, glaring at

Sam. But Robert's still nowhere to be seen. "Your Honor! Please accept my apology," Peabody says as he wipes his brow with a hanky. "We need to revisit the civil suit. I ask to meet with you and counsel in chambers."

Friday looks at his watch and growls, "This better be good, Mr. Peabody. Court's in recess." He bangs the gavel, a little harder than he needed to.

Friday stands and motions for Joan and Peabody to follow him to his chambers.

"Okay Mr. Peabody, what the hell's going on here?" Judge Friday demands. "I'm sure Ms. Adair would like to know, too."

"Um. Well, it seems the evidence we had is missing." Peabody clears his throat. "Umm, the evidence that will prove Sally Hunter and Sam Ryan worked together to coerce my clients' father out of his team of horses."

The judge sighs, "We're all going to find out anyway. What is this evidence?"

Peabody puffs up, confident. "Photos of Mrs. Hunter and Mr. Ryan…in bed together!"

"Where did these photos come from and where are they now?" the judge demands.

"I'm not exactly sure who the photographer was, umm…" Peabody shifts nervously and tries to loosen his collar, sensing the hole he's digging.

"Answer the questions, Mr. Peabody," the judge states, as he leans onto his desk with hands clasped.

"Well, you see…Robert says Mr. Ryan stole them from him. Came to his house with a gun and broke in…"

Joan tries her best to sit quietly. Her eyes are wide as she watches Peabody backpedaling. This is news to her.

"And you can prove that?" the judge asks, his eyes narrowed.

"Well, yes! Robert will testify to that!"

"Again, I ask: *Can you prove that?* Are you sure you want to go anywhere near that? Your client is sneaking around taking pictures of people in their bedrooms? Is he really going to admit to that? How do you think the board in St. Paul will feel about you advising your client to admit to that?"

"Let me put Ryan and Mrs. Hunter on the stand!" Peabody sputters. "They're upstanding people. Well, except for their extramarital affair. Point is, they won't lie about that!"

"Mr. Peabody," the judge explains calmly, "they dissolved some small clots in the arteries of my brain, but they didn't give me a lobotomy! Even if you find such photos, and you can somehow slither around implicating your client as the Peeping Tom who took them, do you really think there's a judge in this state who will give those horses to the brothers, without first proving their father was incompetent when he gave them away? Got any evidence along those lines?"

Peabody gazes at the floor and shakes his head, no.

The judge continues, "I'm going to do you a favor. I'll have Ms. Adair draw up a Summary Judgment to get those horses back where they belong and award her clients the fees and expenses she mentioned in Court. Then your clients won't have to pay all the way around for another hearing, just for me to throw the case out. Agreed?"

Peabody nods without looking up at the judge.

"And another thing. As long as I have you two in here, let me remind you: Minnesota is a no-fault divorce state. I won't be entertaining ANYTHING in my Court that is of a personal nature between the two parties. Nor will I entertain any 'evidence' concerning a property settlement that deviates from conventional guidelines, unless you can prove it within about two minutes of my time.

"OK, I've got a schedule to keep," the judge declares as he stands. "Let's get back in there."

"All rise."

As Joan reenters the courtroom, her eyes immediately seek out Sam. Her face reveals part disbelief, part surprise.

Peabody doesn't seem to have much wind left in his sails. When he stands in front of his chair awaiting the judge's order to be seated, his shoulders slump. Bill's jaw is set and he's shaking his head rapidly as he tugs on his attorney's coat sleeve. Peabody ignores his client and folds his hands in front of him as the clerk announces that further hearings on the civil suit are cancelled because the plaintiffs, through their attorney, have agreed to drop it. She schedules the next divorce hearing in its place.

Bill cups his hands around Peabody's ear and barks, loud enough that everyone in the courtroom can hear, "What the fuck?"

Friday shakes his head.

But Peabody is already on the move and beats his client out of the courtroom. Bill chases after him like a banty rooster, shouting and cursing at his attorney.

The bailiff asks Friday, "Want me to break that up, Judge?"

Friday actually smiles. "Break what up?" He appears to be stifling a giggle as he disappears into his chambers.

Joan, Maureen, and Sam wait in the courtroom for the commotion to move outdoors. The women can barely contain themselves, waiting to question Sam about Robert and the photos.

Whispering, Joan demands, "What the hell did you do?"

Sam shrugs, leans back casually, and says, "I haven't a clue what you're talkin' about."

"What's going on?" Maureen asks anxiously.

Joan looks skyward and shakes her head in disbelief. "Judge Friday threw out the civil suit and gave us all the costs. Seems like Friday didn't mind someone stole their evidence at gunpoint."

Maureen gapes at Sam.

In his best Sargent Schultz impression, Sam says, "I… knowww…NOTHINNNNG!"

Joan dials her cell phone and hands it to Sam. "It's Sally. Here, tell her the good news."

Joan and Sam have other business in the courthouse. They meet with the county attorney, Jill Abernathy, over Angie Wilson's charges of Sam molesting her daughter. The forensic interview of Missy is complete, and Angie has provided her affidavit.

"We're not filing charges," the county attorney informs them. "I'm really sorry, but we do have to look into these things, just in case."

"I understand," Sam says. "If anyone brought that kind of talk to me about a kid, I'd blow the whistle, too."

Joan asks, "But what about Angie Wilson's statement? What happened there?"

"The timing is suspicious, but we're not going after her for making a false claim—she's got enough problems. She recanted everything, right after Peabody couldn't get her off her drug charge with only a slap on the wrist like he'd promised. She realized then that she really needs help, after ruining your career and reputation, Sam. Missy's going to live with an aunt and uncle, and Angie is doing 30 days plus in-patient treatment afterwards. Here's a letter she wrote to the *Stone Creek Record*. It will be in today's paper."

The county attorney hands it to Sam. It's a photocopy, handwritten on lined spiral notebook paper.

To Stone Creek and Sam Ryan,

I made a horrible mistake. Well, more than one. I was messed up with drugs and desperate, and I lied about Sam. He never did and never would do anything to hurt a child. My Missy said some big kids told her they heard that Sam had hurt her. She cried and cried—said she and her friends miss Sam so much. He's the only bus driver who'll give them a hug on the sidewalk after a long day at school. Hugs are good.

So Stone Creek, please forgive me for taking your bus driver away from you. And let him back to work at the school, right away. The kids need Sam. With me being gone for a while, Missy will need his hugs more than ever.

I am so sorry.

Angie Wilson

Later that evening

"Sally, you know I'm gettin' Elvis and Roy back. Also, I got my job, my dad, and my sanity back. There's only one thing missin' from my life right now—you. Please, please come home. I love you!"

"I love you, too. But if I come home right now, I'm not so sure you'll still love me."

"There's nothin' in this world that could make me not love you," Sam pleads.

"What if there *is* something? Something just as troubling—like if I was carryin' Bill's baby?"

"Even then, I would love that baby more than anything, because he's part of you. What is it, Sally? What could be so wrong?" Sam asks softly.

"Correction," Sally says quietly. "Because *she's* part of me. It's a girl. She's due in March, the month with the aquamarine birthstone. Remember the angel you gave me?"

Sam bites his lower lip and tears begin to flow. He sniffles into the phone.

"See?" Sally concludes tearfully. "You don't wanna be with me anymore, do you?"

"Sally, I want you and this baby girl here more than anything in the world."

"I couldn't go through with the abortion. I was on the table. It was like a tiny voice was urging me, *Please don't, please don't*. I know it was her whispering to me, my baby."

"God bless you, Sally," Sam whispers through his tears. "And you, too, little angel."

"I met this nice couple in the Black Hills—Hill City. He's a doctor. They took me in. Their daughter runs a battered women group. I've learned a lot. I planned to have the baby and give her up—never telling Bill or you…or anyone. But then you gave me the angel necklace…"

"We'll deal with Bill. He won't get near you. I think I got both his and Robert's attention pretty good."

"But now this baby is gonna know who her father is. What if Bill wants a place in her life?"

"I guess any child deserves that. If her father truly wants that with her. Lotsa folks out there are shitty partners, but still good enough parents. We'll just love her all we can."

Sam asks, "Are you ready to come home? I'll come get you. I'll catch a flight from Fargo. I better hurry up and check on that."

"Maria already did. She said she knows you'll love this little angel with all your heart."

Sally's crying. "A flight leaves Fargo at 10 a.m. tomorrow mornin'. Doc, Maria, and I will see you an hour later. I'll be the one with the big belly and swollen ankles. Oh yeah, I did somethin' to my hair…dyed it back to my real color, light brown."

Sam laughs. "Yeah, I know what your real hair color is, remember? One more thing. Exactly when's the little angel due?"

"March 20th."

"That's three days after Marsha's due. Remind me to stock up on O.B. kits. And put a short leash on your sister that week."

Sam suggests, "You wanna do the honors, call Maureen and tell her she's gonna be an aunt? And that she and I need to be outta here for the airport by 7:00 or 7:30 a.m. at the latest. And one more thing—you can't *believe* how much I love you!"

Sam tries to wipe his eyes dry with his sleeve, but it seems he can't control the waterworks. His hands shake as he dials his dad through the moist veil. Wrong number. And then a second misdial. "Calm down," he instructs himself as he grabs a paper towel and leans back into the kitchen counter.

"Dad, can you get right up here?" Sam gushes into the phone. "I mean, like, *tonight*…or by eight or so tomorrow mornin'? But I'll already be gone."

"Hold on. Hold your britches, Son. What the hell's goin' on? They runnin' you outta town?"

"No. Hell no! No, I got my job back. It's Elvis and Roy. I need somebody here when they get home tomorrow. And to watch Deja."

"Slow down," his dad orders. "Where…are…you… GOING?"

Sam is pacing in front of the old wood kitchen stove, running his hand through his hair. "I'm bringin' Sally home! From the other side of Rapid City. She didn't have an abortion after all. It's almost like I'm gonna be a dad again myself…"

"That's great! Weather's gonna be good. I'll be outta here before five. By the way, how'd you get Elvis and Roy back?"

"It's a long story. I'll have Maureen fill you in. Lotsa calls left to make before I pack."

"Well, wait a minute. You gonna drive home right through? You need some help, cash? You just get it done. I'll cover it when you get home."

"I'm sure we'll stay at Sally's place tomorrow night. Maybe another night. We'll take our time—got the horses to haul. Be home Thursday, by supper for sure!"

"How far along is she?"

"Not quite seven months, so I don't think I'll need to pack an O.B. kit. Hmm, unless some other kid along the way wants mine to be the first ugly mug it sees. Yup, better pack it. Thanks, Dad! Oh shit. Better make sure I can get a plane ticket first. I'll call ya back if I can't. Otherwise, see you Thursday!"

"I'm sorry, sir. The flight from Fargo to Rapid City is full. We had a cancellation, but the seat was sold just five minutes ago."

"Oh, crap!"

"Wait. Hold on. Your phone number on my caller ID…it's the same one I am supposed to call to confirm the ticket. Are you…Sam Ryan?"

"Yes!"

"Compliments of a Maria Nagel," the agent says. "Just be at the gate half an hour early."

CHAPTER 16

THE POWER OF PRAYER

Sally and her entourage wait for Sam outside the airport security gate. Doc is the first to see him hurrying down the concourse.

"That him?" he asks, pointing to a man with a carry-on bag slung over one shoulder and a wool coat over the other.

Sam anxiously scans the signs directing him to the exit. He stops suddenly when he realizes he almost passed the exit gate. He turns and looks around anxiously. Sally is there on the other side of the gate, more beautiful than ever, her smile even more radiant than he remembers.

She's surrounded by at least a dozen people. He soon learns they are Doc and Maria, some of their kids and their spouses, and grandchildren. The couple appears to be a little beyond 60.

Maria is Hispanic, with perfectly coiffed medium-length gray hair and bright red lipstick, smiling widely, her hands on rosy cheeks. Doc is white, stocky, about his wife's height, with a handsome thatch of wavy, gray hair. It's obvious who their children are, beautiful with olive skin and dark hair.

The other adults are a mixture of skin tones. Two pretty little dark-haired, dark-eyed girls, about three or four years old, cling to Sally's hands. She looks perfectly natural with the children hanging onto her.

Sally wears jeans and a satiny white blouse. The angel necklace sparkles just below her neck. Her face looks the same as Sam remembered, except her hair's a little darker. She carries the baby out front beautifully.

A little boy about two years old holds a cardboard sign that reads *Sam Ryan* upside down. Maria is crying. Doc, however, is grinning from ear to ear and nodding.

Sam and Sally walk slowly toward each other, as if in a dream. Neither can speak. They meet at the gate, their eyes shiny, welling up. Sam carefully places his hands beside Sally's shoulders, like she's going to break if he hugs her as hard as he wants to. He still can't believe it's her, that they're finally together.

They kiss lightly, then lean back and look at each other. They kiss again. This time they don't let go right away.

They're blocking the exit, but the security guard lets them be. The other travelers who are exiting through that gate wait patiently and watch the reunion.

Finally Sam whispers, "Oh God, I love you," and kisses Sally again on the forehead.

"I love you, too." She stands on her tiptoes and gives him another kiss on the lips, lingering for several heartbeats.

They both look around, embarrassed, Sally dabbing at her eyes with a tissue from her pocket. At least 50 strangers are watching quietly. Apparently that kind of love *can* stop the world—or at least the flow of pedestrians in the Rapid City airport.

"Hey!" Sally says. "I got some folks for you to meet."

Arm in arm, they turn toward the others, her head nestled on his shoulder. Someone takes a photo. She takes his free hand and places it on her belly.

"Sam, meet my little angel…Angel, meet Sam."

"Angel? Is that her name?"

"You named her! When you called her a little angel over the phone, I swear she jumped for joy in here. The little rascal almost made me pee my pants! What do you think of that name?"

"Perfect. Just perfect."

The gang cheers and suddenly breaks ranks, surrounding the two of them. Sally attempts introductions between hugs and kisses. Other than Doc and Maria, who seem vaguely familiar, Sam isn't having any luck connecting names and faces. Sally hangs onto his hand for dear life. The two little girls and the little boy dash through the security entrance and are pulling Sam's heavy bag by the strap.

Doc and Maria's children load their own into their vehicles. Sally and Sam ride with the old couple. They make a caravan out of Rapid City, south on the road to Mount Rushmore. Doc and Maria are quiet in the front seat, letting Sam and Sally be.

"It's pretty, isn't it?" Sally whispers, gazing out the window.

"Yup. It's been a while."

"A while?"

Sam smiles. "I probably never told you. Just about every spring for 15 years, I came out here turkey huntin'. Last time was about nine years ago. I came back out for two months that summer. Built a stone fireplace in a gorgeous log house in a pretty valley. Lived in my camper by a creek. The first time Karen and I were separated."

"Where?" Sally asks, her hand on Sam's shoulder.

"West of Hill City—Deerfield. You know it?"

Sally sits up straight. Maria turns and looks surprised. Doc is smiling in the rearview mirror.

"What?" Sam asks. "I didn't realize it until I washed the fireplace rocks with acid when I was done, but a big piece of rose quartz in the center above the mantel about two feet had the perfect image of an angel in it."

Sally gasps. "Wings spread…even a halo."

"That's *your* house?" Sam asks incredulously, looking at Doc in the mirror.

Doc smiles widely. "I knew I'd seen you someplace before. You're the rock savant."

"The what?" Sally asks.

"Drove the general contractor nuts!" Doc laughs. "Sam picking through the piles of rock—keeping just one rock for the helper to haul into the house, while tossing 10 or 15 away. 'They're just rocks!' the contractor would holler, as Sam would heft each one and look it over in silence—as if he was inventorying each rock into his head. When he came to a tough spot, he'd stop for a little bit, then walk right to the perfect rock…every time."

"I can't believe it," Sam whispers.

He kisses Sally on the forehead. "How many times have you gone to the top of Hat Mountain?"

"At least 20."

"Me, too. Now I know what I was lookin' for. I was just there at the wrong time."

She nestles into his chest, then gazes at his face. She kisses him on the lips and contentedly falls asleep in his arms.

The day Sam arrives in the Black Hills is the beginning of three days of Chinook winds. No place on Earth that far north can be so warm and inviting in the middle of January. The southern breeze is like a mother's kiss, warm and gentle. The sun reflects brilliantly through the thin air on the new snow, almost blinding a person. The ponderosa pines and Black Hills spruce catch the sun's rays, and the trees hum gently in the breeze. Streams open and run merrily. Even at 6,000 feet, the temperature soars that day to nearly 60 degrees. The snow melts before their eyes.

Sally and Sam saddle up Sparky and Dakota.

"You sure you should be ridin'?" Sam asks anxiously.

"I'll take Sparky. She's never done anything stupid. Besides, Angel loves to ride. I promised her one more ride to Hat Mountain."

They ride toward the mountain from the west, through a broad pasture, a grassy valley. Hat Mountain looks like a long-dormant volcano—or a funnel with its blunt spout pointing skyward—the uppermost reaches treeless.

They halter and tie the horses on a plateau under the south rim, a hundred yards below the top, and climb the last of it on foot.

It's flat as a table top up there, fractured reddish-brown rock, an oval, north to south a hundred feet, east to west half of that. Initials and words are scratched into the soft rock here and there. An Indian vision quest pit has been chipped out near the southeast rim.

Sally holds Sam's hand to make those final steps up over the rim. She wraps her arms around him and kisses him, breathing through her nose, inhaling his scent. They stand under the Black Hills sun, embracing for several thousand heartbeats. A golden eagle cries from below the north rim.

She whispers, "I want to show you something."

She leads him to the north rim, where small pieces of rock have been laid out to form the words *Wope La*.

"I made that. It's Sioux for…"

"…thanks to the Creator," Sam finishes.

They ask at the same time, "How'd you know that?"

"You first," he says, laughing.

Sally points to a ravine halfway to the creek valley, about two miles away.

"Rose quartz in that ravine. I found those words made out of rocks the size of apples. Went back to the ranch computer and figured it out. I love it down there in that protected little valley. So does Angel—we went back twice."

Sam says, "On a rock outcropping facing south, above a little waterfall. I shot a big tom behind there. I always write *Wope La* in the soil or carve it in a tree or make it out of rocks or pebbles when I take a turkey or a deer. Those rocks are still there from nine years ago?"

He holds her from behind, hands folded over her belly. "Just a hunch," he whispers into Sally's ear. "But I'd say we are meant to be. All three of us." He pats her belly gently.

The Power of Prayer   247

She turns to him and smiles. They embrace, standing in happy, thankful disbelief for several minutes, tears soaking each other's shoulders.

───────

Doc and Maria have a party for them that night. The entire family is there. And there are neighbors, and there are friends, and the children and grandchildren that Sally has schooled on horses—more than 30 guests in all.

A feast, tables crowded with food. Doc and Maria's sons are grilling steaks. Sam had a hunch before he'd left Stone Creek that they might appreciate his wine. His traveling bag contains only one set of clothes and two sets of underclothes…but six bottles of wine.

They play Mexican music and dance. Little kids cling to Sally like she's their favorite blanket or doll. The bigger ones ask anxiously when she's coming back. Maria confides in Sam that she has prayed and prayed for this day.

After supper, Maria herds the two of them into Sally's bedroom. Everyone in the crowd is smiling, murmuring.

"Don't come out 'til we tell you!" Maria orders through a big, red lipstick grin.

They can hear muffled talking and giggles, parents shushing kids, furniture moving.

"What do you s'pose this is all about?" Sam asks Sally.

"I haven't a clue, but nothin' will ever surprise me again!"

Finally, the two little girls knock on the bedroom door. Grinning, they wedge themselves through the narrow opening of the door barely open so Sam and Sally can't see out. The girls giggle and tell them to put on blindfolds, then lead them carefully by their hands out into the living room. The girls direct them to face the fireplace.

"Okay!" Maria shouts. "Take off the blindfolds!"

"OH MY GOSH!" Sally cries.

Sam is speechless. He bites his lower lip to keep from sobbing.

The room glows pink with balloons and streamers. Cutout angels are everywhere. A banner proclaiming *It's a girl!* hangs between the two chandeliers. A huge cake with *Congratulations, Sally and Sam!* in fluffy, pink icing. A baby crib with a giant pink bow is overflowing with gifts.

"You don't give a person much warnin' when you're gonna pack up and move on," Doc teases. "The crib still needs another coat of paint!"

Sally had wondered what Doc had been up to in his shop the past month, warning her not to go in there and breathe the fumes. He'd known in his heart she would never give her precious baby away.

Doc hands Sam a glass of his own wild grape wine. He gives a glass to Sally, too, with only a tiny sip in it.

"A toast!" Doc declares, holding his glass high. "To Sally, our adopted daughter—our bearer of love, riding lessons, and a little angel. To Sam, who finally got it figured out, so I didn't have to personally drive to Minnesota to kidnap him and convince him how much this woman loves him! And to my beautiful wife, who has given me a newfound belief in the power of prayer."

Maria bites her lip. Tears flow down her rosy cheeks. The room erupts in applause.

Later, after all the guests have left, and in spite of the long day, neither of them can sleep. It feels too good, too heaven-sent. To hold each other, to feel the baby move, to gaze at each other. To whisper and run their hands slowly, carefully, over each other's bodies. On their sides, they hug and hold each other.

"You were right," Sally whispers. "There was nothin' on Earth like that night we had together. Until tonight…"

Doc arranges a quick appointment with his partner at the clinic, so Sally can have one last checkup before she leaves. Sam goes along, so the doctor performs an ultrasound for his benefit. Angel is sucking her thumb. Her profile is just like Sally's. The doctor talks to them as if they're a couple, like they have been forever.

That night is much quieter at the ranch. Only Doc and Maria are there with Sally and Sam. A couple of the neighbors had helped Sam pack the trailer with Sally's things, the gifts, and the horse tack that afternoon. The last coat of paint had been put on the crib before Doc went to the clinic. It would be dry enough to load by the time they left, early the next morning.

They are excited to get home but anxious, too, over facing Bill and Peabody. At 4:00 a.m., tearful promises to stay in touch and to visit are exchanged. Thanks are given. Sandwiches and a thermos of coffee are stowed in the backseat of Sally's truck. Two bales of hay, a pail of grain and two empty buckets to run water into are placed in the truck bed, in case they have to stop for the night. Normally a 10-hour trip, it will probably be 12 hours with the trailer and horses. The Chinook wind still prevails from the southwest. It will gently push them home.

Sam knows the route, the landmarks. Up the long hill into the Reynolds Prairie. Flag Mountain on the left. Winding down to Rochford, then back up to the road to Lead. Down into Deadwood. Winding again to Sturgis. Bear Butte looms beautifully against the inky eastern sky, blotting out the stars with its ancient profile. Then north through the rolling prairie of northwestern South Dakota. The sun starts to rise as they near the border of North Dakota.

The reality and the ugliness of the issues back home have not been forgotten. They decide to have Joan tell Peabody that Sally's back and living with Sam. They figure the best way to do that will be in a restraining order.

They stop in Fargo at the women's clinic. The day Sally had been there, the staff had taken photos of her injuries to facilitate her pressing charges against Bill. But, instead of going back home to do that, she had headed west.

The photos are still in her file. Sally herself seems disconnected from them as she looks them over. Sam isn't sure what he's feeling. His heart aches for the damage Bill inflicted, physically and emotionally. But something else twists his gut.

Those two brothers had brought out the worst ever in Sam—drunk and wrecking the cousin's truck with a hammer, taking the rifle to Robert's and kicking the shit out of him. He worries that if Bill does something else stupid, he'll do something maybe even more stupid.

They clear Fargo around 2:30 in the afternoon. Highway 10 is busy with afternoon traffic. It has been a long day. Sally lays her head on Sam's shoulder.

"Honey, I love you so much," she says softly. "I didn't think this would ever be possible. Thank you for helping me get through the tough part ahead. In the meantime, we've got a baby to get ready for!"

As the horse trailer pulls in, Elvis and Roy charge to the gate and whinny, posturing and jostling for position. Sparky and Dakota whinny back—old pasture-mates saying, *Where the hell have you been?* When Sam brings the truck to a stop near the gate, the horses in the trailer begin kicking and bouncing.

Sam's dad hurries out of the house, pulling on his jacket. Deja rushes past him. The gangly teenage dog runs to Sally first.

"Saw ya drive in!" Dad hollers. "Already called Maureen!"

Dad hurries to the truck. Instead of attending to the antsy horses, Sally walks up to Sam's dad with her arms open.

"When Sam said you were beautiful…I had no idea!" the old man teases.

She embraces his father. "It's so nice to finally meet you. Can I call you Dad?"

The old man smiles. "You can call me anything you want—from anywhere, anytime. But yes, please call me Dad."

Sally pats her belly, "And this little angel will call you Grandpa."

They sit around the kitchen table that evening—Sally, Sam, Dad, Maureen, and Joan—discussing their legal options.

Sally admits, "I have no idea what Bill will say or do when he finds out I'm still pregnant. I'm scared of him." She shakes her head and tears well up.

Joan agrees, "Don't worry, we'll get the restrainin' order. Stop into the office. We'll write up your affidavit and include the photos. I'm sure the judge will make you appear personally. Yup, the cat will be out of the bag then."

Sam asks, "Will Peabody be able to make any hay now concerning Angel?"

Joan shakes her head. "The reality is, Bill has a right to access the child, to parent Angel in some way. Don't worry, he'll never get custody, but I'm sure Peabody will make all kinds of noise about it. And about you, Sally, living here with Sam. The thing with Roy and Elvis—getting the team back here—no doubt has made 'em even more likely to fight dirty."

CHAPTER 17

PEABODY'S WHEELS ARE TURNING

Friday, January 23, 2004

Sam and the three women drive up to the courthouse an hour early for the restraining order hearing, wanting to avoid any possible contact with Bill in the lobby. But his truck is already parked out front. That doesn't surprise Joan; she's represented many battered women. What's surprising is that those guys always think they just invented a sneaky way to get to the women they beat up, to try and talk them out of pressing charges.

Joan calls court administration. "Yes, he's here already. Could you please call the jail so we can come in that way? Also, can we have the conference room behind the courtroom? Thanks."

Right on time, at 3:00 p.m., the clerk raps on the conference room door.

"We're ready. Everybody's in there. You know the way through the jury room. Mr. Ryan, come with me. You'll have to enter through the foyer because you aren't officially a party to this."

When Sam opens the door into the courtroom, Peabody and Bill swivel to glare at him. They both hold threatening gazes for longer than necessary. Judge Friday is already seated. He doesn't look up from his paperwork. Only one person sits in the gallery, a woman. Sam doesn't recognize her. He sits two seats away from her. Bill looks back again, frowning at the woman and indicating with his head emphatically for her to move away from Sam.

The woman is young, probably around 30, skinny and frail. Her long, black hair is stringy, and blackish rings under her eyes dominate her makeup-less face. She has a frozen, deer-in-the-headlights look when Bill directs her to change seats, like she doesn't know which ditch to jump into. She scurries around three rows and takes a seat in the back corner.

The door to the jury room clicks. The clerk heads behind the bench toward her post to the left of the judge. Joan enters next, her expression firm and serious, followed by Maureen, who looks straight ahead, then Sally, whose eyes are cast downward. She doesn't take a look at Peabody and Bill either. Had she done so, she would have seen their jaws drop in unison over her condition. Peabody flashes an evil grin, his wheels turning. Sam glances over his shoulder at the woman tucked into the far corner of the gallery. Her mouth is agape.

Friday removes his reading glasses and raises his eyebrows as Sally crosses in front of the bench, following Joan and Maureen to their table.

For a change, Peabody isn't a jack-in-the-box. He's too busy plotting.

Judge Friday invites an explanation, "Ms. Adair?"

"Your Honor, obviously, my client has returned to Minnesota. I know it's a different file, but the first order of business will be to excuse her sister, Maureen Novotny, from her duties as trustee and power of attorney."

"So ordered," Friday says. "I have that file right here." He quickly signs a document.

Joan waits for the judge to finish, then recites for the record the charges and evidence that Sally had been beaten by Bill. She requests that Bill be prevented from any sort of contact with Sally and from coming within a mile of her residence. And she asks that should they, by coincidence, find themselves in the same location, Bill would have to leave immediately.

Friday asks, "Mr. Peabody?"

Peabody stands and pleads, "Your Honor, there is no conclusive evidence that ties the injuries shown in the photos to my client. Who knows what kind of situation Mrs. Hunter got herself into when she suddenly left her husband. There are no witnesses who can testify she left the farm in that condition, other than the husband and wife themselves. But, we are not here to argue who is telling the truth and who isn't. We only ask that there be no finding of battery and that the restraining order is mutual."

He starts to sit, then raises a finger for one last request. "Oh and one more thing—we ask that Mr. Sam Ryan be excluded from contact with my client. Thank you."

A pretty benign speech from the likes of Peabody. Joan wonders what he's up to.

Friday orders, "No findings of battery at this time. The restraining order is mutual. William Hunter will agree to vacate the premises should he accidentally find himself in the vicinity of Ms. Hunter. As far as Mr. Ryan is concerned, that will have to be a separate matter, brought by your client. You know the procedure, Mr. Peabody."

Peabody stands.

"Your Honor, I'd like counsel to approach the bench with me," he requests as he glances over at Joan.

Friday shrugs, then motions Peabody and Joan to approach the bench.

Peabody whispers, "The condition of Mrs. Hunter is quite a surprise. This sheds new light on the divorce proceedings. Now it seems we have a custody issue. I would like to immediately make a motion on the divorce file to have a custody evaluation performed. It's only two months until the divorce trial. We should probably address this today. That is, if the Court sees fit and Ms. Adair agrees…"

Friday asks, "Are you even sure this is your client's child? What about that business where Robert said he saw them in bed together?"

"Ms. Adair, what do you say?"

"My client says the baby is Mr. Hunter's. She should know."

Friday asks the clerk, "This is the last hearing today, right?"

The clerk nods.

"Mr. Peabody, I assume you haven't talked to your client about this. Do you need a few minutes? And you, Ms. Adair?"

Both attorneys nod.

"Good," says Friday. "Ms. Adair, you may use the conference room. And Mr. Peabody, the jury room. See you both back here in 15 minutes."

"Court is in session on the divorce file," Friday notes. "Ms. Adair, are custody and parenting time going to be issues?"

"We hope not, Your Honor," Joan replies. "Of course, my client desires sole physical custody, but certainly sees the value in the child having a relationship with her father, on a parenting time basis."

"Mr. Peabody?"

"It seems we have a disagreement, Your Honor. My client desires to have sole physical custody of the child. However, we would agree that the child does deserve to have some sort of limited ongoing relationship with its mother."

Sally gasps and her head drops to the table. Maureen puts her arm around her as she sobs quietly.

Raising her head suddenly, she screams at Bill, "What do you know about a little baby? Jesus, Bill!"

"Order!" Judge Friday bangs his gavel. "ORDER!"

Joan stands and addresses the judge, "Your Honor, I apologize to the Court for my client's outburst, but this posture by them is obviously contrived solely to heap more abuse and anguish upon my client, Sally Hunter. I implore the Court not to entertain the notion that Mr. Hunter could possibly be considered for sole custody!"

Judge Friday inhales deeply. In a monotone, he gives the speech he has spoken many times. "The statute is clear. Rather than a custody evaluator, I am ordering that a guardian ad litem be assigned to the unborn child, as a party to this case. A guardian ad litem is the proper appointment due to the allegations of abuse. The guardian ad litem will interview all persons who will potentially have a significant role in the child's life and perform criminal background checks on those people, visit the proposed homes, and explore collateral sources as the guardian ad litem sees necessary, including medical and psychological records, in order to provide the Court a recommendation on the child's behalf, relative to permanent custody and parenting time for the non-custodial parent. The guardian ad litem fees will be shared equally by the parties."

The woman who had come in with Bill clasps her hands over her mouth. Quickly, she turns away to hide her reaction.

Court is adjourned, and the judge orders Peabody and his client to leave the building first. The woman's expression as Bill approaches is part incredulous and part fearful. He glares at her, and she obediently drops her gaze to the floor and stands to follow him.

Bill and Peabody pat each other on the back as they leave the courtroom. Peabody offers loudly, "Congratulations! You're going to be a father! And a darn good one!"

Once the judge leaves the courtroom, Sam rushes through the swinging gate. Sally is sobbing uncontrollably into her hands. "Oh Jesus! Oh Jesus! My Angel…I'm gonna be sick…"

Sally wretches as Sam quickly pulls tissues from a box. He moves to put his arms around her as she faints.

"This is my fault," he says softly to Maureen and Joan. "All my fault. If I wasn't in the picture, that fucking Bill would just go away."

"No!" Maureen says. "We'll deal with this. If there's a God in heaven, there's no way the judge will allow Bill to have custody!"

"My dad was right," Sam chokes up. "Never get in a pissin' fight with a skunk. Win or lose, you'll get some on you. And now on Sally. Look what I've done."

The guardian ad litem calls the house Monday evening. Sally takes the call. It's a woman, a Ms. Chandler. She insists on calling Sally "Mrs. Hunter" and refers to Sam only as "Mr. Ryan".

Chandler sounds awfully controlling, speaking in short, direct sentences. Instead of asking when would be a convenient time to meet, she simply informs Sally that she will visit their home the following Monday at 7:00 p.m.

Sally calls Joan at home immediately.

"Oh crap! I know her. I have no idea what bridge they found Chandler under."

"Can't we get rid of her? Have the court appoint a different one?" Sally asks, her voice trembling.

"Unfortunately, no. Not without clear cause. The fact that she's an overly opinionated control freak who's not too smart isn't considered just cause. Thankfully, Friday is thinking straight. Even if she recommends against us, Friday will more than likely dismiss her findings. Most judges do, with her."

"So, what is she still doing in the guardian ad litem business?" Sally asks incredulously.

"The guardian business in this part of the world is a good ol' girls club. Chandler and the coordinator, Catherine (the lady who assigns the cases), go way back. Catherine has run off anyone from the program who exceeds her own skill. Which is everyone else who has taken the job."

"Good grief, this is the court system! There's so much at stake here—the children! What about reporting Catherine?"

Joan laments, "The last guardian—who happened to be a male—went up the ladder to Catherine's boss and beyond, and Catherine's boss fired him, even with his complaint at the state level hanging over her head. He never did hear back from the state."

"So now what?" Sally asks.

"Pray that Judge Friday doesn't have any clots break loose in his brain again."

February 2, 2004

Chandler is nearly as large as Peabody. Deja immediately approaches to sniff her, like any young dog does to a new person in its territory. Chandler kicks her away. Deja slinks to Sally's feet and growls, the hair down the middle of her back standing up. Sam orders Deja to her crate, but the pup won't leave Sally. He finally escorts his dog by the collar to the spare bedroom.

Underneath her fake fur overcoat, the large woman wears a heavy sweater over a turtleneck and a long black skirt down to mid-calf. She's wearing some sort of dark blue hose with thick, green, knitted winter socks over them and scuffed, black man-shoes, which she doesn't offer to remove when she enters their home.

Chandler carries a briefcase, the kind with a little built-in combination lock. Her black hair is obviously dyed, and quite poorly. She appears to be 50-something.

If you passed her on the street, you might assume she was a drag queen—except drag queens have much better fashion taste.

Sam listens carefully to determine her attitude: arrogant, indifferent, or both. Whichever it is, it doesn't seem to be good. He asks to take her coat and drapes it on the couch. It weighs a ton.

They invite Chandler into the kitchen, where the three of them sit uncomfortably around the table. Eyeing them suspiciously, Chandler cups her hand over the combination lock to make sure Sally and Sam can't see the numbers as she opens it.

Chandler wheezes as she breathes in, announcing, "These are the rules. I ask the questions. At some time, I'll ask if you have any questions, but don't knock me off my train of thought before then. I will give neither side any information about the other side, except in my final written report."

First she quizzes Sally about her relationship with Bill, from beginning to present. She writes notes furiously, often putting her hand up to slow Sally down. When Sally describes the beatings, Chandler sternly corrects her, "These are *alleged* beatings. I'm only interested in proven facts."

When the subject switches to Sally and Sam, Chandler's tone changes dramatically. She isn't simply questioning anymore, she's grilling. She sits straight up and narrows her eyes, making it obvious she disapproves of their living arrangements.

"How long have you known each other?" she demands. "And you've only been cohabitating less than a week?

Hmm?" Chandler asks while shaking her head. She writes "less than a week" on her pad and circles the phrase three times.

"At which hospital do you plan to have the baby?"

"I…uh…I'm having the baby here, at home."

Chandler stops writing, drops her pen, and removes her reading glasses. "Where, exactly, in here would be suitable for giving birth?" she demands, looking around as if Sam's house were akin to the city dump.

"Don't know yet," Sally admits. "We'll see how it goes. The bathtub—the bed—right here in the kitchen? My sister, Maureen, who lives down the road, is my midwife."

Chandler pages back through her notes. "Let's see. How old are you?"

"38, why?"

"Hmm."

Sam snaps, "What's the problem, MS. Chandler?" He leans forward and folds his hands tightly in front of him.

"Excuse me. I don't recall opening the floor to questions," Chandler advises, sending him a stern look.

The large woman continues glaring at him, as if playing chicken to see who will look away first. He simply glares right back.

"It's time to take a look around," Chandler announces as she stands abruptly. She fetches a small flashlight from her briefcase, then closes it and spins the numbers. "We'll begin here in the kitchen."

Even though the kitchen is well-lit, she shines her tiny flashlight at the electrical outlets above the counter like some sort of crime scene investigator and quickly makes a note.

"What?" Sam asks impatiently.

Chandler informs him smugly, "No ground fault. No plug-in safety covers."

"Jesus! The baby isn't even here yet!"

She glares at him again. "Just doing my job. If you got a problem with that, we can call this custody evaluation over…" She folds the used sheets of the notepad back over the fresh ones.

"It's okay, Sam," Sally assures him, laying a hand over his.

Chandler makes note of every candle and electrical outlet. She sketches a picture of the woodstove. Sam is surprised she doesn't faint when he identifies what's in the carboys in the spare bedroom. Chandler asks how old the house is and the last time it was painted inside. She also asks if Deja lives in the house, and rolls her eyes when informed that she does. Another mark on her form that she circles three times.

An hour later, Chandler is finished going over the house with her fine-toothed comb. Except, thank God, she declines to go upstairs. Not that she'll find stuff up there she likes less than what she's already noted in four pages. Sam's just not sure if the stairs could take it, the way she clomps around in her man-shoes. She summons Sally and Sam back to the kitchen table.

"Before I go, just one more thing. Have either of you ever been in mental health therapy?"

"Geez, who hasn't these days?" Sam answers. He twiddles his thumbs nervously.

Chandler peers over her glasses, eyes narrowing. "Well, me, for one."

"Well, yeah," Sam admits as he shrugs. "I have been."

Chandler finds a form in her briefcase, which she shoves across the table to Sam.

"Fill this out and sign it. It's a release of information so I can talk to your caregiver."

"Bullshiiit!" he yells. "You…have…NO BUSINESS…"

"Have it your way, Mr. Ryan," Chandler retorts as she snatches the form back. "I'll just have the judge sign a special court order to get your records. That certainly won't make him happy at all…"

"What the hell does any of that have to do with who gets custody?" he asks through gritted teeth.

"Were you in court that day, Mr. Ryan?" Chandler snaps condescendingly. "Didn't Judge Friday order me to look into these things?"

Sam nods and he looks away.

"Have it your way." Chandler shrugs her linebacker's shoulders.

"Gimme that," he grumbles as he grabs the form back.

He fills it out quickly so Chandler can get his records from Laura without causing more drama.

Chandler forces a fabricated smile as she stuffs her notepad into her briefcase and locks it. "Well, that's it. Have either of you got any questions?"

Sally's numb. She shakes her head.

"Yes, I do," Sam replies. "When are you gonna interview Bill and his girlfriend?"

"I was already up to Mr. Hunter's place in Grand Forks," Chandler answers curtly. "Last Friday. And I visited Mr. Hunter at the farm yesterday. I suppose I can let you know that Mr. Hunter is already remodeling the spare bedroom into a nursery with a fresh coat of pink paint. *Non-lead* pink paint," she emphasizes as she scans Sam's kitchen walls, her lips pursed in judgement. "For your information, Mr. Hunter does not have a girlfriend."

"Obviously *you* weren't in court that day. And what's the problem with having the baby born at home?" Sam demands.

Chandler speaks like she's an expert in childbirth. "So, 38 years old. First baby. That is considered a high-risk pregnancy and birth."

"That's really none of your business," Sam charges.

Chandler warns, "According to Judge Friday, it most certainly is. As a matter of fact, on behalf of the Court, I have more to say about the welfare of this child than the mother does."

Sally gapes and her entire body shudders.

Sam orders through gritted teeth, "This meeting is over. There's the door!"

Chandler goes back into her briefcase, pulls out the notepad and scribbles several more lines, ignoring Sam. She closes and locks her briefcase with a loud snap and stands up slowly, as if to emphasize her power.

Sam stands and points toward the front door again. "Let yourself out, right now."

She fetches her heavy coat and hangs it over her arm, wincing as she brushes off dog hair.

"See you in court," Chandler promises confidently, as she opens the front door. "We won't be needing another visit. I've got everything I need from *you two*."

They drive right to Joan and Maureen's.

"I was afraid of this," Joan says. "Not just that she's way overseppin' her bounds on behalf of the baby. But it looks like Peabody has gotten to her, got her doin' his dirty work."

"Like what?" Sally asks.

"Goin' after you, Sam. And ignoring the fact that Bill has a girlfriend who has all the trappings of a meth-head and who definitely, according to the statute, should be interviewed. I don't know what she's up to about where the baby's born though."

When Sam sees Laura a few weeks later, she recounts how Chandler had barged into her office unannounced the day after their interview. The bold woman had leveled a number of threats, claiming she had the authority to personally review his entire file—even to copy it if she desired. Laura had emphatically declined and finally had to threaten to call the police in order to get rid of Chandler.

Laura advises Sam of a way he might be able to sidetrack Chandler from personally snooping like that. He could ask the judge to change the order to a written summary for his eyes only.

CHAPTER 18

THE BABY'S NOT AN "IT"

February 12, 2004

Joan, Sally, Maureen, and Sam enter the courthouse. On the opposite side of the foyer stand Bill, Peabody, and Chandler in rapt conversation. Peabody pats Chandler on the shoulder and nods. Looking up, she quickly heads for the courtroom doorway, avoiding eye contact.

Joan hurries to intercept her. "Is there something you need to see me about, too?"

"Oh!" Chandler feigns surprise. "No. Not at the moment. I'll see you in there." She clumps into the courtroom.

"What was that all about?" Sally asks.

"Generally, a guardian is supposed to be truly independent, not camping out with one side or the other. Looked awfully cozy over there…"

The bailiff calls the parties and attorneys into court. Sam takes a seat in the gallery. The only other person in the courtroom is Chandler, who sits in the jury box by herself. Peabody looks directly at Chandler, and she smiles at Peabody.

The formalities complete, Friday asks for any remaining issues.

Peabody stands. "Well, Your Honor, seems the only thing we agree on is that neither Mr. nor Mrs. Hunter want to stay married. The property issues are still unsettled, and further complicated by Samuel Hunter's will, specifically his having given Mrs. Hunter that very expensive horse trailer in lieu of payments from the person who bought his dealership."

Judge Friday interjects, "I'm sure you'll have your arguments ready for trial."

Peabody continues, "Then there's the custody issue. We've exchanged proposals. We're not even close. There hasn't been any movement."

Judge Friday looks to Joan for any additional comments. "Ms. Adair?"

"Counsel has summed it up accurately," she concurs.

"Discovery is done?" Friday assumes, looking at Peabody and then at Joan.

They both nod.

"No late motions?" Friday asks.

The attorneys concur.

Friday addresses the matronly guardian, "Let's see, Ms. Chandler, will your report and recommendation be complete 15 days before the trial? Any problems with that?"

Chandler stands, "No, Your Honor. But there is one other matter."

Friday straightens and takes off his reading glasses.

"May I approach the bench?" Chandler requests.

"Do you need counsel to also approach?"

"No, Your Honor." Chandler approaches the judge slowly, importantly, like Perry Mason did on television. "I'll serve them copies at their tables."

"Copies of what?" Friday asks.

"Your Honor," Chandler speaks as officially sounding as she can. "As you appointed me, I am a party to this case, with all the rights and powers on behalf of the child that the parents have for themselves. And, because of that, I am entitled to bring a motion, which I am doing today."

The imposing woman certainly has Friday's attention. He leans forward to see what she has in her hands. He motions for her to hurry. Chandler hands the original to the judge, then strides slowly and confidently between the bench and the tables, like she's in front of the Supreme Court, her head held high. Peabody places a hand over his mouth in faux surprise, but can't keep the grin off his face. Neither can Bill.

She gives both attorneys their copies. Joan quickly begins poring over hers. Peabody doesn't even put on his cheater specs to fake looking at this "new" information.

"Go ahead," Friday says absently, as he quickly begins reading the motion. "Explain the basis for your motion, please."

"Your Honor, I do not believe that Mrs. Hunter's intention to give birth to the child at home is in the child's best interest. Home birth with a midwife is a default situation that's appropriate only for destitute mothers who lack resources, or when both parents agree, and that is not the case. Mrs. Hunter and the baby are still covered under Mr. Hunter's health insurance policy. And Mr.

Hunter has assured me he is not in favor of such a birth. He, in fact, would prefer to attend the birth, if the Court will allow—which I believe is in the child's best interest, considering Mr. Hunter is going to have an ongoing relationship with the child."

Joan jumps up from her chair. "Your Honor! Why is the guardian ad litem bringing this motion? Obviously, the father has been made aware ahead of time that this motion was forthcoming! If this is truly his concern, he should file such a motion himself!"

Peabody remains seated. He interjects with his hands outstretched, in a posture of compliance, "Your Honor, we certainly will, if need be. Either way, time is of the essence. The baby is due in five weeks. For that reason, I would like to argue this next week."

Judge Friday looks at his clerk. "What have you got?"

"Friday afternoon is open," she replies.

"1:00 Friday then. Anything else?"

Chandler stands up again. "Yes, Your Honor."

"Go ahead."

"It's Mr. Ryan. His therapist has refused to allow me access to his mental health records, based upon the standard court order appointing me."

"And why do you need those?" the judge asks.

"With your permission," Chandler implores, "I would like to discuss my reasons in chambers."

Judge Friday looks around the courtroom. Except for the bailiff, Sam is the only other person in the courtroom.

"Nobody's here who isn't going to hear about it anyway. Carry on."

"Well, it's just...Mr. Ryan clearly has some obvious anger issues. I was treated rather poorly at his home.

I must say I was frightened." Gazing in Sam's direction, Chandler bites her lip and fakes shuddering. "Also, two incidents have been brought to my attention when Mr. Ryan was drunk and became quite violent. If he wasn't already in therapy, I'd be asking the Court for an order to have him undergo a psychiatric evaluation—as a precondition to any possibility of me recommending any kind of contact with the child."

The judge turns to Sam. "Mr. Ryan, do I need to sign an order?"

Sam stands and holds his hands together in a compliant pose. "Your Honor, I'll talk to my therapist. But I don't think it's necessary for anyone to have carte blanche access to my records. May I suggest a compromise?"

The judge nods.

"Would a summary of my condition, the dates of treatment, and prognosis be sufficient? If Ms. Chandler feels that my therapist hasn't been forthcoming with all relevant information, then I would ask Your Honor to personally examine my records."

"It's done," Judge Friday orders, clearly agitated. "Everybody else stay put for now. I want counsel in my chambers. And Ms. Chandler."

Joan looks questioningly at Sally and Maureen and shrugs. She doesn't have a clue what Friday wants to discuss. Peabody does likewise with Bill. Obediently they make the trip, following the judge to his chambers.

Once in chambers, Friday adopts an even more stern posture and tone from his normal professional, unbiased courtroom decor. He leans forward and folds his hands in his desk, making it obvious he is pissed-off as hell.

"Mr. Peabody, Ms. Chandler—don't for a second think I don't know what just happened out there," Friday warns, his face turning red. "This crap you're putting Ms. Hunter through is getting very old. Let me fill you in on something. My oldest daughter is a midwife."

Chandler seems unimpressed with that revelation and stares out the window, as if the judge were invisible.

"Except for the two children she personally gave birth to (with the help of another midwife, who happens to be my wife), she has delivered all my grandchildren, all seven of them. Five of them right in my house. Need I say more?"

Chandler finally appreciates the gist of the judge's speech, turning as white as a very large, poorly dressed drag queen of a ghost. Peabody stares down at the floor like a first grader being scolded by a nun.

He raises his voice and points his finger back and forth between Peabody and Chandler. "If you think there's any way in hell I'm going to let Mr. Hunter interfere with Ms. Hunter giving birth to that child—or be within one mile of that blessed event—then you *both* need to have your brain arteries checked."

"Your Honor," Chandler interrupts, sticking her chin out in defiance. "Then with all due respect I demand you take me off this case! I am a professional, and I am INSULTED that you question the integrity and impartiality of my recommendation. I will never, EVER, show my face in your Court again!"

"I couldn't have said it better myself, Ms. Chandler," Judge Friday agrees in a cordial, even tone, as he leans back in his chair. "In fact, you won't be appearing in anyone's court again once I'm done. I'm relieving Ms. Hunter of liability for her half of your fees.

"Considering you have been working on Mr. Hunter's behalf—I'm no dummy, I saw you and Peabody grinning at each other, and it was pretty damn obvious he knew the contents of your motion before it hit the table in front of him—you can go ahead and send your bill directly to him. Your boss, and your boss's boss, are going with you down the road if I have anything to say about it. It's time the guardian ad litem system becomes about the kids and not about a bunch of leeches propping each other up, sucking the system and parents dry."

Chandler turns abruptly and storms out of the chambers, slamming the door shut behind her.

"Mr. Peabody, make no mistake. If you do anything else to interfere with this mother preparing for the happiest day of her life, I'll turn my file on you over to the board that very minute. I'm giving you a chance to make these things right."

Peabody doesn't look up, but sighs heavily and shakes his head. Joan looks shocked, her eyes wide and mouth open a bit like she can't find the words.

"Ms. Adair, I'll tell the clerk our little meeting next week is cancelled. I'll see you all in March. And should the trial interfere with the birth of the baby, I still want you both in here. At the least the Hunters will still be getting divorced that day, and I'll determine custody at that time."

Friday waves them out of his office, but then calls after them.

"Oh! I almost forgot. My son-in-law is a guardian ad litem down in the Fourth District. A damn good one. I'll have him look into this."

As Joan follows Peabody back toward the courtroom, she mumbles, "Thank God for free-flowing brain arteries. You ought to try it, Peabody."

Peabody asks, "Do me a favor. Get your folks outta there before I go in and talk to Bill."

"Gladly," Joan agrees, as Peabody retreats several steps so he can't be seen from the courtroom.

She steps through the judge's entrance to the courtroom and motions for Sam, Maureen, and Sally to follow her. As the two pass in front of Bill's table, he begins singing in a mockingly sweet voice, as if holding and swinging a baby in his arms, "Lul-la-byyyy…and good night…"

Sally covers her mouth and hurries toward Joan. Sam stops and turns slowly, only two steps from Bill, who's still singing. The bailiff, who has been watching carefully from between the two counsel tables, steps between the two men. In a whisper, he informs Bill, "Shut the fuck up.

"You piece o' goddamn horseshit!" Bill screams at his attorney. "If you think you're gonna get a nickel out of me…if you think I'm gonna lose my slut wife to that goddamn Sam Ryan without him payin' for it…or have anything to do with my kid…"

"We've just got the trial left," Peabody says blankly, as he stuffs papers into his briefcase. "What are you hoping to get? Do you really want anything to do with this baby?"

"Fuck the kid," Bill spits. "I just wanna watch Ryan squirm every time I come see it. That fucker took my wife *and* my horses."

"The baby's not an *it*," Peabody informs his client, as they continue to the courthouse foyer. "She's a girl."

"So what do we have to do between now and then?" Bill demands.

"Financial records. For child support. Trust me, you won't be getting custody."

"You're givin' up, you cocksucker," Bill shrieks. He dashes in front of Peabody and gets right up in his face. Drops of angry spit land on Peabody's face and glasses. "Who's gonna be payin' who?"

"Let this go," Peabody suggests as he brushes past Bill and out the door. "My fees. Forget it. I'm done—I'm withdrawing as your attorney. Sue me."

Peabody trudges down the sidewalk like a zombie. Bill stalks closely behind his former lawyer and, once in the crosswalk, jumps in front of him—circling, cursing, and spitting—challenging the attorney to show some balls. Peabody acts as if Bill is invisible, except to step around him.

The attorney stumbles across the parking lot, as if drunk, to his sedan. Bill continues to denigrate him like a rabid terrier, all the way.

"You fuckin' piece of dried-up cat puke!" Bill kicks the Cadillac's left taillight, smashing the red plastic into dozens of jagged pieces. Peabody doesn't respond; he doesn't even seem to notice. Bill smashes his fist onto the roof of the car so hard he dents it and cracks the back window. "You piece of goddamn shit! Listen to me!"

Peabody continues to ignore Bill and slumps into the front seat, his legs still outside the car. He is pale, and his head hangs low.

Bill races across the parking lot to his truck, jumps in, and revs the engine. Jamming the gearshift into reverse, he shoves the gas pedal to the floor, spinning the rear wheels and sending gravel flying, spraying the fence like buckshot.

The tires screech and Bill slams the rear of his truck into the trunk of Peabody's sedan, crushing the trunk lid all the way to the rear window as if it were aluminum foil. The side of Peabody's head slams into the headrest, but he still he seems unaware of what's happening, staring blankly ahead.

Finally, Peabody pulls his legs in, shuts the door, and drives forward through the empty parking spot ahead of him, taking a left out of the lot. The courthouse windows that face the parking lot are now filled with county workers watching the carnage. The bailiff hurries outside, pausing briefly on the sidewalk to radio the sheriff dispatch center.

Bill again spins his tires as he speeds toward the street, intending to T-bone Peabody's car as it passes by the east lot entrance. Instead, Peabody slams on his brakes, so Bill swerves and only clips the bumper. Propelled by inertia, his truck jumps the curb and speeds head-on into a 100-year-old oak.

Bill has to stretch across the seat and kick at his door to get it open. When he slides from the seat, his jaw is set and his eyes are angry slits. Blood is trickling from a gash on the right side of his forehead down into his eye. He staggers back toward the street. Peabody stands waiting for him, 20 feet away.

The bailiff, gun drawn, runs toward Bill to keep him away from Peabody. "Hold it right there, Hunter!"

But Bill ignores the bailiff and continues stumbling and lumbering like a drunk toward Peabody. The bailiff has his service pistol pointed at Bill's chest.

The two men are only 10 feet apart when the bailiff notices Peabody has a small pistol aimed at Bill. They meet at the curb, the attorney's pistol now aimed—only an arm's length away—at the middle of Bill's forehead. Through the blood and grime running down his face, Bill smiles an evil grin and lifts an arm to swat the gun.

This is Bill's last misguided effort on Earth. Peabody's aim is accurate. Bill slumps to the ground, blood pouring from his forehead.

Peabody, in a daze, slowly turns and levels the pistol in the bailiff's direction.

Another shot rings out. Two deputies sprint from around the corner of the courthouse, their guns drawn. By the time they reach the sidewalk, it is over.

Peabody has fallen over backward. Gasping twice, his eyes glaze over, and he's dead.

The funeral director calls Sally. It is a short conversation. He says he'll arrange a private viewing for her if she wants one, on Sunday evening. According to Robert's wishes, there won't be a funeral, only a viewing Monday evening. Not even a prayer or graveside service. The funeral director admits that it's hard to tell how Robert's doing. He had turned the whole thing over to them, said he probably wouldn't even attend.

Sally tells Sam she'd prefer to be alone when she goes to see her husband one last time.

He holds her tightly. "I'll be here when you come home. I love you."

Sally asks the funeral director to open the casket. He warns her that they hadn't prepared Bill for a viewing. They had changed him out of his bloody clothes into an outfit that Robert brought and bandaged the bullet hole and gash—that was all. There's no makeup to cover the cuts and bruises, or to mask the pallor of death.

But Sally insists in a firm whisper.

The funeral director brings the sisters two chairs. They sit as he slowly opens the casket. Maureen covers her eyes, but Sally stares at Bill—expressionless, stone-faced, dry-eyed. From her chair, she can only see his face and his hands. So she stands and walks up to the casket to look down at him one last time. Angel is calm inside her belly.

Sally sits back down and closes her eyes tightly. A tear escapes from the corner of each one, but she doesn't wipe them away. The sisters stay for about 10 minutes, without speaking a word or looking at each other. Sally will never tell a soul what she was thinking during the viewing.

She is quiet during the drive home, too, until they pass the Halfway Bar. Robert's car is there—the only car in the lot. Sally motions for Maureen to turn in.

"Are you sure?" Maureen asks, concern lining her brow.

"Yes. I want to see him."

Robert, unshaven, his hair greasy and hanging in clumps from under his hat, wearing his work shirt with the tail hanging out, is slumped over the bar, a lowball glass half full of liquor in front of him. He doesn't turn to look when the door bangs shut and the bell rings. The bartender says quietly, "Hey, you got company."

Robert turns and begins sobbing like a little boy. He wipes his mouth several times before he can say her name.

"Saaalllly," he cries, holding his arms out. She stops two steps away from him and holds her hand out in front to keep him from getting near her.

Robert is a pathetic sight. Tears form in the corner of Sally's eyes. There was always a part of him she had pitied, in spite of it all. But she's determined not to let tears fall today.

"Sally, what am I gonna do now? I don't know nothing 'bout runnin' the campground, except to clean up."

She replies without emotion, simply shaking her head, "I don't know, Robert. I don't know."

It hasn't occurred to her until this moment that the campground and four-wheeler course are two-thirds hers now.

"I've talked to your ex-wife. The damage you did to those little girls…it's showin' up now. Frankly, I don't care if you blow your brains out or run away, but Marcy's goin' public. So I'm quite certain the county'll press charges now.

"You know, I don't blame you entirely for the way you turned out, but it's up to you now to make it right. For one thing, you're gonna help me give the 240 acres to the school for a natural history area. We're gonna sell the other 80 with the house and farm buildings. Some of that money'll go toward Marcy's girls. Some'll go to a foundation that helps create effective sex offender laws. And you will turn yourself in and cooperate with the court.

"It's that simple, Robert. You are never gonna hurt anyone again. I wish I had sympathy for what's ahead for you, but Sam and I have got a little girl we're bringin' into this world. Not only do I pray she never crosses paths with anyone like you, I'll do my best to make sure of that by helpin' to keep people like you under control."

He nods and sobs into his hands, "Yeah. I been real bad. I'm so sorry."

When Robert looks up, Sally is gone. The door bangs shut and the bell jingles.

She slides into the passenger seat with a huge sigh of relief. "Now, let's get home…and on with the rest of our lives."

CHAPTER 19

KIND OF BUSY

March 22, 2004

It is Monday morning. A young woman enters the courthouse foyer, grasping an envelope. She looks around, confused, at the empty hallway. The double doors to the courtroom are locked, and she can see through the crack that it's dark inside.

"Excuse me," she says to an administration clerk behind a glass partition. "I must have the wrong day. The divorce trial? Bill and Sally Hunter?"

It just so happens that Judge Friday is at the counter signing papers. The clerk defers to the judge.

"You haven't heard?"

"No. What?"

"Ah. You're the woman who was with Bill Hunter in Court that day."

She nods.

"And what brings you here today?"

"I couldn't let Bill do that to her, let everyone think…" she stammers.

"Let everyone think what, ma'am?" Friday asks in a patient, understanding voice.

"Think that baby's his. It ain't. I was gonna tell you that in Court today."

"How do you know the baby isn't Bill Hunter's?" Friday frowns.

"Because I'm Bill's fiancée, from Grand Forks. He always said he couldn't have no kids, had that taken care of a long time ago after he got another girl in trouble. When Sally got pregnant, he went in for a test."

The woman holds up the envelope. "Couldn't have been him…"

"May I see that?"

"Yes, sir. You can have it." She hands it to the judge. "But where is everybody?"

"Well, where have you been the last month?"

"In a shelter, recoverin'. Bill tried to beat this envelope outta me."

Friday informs her solemnly, "I'm afraid, dear woman, that Bill Hunter is dead."

The woman stares in disbelief and cries, "What? NO! He can't be dead! I love him! We're gonna get married…"

She stumbles out of the office, sobbing.

Friday forgets the paperwork he was signing and hurries back to his office. His hands tremble as he thumbs through the phone book, searching for Sam's phone number.

"Hello?"

"This is Judge Friday, Sam. I need to talk to Sally—right now!"

"Sorry, Judge. She's kinda busy!"

"With what? This is quite important!"

"Umm, she's havin' the baby! And so's my daughter-in-law!"

"Well, if she can listen at all, she's gonna want to hear this. Take the phone to her, please," the judge insists.

"Judge," Sally says through clenched teeth, in the middle of a contraction. "Excuse me, but you caught me at a bad time."

"No, my dear—I caught you just *in* time!"

"What?" Sally breathes, panting.

"I've got proof here!" Friday exclaims. "Bill was sterile all along! And he *knew* it. The baby isn't his!"

"OHHHH!" Sally cries into the phone as another contraction begins. "Thanks…gotta go…"

"You're welcome. You're so welcome."

"Sam!"

She stands, leaning with one hand on the kitchen counter, the other on the table.

"Do you still have those other two condoms?" she blurts.

That gets everyone's attention—Maureen, Dad, Matt and Marsha, Marsha's folks.

Sam laughs nervously. "Umm, well…one of 'em. Honey, ain't it a little late for that?" he jokes.

Sally growls, "I'm not even gonna ask where the other one went. Just…go…get…the… goddamn CONDOM!"

He dashes to the bedroom. When he returns, Sally's squatting over some large pads.

"Take it out!" she growls.

He fumbles with the wrapper and finally holds the condom up. "What's the expiration date?" Sally asks, biting her lip.

Sam stammers, "J-June 2000."

"Put it on the faucet—fill it like a water balloon. Ohh-hhh!" Sally cries out in pain.

Sam, confused but willing to do anything her heart desires, obeys again. Everyone gathers around to watch. Even Marsha gets off the couch in the living room and shuffles into the kitchen.

The condom fills to about a cup and sags, so Sam has to hold it onto the spigot. Suddenly, it sprays water out of dozens of tiny holes, like a fountain in the town square.

Sally grits her teeth. "Friday's got proof. Bill couldn't have kids. Next time you screw some guy's wife, you better check the expiration date on the condoms. You're about to become a father…Ohhhhh!"

At that moment Angel's entire little head presents. Maureen helps Sally to the floor and kneels in front of her sister. She syringes the baby's nostrils and mouth. Dad, still the scientist and keeper of records, fumbles for his pen and paper to record the time of birth.

"Does this count? 9:18?" Dad asks excitedly.

"Close enough," Maureen answers.

She coaches Sam, "Come on, now! Get down here! This YOUR daughter!"

Sam's in shock but obeys, kneeling and holding a small blanket under the baby. Sally pushes again, and little Angel is born into her father's shaking hands. Matt helps Sally sit back on some pillows to rest with her back against the kitchen cupboards. Sam gently places Angel in Sally's lap.

Sally sighs through her tears, "Really, Matt! This is your little sister, not your dad's stepdaughter. Can you frickin' believe it?"

Marsha's folks, Gary and Amy, are helping their daughter back to the living room, when she suddenly cries out. Matt leaves the kitchen and runs to her.

"It's happenin'…right now!" Marsha cries.

Maureen is busy unwrapping the clamp for the umbilical cord. Sally and Sam dab at Angel to dry her off. Their baby stretches and cries, then nuzzles at Sally's breast, while Maureen clamps the umbilical cord. Sam cuts the cord and dabs at the trickle of blood with a cotton gauze.

The others have gotten Marsha to the couch. She leans back and cries out.

"Somebody get in here!" Matt yells in a panic.

"Go ahead," Maureen urges Sam.

Just like a doctor, Sam deftly removes his latex gloves by turning them inside out and shoots them into the wastebasket by the woodstove. He snatches a fresh pair from the kitchen table among the boxes of gauze, sutures, and other childbirth supplies as he hurries past.

"Gary! Come grab some pads and blankets—and a fresh syringe," Sam orders.

Little Sam Anthony is already crowning when his paternal grandfather kneels in front. Marsha is between contractions, but in a great deal of pain.

"Breathe, help her breathe, Matt," Sam suggests. They puff in unison.

In a minute, Marsha's back arches and she cries again.

"This is it," Sam informs her calmly. "You can do it… all you got…"

And Sam Anthony's head presents.

"A little more. Come on, Marsha!"

She bears down hard and Sam Anthony's shoulders appear. Gary hands Sam the syringe.

From the easy chair by the front window, Dad announces hoarsely through his tears, "9:20!"

"How's it goin' in there?" Maureen hollers from the kitchen.

Sam Anthony answers her with a tiny cry.

Seemingly effortlessly, the rest of Sam Anthony delivers into his grandfather's waiting hands. Matt places a blanket on his wife's belly. Carefully, Sam hands them their son.

He shows Gary and Amy where to clamp the cord. Matt cuts it.

"Come on, you guys," Sam urges the other grandparents and Matt. "Dry 'im off and introduce yourselves."

"Hey, Grandpa," Sally hollers from the kitchen. "Grab a fresh blanket for your lap. Somebody wants to meet you."

Sam hurries back to the kitchen, flicks off his gloves, washes his hands carefully, and gently picks up his daughter, all folded up in a fresh blanket. So small and pink, making tiny grunting noises. Dad seems apprehensive, sitting in the chair with a fresh blanket on his lap. Shakily, he receives his granddaughter, like she'll shatter if he isn't as careful as he can be. A tear drops onto Angel's nose, and she flinches. The onlookers laugh, and Angel's grandpa smiles.

"And your great grandson," Matt offers, nestling Sam Anthony into the crook of his other arm.

The old man sits proudly, tears running like rain. Amy grabs a fresh gauze pad and dabs at his eyes gently.

"Mom, get your camera," Gary suggests. Matt fishes his camera out of his shirt pocket and snaps a picture from the couch.

Sam helps Sally to her feet. With his arm around her waist, she shuffles into the living room. Maureen attends to Marsha, while Matt embraces his wife tightly.

"Okay!" Dad the scientist suddenly blurts. "We better get these two weighed and measured. Now where's my pen and notepad?"

CHAPTER 20

MISSION ACCOMPLISHED

Memorial Day

Sam's dad drives Judge Friday in the golf cart up to the fire ring. It is near noon, a perfect late spring day. The rain from the night before has left the woods smelling fresh and alive. Robins gathering worms for their fledglings off the dirt ruts of the trail protest noisily at being disturbed. Warblers and finches bob and flit among the low branches. The patch of yellow lady slippers is in full bloom—hundreds of yellow flowers among the new grass on the open hillside down from the trail. The men proceed slowly, each sipping a plastic bottle of wine.

The rest of the guests are already at the fire ring, where a small fire burns. They sip wild grape wine and visit. The women stand to one side. Joan holds Sam Anthony, cooing at him. Marsha and her mother laugh at something. Maria has Angel nestled in her arms, while Ellen tries to coax a smile from her little sister. Maria's two little granddaughters dote over Sammy Bob, who spends as much time on his butt as on his feet.

Johnny's son, Mike, under the watchful eyes of Josh, tends the fire and pours the wine. Johnny and Mack are chatting with Gary and Keith; Friday and Dad join them.

"Here they come!" shouts Josh, pointing to the trail that comes from the house.

Matt drives the team, his father next to him. Even though Matt sits half a head taller than Sam, you can tell they are father and son. Their posture and the way they talk with their hands leave no doubt. They both wear new jeans and tweed coats over light-blue shirts, and shiny Western boots.

"I wanna ride with Grandpa!" shouts Josh.

The little guy tugs at Mike's hand. They run down the hill. Mike lifts Josh aboard and into Grandpa's hands. Little Josh squirms to the seat between his grandpa and uncle, where he sits proud and beaming. He places one little hand on a rein and looks serious, like he's driving the team himself.

"Giddup!" the little driver orders his team.

Matt turns the team up the hill. The guests gather and clap as the men and Josh climb down from the wagon seat.

Elvis and Roy suddenly stare to the east, their ears alert. Roy whinnies, and a horse in the distance whinnies back. Soon, far down the trail, appears Maureen on Sparky. Right behind is Sally on Dakota.

She has kept her outfit a secret from Sam. Her new boots are black with fancy red stitching. Her black jeans are elaborate, a red rose embroidered on the bottom outside of each leg, with shiny silver rivets. Her wide belt bears the silver and red buckle she'd won at the rodeo. It is her blouse, though, that takes Sam's breath away. Satiny, white, and fringed along the sleeves. When Sally moves, the sun reflects and dances on the fabric. The buttons are red set in silver, matching her necklace and dangly earrings.

"Pinch me, Matt. No, don't. If this is a dream, I don't ever wanna wake up."

Judge Friday takes his place behind the north rock. Sam stands to the judge's left, with Matt alongside him. Johnny and Mack meet the women riders. Pop's two best friends hold the horses as the bride and maid of honor dismount. Maria, as Sally's personal attendant, quickly checks their makeup and hair. Joan hands them each a long stem red rose tied with a white silk ribbon.

Maureen leads. Sally follows three steps behind with Johnny and Mack, one on each arm. Proudly, they escort Sally to Sam.

He whispers, "You are so beautiful."

She touches a tear on his cheek and gently wipes it away. "So are you."

Friday pipes up, "I hate to break this up, you two, but I have a marriage to perform. Now everybody come up closer." He waves them forward.

"As is the custom these days, Sally and Sam have written their own vows. Sam, you first."

His hand shaking, he reaches into his breast pocket, then cringes. He covers his eyes and mumbles, "Oh, shit."

"No! No!" Sam corrects himself, to the laughter of the guests. "That's not part of it! Lemme see…"

He closes his eyes for a moment, trying to remember. Instead of attempting to recall the vows he'd written word for word, he speaks from the heart.

"Okay. Sally, I'm askin' you to have me as your friend and your husband, forever. I promise to love you and myself as one. And I promise to honor you as the most beautiful and unique soul you are, who I still can't believe I know and love. I don't want you to change a thing about yourself—unless you want to. And then I'll support you with all my heart and soul."

The guests give a collective sigh for such sweet sentiments.

"Here's what else I promise: to not keep secret my morel mushroom haunts, to not tip the canoe over, and to not skin deer on the kitchen table. But I do reserve the right to clean fish there!"

Now, folks are starting to giggle—Sam has lost his train of thought. He squeezes his temples, trying to remember what else he wants to say.

"Um…I guess that's it," he tells Judge Friday. "Except…except…will you take me to be your husband?"

"I will. Yes, I will!" She squeezes his hands.

"Matter of fact, I forgot to bring my vows, too. But here's what I promise. If you'll have me, Sam Ryan, as your best friend and wife, I promise to honor you—the most unique and beautiful soul you are. We are one, forever, which is what I want and promise to be. Don't change a thing about you for me—unless you want to. And I'll be by your side the entire way.

"I also promise never to move to the other bedroom because of your snoring and other nocturnal sounds. And I promise you a foot rub for every time you shave my legs."

"Hold it!" Judge Friday orders, as the guests laugh. "That's a little more information than we need to make this marriage official!"

Sally blushes. She turns and looks out among the guests, winking, and offers giddily, "But, ladies! You should let your guys try it sometime!"

Composing herself, she turns back to Sam. "One more thing. Sam, will you let me be your wife?"

"Yes...yes...I will!"

The good judge finishes with the formalities.

"By the power vested in me by the State of Minnesota, I now pronounce you husband and wife."

The crowd claps wildly, while Sam and Sally turn to face their guests. Judge Friday gestures with open arms. "Ladies and gentlemen...babies, kids, horses, dogs...I present you...Sally and Sam Ryan!"

As everyone begins to gather near, Sam holds up his hands to quiet them. The guests obey, inquisitive looks traded among them, including from Sally and the judge.

Sam clears his voice nervously. "Ahem. Unless you happened to be in the muni for karaoke one snowy Saturday night about three years ago, when only about four people showed up and we were all well into our cups, you've never heard me sing. Not that what I was doing that night could be considered singin'."

He bites his lip. "There should be a song at a weddin', even if it's badly done. I'm sure it wasn't an accident that this CD fell outta Sally's trailer cupboard and smacked her in the head...and then a voice—little Angel's, I'm sure—told her to give it to me."

Angel squirms in Maria's arms and cries softly. Sally motions to Maria to bring their baby to them.

Sam nods to Mike, who pushes the button on the CD player set up on the big jack pine stump. During a few seconds of instrumental prelude, Sally's eyes moisten and she kisses Angel on the forehead.

Sam's eyes smile and tear up at the same time. His two hands hold Sally's and Angel's. He inhales on cue and covers the woman's voice an octave lower, in perfect pitch.

How could anyone ever tell you
You were anything less than beautiful
How could anyone ever tell you
You were less than whole
How could anyone fail to notice
That your loving is a miracle
How deeply you're connected to my soul.

Sally joins in the second verse. Those with tissues or hankies are using them and sharing them. The guests gather closely around them, everyone arm in arm encircling them and swaying, singing the third verse with them.

Little Angel falls asleep.

"Sally, Sam," Maria says, "Open up Angel's blanket, please. I made it just for her."

Sam peels the folds back. Angel's nightie features a cherub flying through the heavens. And above the angel, embroidered in the clouds, are the words *Mission Accomplished!*

This night, after all the guests have left, Sally and Sam lie in each other's arms and listen to Angel softly stirring in her crib next to their bed.

Sally whispers, "The spring equinox, two days before Angel was born—what did you say to God up at the fire ring?"

"It had worked so good the year before, I just said, *God, surprise me again.* And then I got the fluttery feeling up and down my spine; I felt like I wasn't up there at the fire alone—just like when I canoed the river the day after we made love, and so many times since then. Even Deja was looking around up in the air like she did that day on the river. I swear I heard a tiny voice in my mind say, *Hang onto your hat!*"

"Our Angel..." Sally whispers as she snuggles tightly against Sam's chest. "You ready for one more surprise?"

"Already had my surprise for this year..." Sam says as he kisses Sally on the forehead.

She lifts Sam's hand and places it on her belly. "I stopped at the drugstore. We'll see first thing in the mornin', but I'm pretty sure..."

She snuggles in tighter. He pushes her hair from her face and kisses her lips.

"I hope so."

She runs her hand down his side to his hip. "Honey? Um, just in case we're not pregnant..."

"Well, I'm not gettin' any younger..."

A coyote howls from up near the fire ring, starting a wild canine chorus across the hills that Sam, Sally, and a baby Angel call home.

ACKNOWLEDGEMENTS

Again I must thank the "team", who truly were collaborators in this venture:

My editor, Julia Willson, whose expertise with language, and keen eye for good story telling makes me appear skilled way beyond what I really should receive credit for.

My producer, Julie Anne Eason, who crafted my manuscripts from computer files, into real books for the shelves, not to forget her tireless efforts at promoting my books and me.

And my cover artist, fellow Nevis-ite Amelia Woltjers, who again not only grasped my vision for the cover, she took it several steps further.

Above all, I must thank these three ladies for their saintly patience with me!

ABOUT THE AUTHOR

A handful of years ago, my son mentioned to my first ex-wife that I had retired.

Curiously she asked, "From what?"

My path through life has been akin to floating down a winding river—around every bend there's a new view, an unknown place to explore, and people I've never met. Along the way I've been blessed with a multitude of jobs, and I've witnessed such an expansive spectrum of humanity–from the sublime to the not so. My last job before retiring was writing, editing, and producing our small-town weekly newspaper.

I grew up just north of the Minneapolis city limits, when the north end of Anoka County was still *country* (and you could actually make it to Minneapolis in half an hour). There I hunted, swam, canoed, played ball and fished to my boyhood heart's content.

I stayed put for a while into adulthood, but upon approaching middle age, I realized the suburban sprawl had crept up and surrounded me. Home had become someplace claustrophobic. I joke that one Friday in 1984, I went "up north to the lake" and decided never to go back home. (Actually though, it was a planned move for our whole family.) I spent the next eleven years in west-central Minnesota–away from the big city traffic jams and with my beloved outdoors just steps away.

But the river of life beckoned. Twenty-one years and two divorces later, I looked around the next bend in the river, and found the quiet, friendly little burg of Nevis. It was smack-dab in the middle of northern Minnesota's beautiful rivers, lakes, forests, and hill country–the kind of place I'd always dreamed about living. I didn't realize it then, but I was finally home. For good.

There's no better place on earth to live. And write.

You can catch up on all my adventures at www.CanoesInWinter.com